Reviewers on *Nicholas:*

"... the leading man is the sexiest one this reader has seen in a long time!"
—*Romantic Times BOOKreviews* (Rhomylly Forbes)

"Everything about this story and the elements within worked ... a wonderful book that did not disappoint!"
—*Paranormal Romance Reviews*

"I really didn't want this book to end, and when I finished I knew that this book would stay with me ..."
—*TwoLips Reviews* (5 lips; Reviewer's Choice; Recommended Read—Julianne)

"... kept me spellbound and wanting more ..."
—*Joyfully Reviewed* (A Recommended Read—Amelia)

"... engrossing and easy to read in one sitting ... the sex is knock-out hot ... sure to please any erotica fan."
—*Just Erotic Romance Reviews*

"... on my top ten favorite erotic books list. .."
—*Night Owl Romance* (5 stars—Tammie)

"I couldn't put this book down until I finished every delight-fully wicked page! ... Beautifully written ..."
—*Romance Junkies* (5 stars, Chrissy)

"... This is a page turner from start to finish!"
—*Fallen Angel Reviews*

" ... a steamy, hot tale that scorches the pages."
—*Coffee Time Romance*

Reviewers on *Raine:*

"One of the the strongest heroines I have ever read ... great, erotic sex."
—*TwoLips Reviews* (5 lips; Recommended Read—Julianne)

"... without question the best historical paranormal erotic romance this reviewer has ever read ... This is a must read book for 2008!"
—*Paranormal Romance Reviews* (Jan

Also by Elizabeth Amber:

LYON: The Lords of Satyr

RAINE: The Lords of Satyr

NICHOLAS: The Lords of Satyr

Coming soon:

DANE: The Lords of Satyr

DOMINIC:
THE LORDS OF SATYR

ELIZABETH AMBER

APHRODISIA

KENSINGTON PUBLISHING CORP.
http://www.kensingtonbooks.com

APHRODISIA BOOKS are published by

Kensington Publishing Corp.
850 Third Avenue
New York, NY 10022

All Kensington Titles, Imprints, and Distributed Lines are available at special quantity discounts for bulk purchases for sales promotions, premiums, fund-raising, and educational or institutional use.

Special book excerpts or customized printings can also be created to fit specific needs. For details, write or phone the office of the Kensington special sales manager: Kensington Publishing Corp., 850 Third Avenue, New York, NY 10022, attn: Special Sales Department, Phone: 1-800-221-2647.

Aphrodisia and the A logo Reg. U.S. Pat & TM Off.

ISBN-13: 978-0-7582-2581-8
ISBN-10: 0-7582-2581-4

First Trade Paperback Printing: March 2009

10 9 8 7 6 5 4 3 2 1

Printed in the United States of America

Contents

DOMINIC

1

Temple of Bacchus
ElseWorld, 1837

"Her name is Emma."

The Facilitator's voice echoed off the ancient stone walls, lending his words authority as he directed Dominic's attention to the large, mirrored disk positioned prominently in the middle of the temple's bloodied floor.

The image of a woman, who existed somewhere in a neighboring world, was reflected on the disk's surface like a living portrait. Her countenance was serene, oblivious. For she was unaware she was being watched.

Carved from polished obsidian as black and impenetrable as the night, the six-foot mirror was encircled by nine more disks of lesser circumference. Each was concave and had been shaped from a disparate exotic stone intended to represent one of the lunar phases. All were set at an angle meant to capture the moonlight streaming in through an aperture in the roof and to direct it toward the central mirror where the woman was on view.

"You expect me to rape her," Dominic stated, his voice flat.

The woman's hand moved, and a page flipped. She was reading.

"We expect you to do what is necessary. As always," the Facilitator replied, speaking for himself as well as the two silent Acolytes who flanked him.

At first glance, the woman appeared to be plain, unremarkable in every way. Dominic judged her to be a quarter of a century old like himself, perhaps a little older. Except for the occasional movement of her hand, she was utterly still. Her head was bent intently over a tome entitled *The Fruits of Philosophy*, which lay before her upon a polished desk.

She wore spectacles, and her profile was half turned from him, so that the shape of her delicate cheek was limned by flickering candlelight. Tendrils of ash-brown hair curled along a vulnerable nape.

The garment she wore was stiff and lengthy, and it almost completely hid her body from view. He'd heard that Earth-World females sheathed themselves in swaths of fabric impermeable to the masculine eye but until now had believed this to be only a rumor. Her breasts were full and her figure shapely. Why did she hide it?

"You'll bow to Our Will in this matter?" prompted the Facilitator.

Dominic grunted a grudging assent. His hard, quicksilver gaze flicked over the woman again. He'd been required to do worse in his life. And he had little choice.

From the corridor behind them came the swishing sound of the votaries' brooms. Solemnly they swept the sacred remnants of what had been a colossal statue of Bacchus into vessels that would later be placed in reliquaries.

Rage simmered in him. This hallowed sanctum—his home—

had been brutally attacked. And to think that just hours ago he'd been out fighting the very beings who had taken advantage of his absence to defile it!

He resided here, alone for the most part, sleeping in an alcove with few creature comforts. Like a bird of prey, he swooped down on the enemies of his people by night and returned to the relative protection offered here in the temple to roost by day. But this attack had altered his schedule.

"Seven were killed in the strike here last night," the Facilitator informed him, though he hadn't asked. "And the amulet in the statue has gone missing. We can only thank the Gods that the time involved in its removal prevented our enemies from reaching these mirrors."

"Our 'enemies,' " Dominic mocked, shooting him a cynical look. The stench of demons was everywhere, yet the Facilitator adamantly refrained from referring to them directly, as if doing so might somehow raise them in the flesh.

"They weren't 'prevented,' " he informed his elderly companion. "They came here with specific intentions. They destroyed the statue but painstakingly hacked its genitals and right hand off. The fact that they left only those pieces undamaged and to be discovered by us in this mess was no accident."

It had been a message directed at him, for those were his susceptible points.

The Facilitator's placid gaze didn't alter.

"It's widely known that these scrying mirrors allow us to see into the adjoining world," Dominic persisted. "They were purposely left intact so that we might continue to do so." He jerked his jaw toward the woman in the mirror. "Let me postpone this new duty until I can find out the reason behind this attack. Until I can hunt down the demons who were responsible."

The two Acolytes on either side of the Facilitator stirred for the first time, murmuring in distress. Whether in response to his suggestion of postponement or to his profanity in calling the demons by name, he neither knew nor cared.

The Facilitator calmed them with the lift of a hand, and then shook his head at Dominic. "No. You will do as We have directed."

Dominic heaved a frustrated breath and stalked away. Standing in the arched entrance of the chamber, he watched the votives at their work. The twelve marble statues that ringed the room regarded him coldly, unspeaking. Accustomed to their unwavering, brooding gazes, he ignored them.

Slamming the side of his fisted, gloved hand against a limestone column, he felt the familiar bolt of lightning zap up his arm, a cruel reminder of his duty. Free will was a luxury he had not enjoyed since the age of ten. The three males behind him ruled his sect, and he would obey their directive.

"How am I to get through the gate?" he gritted after a moment.

"Ingratiate yourself with her husband. Cajole him into offering you safe passage. He's one of the EarthWorld Satyr, but he serves here in our regiments."

Dominic's brows rammed together, and he whipped around toward the female in the mirror.

"She's wed? To one of our fighters?" he demanded. "And you would have me usurp his rights with her?"

Another page flipped under the touch of a feminine hand, reclaiming everyone's attention. Gold flashed on the woman's finger. She wore a wedding band.

"She's not of our blood," he was hastily assured, as if that would render the unsavory task he'd been assigned perfectly palatable. "Her sister is King Feydon's offspring. One of the infamous half-Human, half-Faerie brides wed to the three EarthWorld Satyr lords. But this one—" he tapped the mirror with a gnarled finger, causing the woman's image to undulate for a few seconds, "this one doesn't share the deceased king's blood."

"How strong is the blood of her husband?"

"Him? He's hardly fit to call himself Satyr," the Facilitator scoffed. "He boasts that he's a quarter blood, but We believe him to be less. And he doesn't 'fight,' as you assume. No, he serves himself up to the other soldiers in a base manner, as one of the *cinaedi*. You'll find him in the regiment camped closest to the gate. He chose to be stationed there so that he might easily return to his world regularly at Moonful."

"To fuck his wife," Dominic conjectured. "As you would have me fuck her. Why?"

The Acolytes whispered again, gently rebuking his plain speaking. The Facilitator overlooked it, preferring as always to gloss over the more sordid details of the sequential duties that made up Dominic's existence.

"She's newly plowed. Her husband lay with her last evening," the elderly man remarked significantly.

At that, Dominic returned to stand before the woman, his eyes dropping to her waist. He opened himself to her for the briefest of intervals, learning what he could.

Her belly was not yet rounded, but even with a world of distance between them, his instincts quickly informed him that she did house another man's seed within her womb—seed planted there only last night.

On the heels of that realization, another struck him with the impact of a giant fist. He staggered back from the mirror, his accusing gaze flying to his companion.

"Yes," the Facilitator affirmed, refusing to meet his eyes. "She's with child."

A heartbeat of silence passed. Then another and another.

"Not just any child, though, is it?" Dominic inquired with soft menace.

His right hand vibrated as if the evil that dwelled in its palm had been agitated by his suspicions. He raised the hand between himself and the other man and carefully flexed it within its silver-threaded glove.

The Facilitator shifted uncomfortably. Darting a glance at the glove, he subtly distanced himself from it.

The Acolytes began to hum. Nervously they cupped their long-fingered hands together, catching the rays of the moon overhead in their palms—an act believed to ward off demons.

Dominic's lip curled, cruelly voluptuous. His lashes lowered to shadow the slits of his eyes. And for just a moment he savored the latent power that made others—even these influential beings—fear him.

"As you . . ." The Facilitator cleared his throat in a rare display of uneasiness. "As you've no doubt guessed, the child will be a Chosen One. Your successor."

A chill crawled up Dominic's spine. He stared at the Facilitator, thunderstruck.

"This can come as no surprise," the Facilitator rambled on. "You were aware your replacement would be selected one day."

Yes, he'd known. But he'd been too engrossed in the never-ending hunting and killing that comprised his nightly routine to dwell on the matter. This news had taken him completely off guard. Did it imply that his death was imminent?

"Now, then, you have four weeks," the Facilitator informed him crisply. "With the coming of another Moonful, it will be imperative that you mate her in order to endow her child's powers. Four weeks. Is it time enough to find her husband and secure an invitation to his world?"

Dominic nodded slowly, his fascinated gaze returning to the mirror where it resettled on the woman. On the delicate blush of her cheek. On the inviting slope of her shoulder.

On her flat belly.

Like his own mother, she would have no inkling she was to bear a Chosen One. Wouldn't be informed of her child's destiny until Dominic's eventual death.

His own predecessor had been unknown to him, for the demonhand—quite literally a hand that held demons—didn't pass to a successor through bloodlines. It selected its hosts seemingly at random, one after another. Only once in a generation was a single child given the power—the curse—that had been bestowed upon Dominic as a boy. A mirrored palm.

"Excellent." The Facilitator nodded to his two companions.

Snap!

At the sharp sound, the woman's image wavered as if it were a reflection on the surface of a pond that had been abruptly disturbed. Then it shrank to a pin light. And then she was gone.

The distant, tranquil scene had evoked a peculiar fascination in Dominic, and he found himself strangely sorry to see it go. His own world was in constant turmoil. Perhaps this woman's son might be the one to ultimately bring peace. Something Dominic had failed to do despite his dedication.

The two Acolytes extended their right hands to the Facilitator and then to one another. Palms came together in the traditional way that served as both greeting and farewell.

"As the moon reflects the sun," their three voices droned in harmony, signifying that this meeting was at an end.

No one offered such a gesture or valediction to Dominic, nor did he expect it. No one ever touched him voluntarily. Not once they realized what he was.

Without another word, he turned and made his way outside. Soon his boots were striking the nine marble steps in front of the temple with determined, resigned thuds. The votaries scurried from his path, dropping their brooms and falling over themselves in their efforts to avoid him. Though he disguised himself from the rest of the world, members of his own sect recognized him for what he was.

The fact that they so obviously spurned him—they whom he protected with his very life—might have destroyed another man. Fortunately he'd been hardened to such scorn long ago. But with the coming of this new child, he was reminded that his time as protector would one day draw to an end.

At any moment, he could be demolished by demons—like the statue that had stood for centuries before this temple, the remains of which now crunched under his boots. Then, like the statue, he would simply be swept away. In favor of the next Chosen One.

Until such time he would continue to be a repository of evil. One of a kind. The most valuable, dependable, and vicious weapon his people possessed.

And like any well-honed weapon, his thoughts now trained themselves on reaching their assigned target, the woman in the mirror. The woman whose unborn son would someday wear the glove.

His right hand clenched tight. When it uncurled, the single, fingerless glove he wore seemed to melt away, revealing a mirrored palm instead of flesh. He closed and reopened his fingers again and the slick mirror that shielded a cache of terrible evil disappeared from view as well.

He raised the disguised hand in a brief salute to a soldier he passed and received an easy wave in return. Pausing a mile or so later, he assisted a farmer in righting a wagon with a load that had slid askew and threatened to topple it. Afterward he was heartily thanked. The man even went so far as to attempt to shake the camouflaged hand, a gesture Dominic evaded.

Satisfied that it appeared to everyone save himself that he was an ordinary Satyr, he made his way toward the region just this side of the interworld gate.

His features remained undisguised. But he'd bespelled them as usual in such a way as to leave a vague impression that none who saw him would later be able to recall. So that no portrait or depiction of him could ever be created and given over to hands that would do him harm.

Within two hours, he'd located the regiment fighting closest to the gate. Within three, he'd traded his pants and jacket of black leather for their gray woolen uniform.

At sundown, he met the woman's husband, and within the week the man was indebted to him for saving his life.

By the time Moonful neared, his new acquaintance was half besotted with him.

Though his new comrade rarely spoke of his wife, Dominic continued to carry within him the image of the tranquil scene he'd viewed in the obsidian mirror.

Emma.

She'd roused something in him he'd thought long destroyed. Something he'd pushed deep within himself where his enemies couldn't exploit it.

A longing.

Though he knew such an emotion weakened him, the desire to view her face and her body in the flesh and to hear her voice increased by the hour. With each kill—with each battle he undertook—his anticipation of the night he would at last touch her clean, soft sweetness grew ever stronger.

She had no idea what was coming.

2

Satyr Estate in Tuscany, Italy
EarthWorld, 1837

"Damned beasts."

It was Carlo.

Emma had been listening for his arrival. She'd monitored his forward progress by the staccato sound of his sneezes. He was allergic to Lyon's panthers.

They'd never warmed to him either. Not in the entire year and a half since Nicholas had found and brought Carlo to the estate. Even now, the sleek black animals paced just behind her husband at the edge of the tree line, grumbling as if to warn her of his approach.

"Liber. Ceres. Away," she ordered softly. At the sound of her voice, Carlo's head lifted. His eyes narrowed on her where she stood in the doorway of their home.

The hopeful thrill that had always zinged through her when she caught sight of him was missing this time. Yet she'd waited for him tonight as anxiously as always, half fearing he wouldn't come. Her relief now that he had shown himself was tinged with dread. It was a curious reaction, and one for which only she and he knew the reason.

Carlo stepped out of the late afternoon shadows and next to her beneath the portico of the carriage house. Adjacent to that of her sister's lavish *castello*, it had been converted into their home upon their wedding. But though Emma resided here, her husband had visited only twelve times during the entire year of their marriage. Once a month, like clockwork, he'd returned to bed her. As he would do tonight.

Their eyes met—hers a wary ash brown, his a boyish, confident blue. His smile was warm, false, familiar. Frightening.

"I've missed you," he said, reaching for her.

So he thought they would both pretend.

She pulled away. "Don't touch me," she warned coolly. "Except as necessary. Later."

He feigned astonishment. "What's this? Where's my usual affectionate welcome? Do you wish me gone again? Shall I leave?" He turned on his heel as though to depart.

"No!" She took a hasty step forward and put a staying hand on his sleeve.

He smirked. "I thought not." Dropping his bag on the porch, he snaked an arm around her, drawing her so close that she felt the hard weapon he wore at his hip.

Cupping the back of her head, he pressed her soft cheek to the coarse wool of his uniform. She inhaled the peculiar scent of that other world in which he dwelled. That world into which she could not trespass. That world she used to despise because it kept him away from her.

Now she could hardly wait for morning, when he would return there.

"Don't." She wedged her elbows between them, trying to nudge him away.

His grip on her tightened, and she winced as the beading along the back of her gown punished her skin.

"I didn't mean to hurt you, Emma," he murmured, refusing to release her. His breath was cool against her neck. "Can't you let it go?"

At his words, hope tried to flicker to life within her. Had his ill treatment of her last month been an aberration? Would this sojourn from the war in ElseWorld signal a new beginning for their marriage? Hope—foolish hope—brightened her heart, just a little. She squashed it.

Carlo drew back, and his satisfied gaze fell to her swollen waistline.

"You've grown fat in the past month," he teased.

"And whose fault is that?" she told him, forcing herself to match his light tone.

An odd expression shifted in his face, gone before she could decipher it.

"Mine, I suppose. But motherhood agrees with you." He found his usual smile once more. The one that made him so deceptively attractive and which had lured her into wedding him.

"Did you tell your sister?" he asked.

"No, Jane noticed my condition without my having to do so."

In a gesture that had become habitual over the last four weeks, she smoothed a hand over her rounded abdomen. It had grown to this size within a single month, the entirety of the period necessary for the gestation of a child of Satyr heritage. The bulge was only half the size of her sister's or of her two aunts' by the time they'd given birth.

"She predicts our first child will be a small one."

"You misunderstand," said Carlo. "I meant to inquire regarding whether or not you told her what happened between us."

Emma arched a brow. "Do you refer to my reluctance to conceive and your insistence?" she asked. She refused to pretend it had been something else. "If so, no. I saw little point. However, you should be aware I'll not tolerate a repeat of your brutality."

"Brutality? Come now, you overstate the case. You know how my blood stirs under a full moon." He pulled her close again and bumped his forehead to hers, his pretty eyes willing her plain ones to offer forgiveness.

She simply stared at him, stunned anew at his refusal to concede that there could be no excuses for what he'd done.

"It's unnatural for a woman to thwart her husband's efforts to beget heirs on her. Why did you do it, Emma? Why didn't you want my child?"

Because this child shackles me to you forever. Makes it more difficult to leave you. Unaccustomed anger surged in her, but she tamped it down. *Just get through tonight,* she reminded herself. *Tomorrow will be time enough for frank words.*

A squeal of delight had them both turning. Emma's older half sister Jane had peeked into the hall and seen them.

Carlo straightened, drawing Emma into the curve of his arm. Making a pretense that all was well.

"You've returned at last, Carlo. How wonderful!" Jane said. "I'll summon the others."

"Do! I've brought news of matters on the other side." Carlo glanced behind himself, through the open front door. The air shifted as her sister departed in a swirl of skirts, and candlelight from the hall sconces rose for a moment, flaring across his throat. Angry scratches striped the flesh there and on his collarbone, spidering even lower within the concealment of his uniform.

"You're hurt!" Emma said, impulsively reaching to inspect his injuries.

"Shhh!" Carlo grabbed her wrist, rejecting her touch. His mood had altered like lightning, transforming him into the monster she'd glimpsed only once before. A month ago.

"He's here!" Oblivious to any undercurrents, Jane had already departed. Her footsteps and voice receded down the corridor toward the dining room.

Emma tugged at her arm, but Carlo held her fast in an intentional show of strength. With his free hand, he fastened his collar over his injuries, firmly shutting her out.

The distant scrape of chair legs against wooden parquet indicated that the rest of the Satyr clan would soon come rushing out to join them. Her time alone with her husband was at an end. At least until they retired together upstairs.

His grip relaxed, and she pulled her wrist from his hold and stepped away, rubbing it and surveying him through downcast lashes. Panic beat its delicate wings in her chest.

Should she speak to Jane? Or to one of the others? Tell them what he'd done to her last month? No. She wouldn't tell them, for the same reasons she hadn't told them before now. Carlo had gone to great lengths to obtain what he wanted of her—a child. It was unlikely he would chance harming it when they were alone.

And, regardless, the rest of the family would soon be incapable of protecting her. When the full moon came, all on the estate would fall under its spell.

"Say nothing of this. There's no need to alarm the family," Carlo instructed. She shot him a sharp glance, wondering if he'd read her mind. But he only touched his throat, indicating his injuries. "We'll speak more of my wounds privately. Later."

He brushed past her, his boot heels tapping across polished Italian travertine.

Jane returned and dashed forward on silent slippers, taking him by surprise and enfolding him in a sisterly hug. He was too well mannered not to allow it. But Emma read the tension in him as he endured the affectionate clasp.

The hall was narrow, and their presence temporarily trapped Emma just inside the front door. Watching them, she fidgeted, smoothing her long, rustling skirts. Jane had insisted that she begin preparations for this momentous homecoming weeks ago, helping her in the selection of this extravagant gown as well as new nightclothes.

They'd spent today together, making sure she would look her best to greet her husband on the night they would become new parents. Emma hadn't had the heart to protest to her sister that she was attempting to make a silk purse from a sow's ear. While Jane was beautiful and skilled at enhancing her beauty, Emma was plain and devoted little care to her appearance.

The splendid taffeta gown she wore was adorned with intricate tatting at its hem and delicate Venetian glass beading at its neckline. It had been designed and delivered earlier that week by the most skilled dressmaker in all of Florence. Her hair had been brushed and styled, with fluted ribbon woven through her brown curls.

All in preparation for her husband's homecoming. All for a man who had no love for her, except as a means by which he could produce his progeny.

"Welcome, Carlo!" The deep, masculine voice belonged to Jane's husband, Nicholas, who'd joined them. He was followed by his younger brothers, Raine and Lyon, and their respective wives, Jordan and Juliette. The entire family had gathered here tonight to wish them well on the night their first child would be born. The other three couples resided in the original *castellos* on the ancestral estate, which made visiting convenient.

As they all crowded into the hallway, Emma allowed herself to be shunted aside. It was natural for everyone to be excited, for they rarely saw Carlo. He had been at war for so long, returning intermittently, only to bed her with a regularity dictated by the carnal stirrings of his Satyr blood.

The last time they'd coupled had been exactly one month ago. It had been a Calling time. The moon had been heavy and ripe, bursting with light. As it would be again tonight.

He'd been tardy in coming to her bed that awful time four weeks ago, waking her sometime around midnight. The moon had risen hours earlier, and she'd long since cried herself to sleep, assuming he'd found another outlet for his passions and would not come. For once dusk fell on a Calling night, rituals commenced that engaged a Satyr male's mind and body beyond all thought and reason.

Because she had given up expecting him, she hadn't been prepared, and he'd—

No, she wouldn't think of that. Not now.

When she'd awoken the next morning, bruised by his cruelty only in places her family wouldn't see, he'd already departed for ElseWorld.

But she hadn't been alone. He'd left her with child. It would be their first, and it would be born at dawn.

Emma moved to shut the door but left it ajar when she saw that Carlo's bag still sat on the porch where he'd dropped it. Her child chose that moment to shift inside her, causing the strange flip-flopping sensation that had become so familiar in the past few days. Her hand found her belly, cupping it in a protective gesture.

The late afternoon shadows stirred unnaturally beyond the steps, pulling her gaze.

A man stood outside, watching her.

3

Twin beams of quicksilver lit the darkness, gleaming at Emma like the eyes of a cunning predator on the hunt—a lone beast lurking in the twilight while others more civilized than he had already sought the warmth of home and hearth with the coming of dusk.

At her gasp, the voyeur stepped over the threshold, immediately commanding everyone's attention. By candlelight, his face was arresting. Its Creator had originally shaped it to be a handsome one. But time and experience had hardened it into something raw and pagan. His voluptuous lips bore a ruthless curve, his hair was a midnight tangle, and a thin scar ran the length of his strong, square jaw.

As tall as Nicholas and as massive as Lyon, he cut a compelling figure—brawny, broad-chested, and soldier straight. Unsmiling, he faced them all with his muscular arms tensed at his sides as if prepared to ward off an attack. Or to wage one.

Nicholas and Lyon were nearest to her, and she felt them bristle with aggression, rallying to protect their family. Strangers rarely visited the compound. Theirs was a small clan with reason to be secretive.

"Stay back," Lyon growled, stepping in front of Jane and Emma.

Emma peeked around him, watching as the interloper advanced into the light. He wore the same gray uniform as Carlo. Austere in design, it had nine buttons aligned down its center, each made of some indeterminate metal mined in ElseWorld. Oblong and plump, they had a sanguine cast and had always reminded her of the grapes on the vines of the Satyr estate. A daggerlike weapon identical to Carlo's hung at his hip.

If this man had been on the same side of the fighting as her husband, surely he was no threat to them. She glanced over at Nicholas and Raine. All three brothers had formed a physical barrier between him and their women, their bearings rife with animosity and suspicion.

"*Entrare, entrare.*" Only Carlo had brightened at the unknown man's approach. There was a lightness in his step as he wove through the assemblage in the vestibule to usher the gentleman— if he could be called that—forward. "Calm yourselves," he told the family. Slinging an arm across the newcomer's back, he companionably hooked his hand at the man's opposite shoulder. Emma stared at that hand, astonished at how easily her normally standoffish husband had embraced this stranger.

"Everyone, this is—"

"Dominic Janus." The deep timbre of the man's voice superseded Carlo's and sent prickles over Emma's skin. His speech was tinged with an accent she couldn't place, and she briefly wondered what his native tongue sounded like.

"Guardians of portals and passageways," she murmured.

Though she'd spoken softly, the stranger heard, and his eyes flashed in her direction. "My sect serves in the way yours does, though we guard the gate between our worlds from its other side."

The secret gate between EarthWorld and ElseWorld, he

meant, for it was hidden deep in the heart of the nearby forest on Satyr land. Nicholas, Raine, Lyon, and their ancestors had secured it against trespass since ancient times.

Everyone visibly relaxed at the news of the visitor's lineage, though something in the three Satyr siblings' expressions remained dubious.

"Come, Dom, and meet my brothers," Carlo effused. Though he liked to call them such, his precise blood tie to the Satyr lords was actually unknown and was likely far more distant than a fraternal one.

After Carlo had presented the rest of the family, Jane surreptitiously elbowed him and nodded her way. Though Emma appreciated her sister's good intentions, her actions had only drawn attention to his oversight.

"Of course, of course. *Scusa*, darling." Belatedly Carlo gestured Emma forward and held her to stand before him so she faced his friend. "And lastly this is my lovely wife . . . Emma." He sounded almost reluctant to claim her, and she cringed inwardly.

"Welcome to our home, signore." Lord, the man was even more imposing up close. She peered up at Dominic through her lashes and found that his gaze had fallen to her most prominent feature—her rounded belly. It seemed to permeate the layers of taffeta and silk, and she fought the inclination to hide the bulge of her unborn child under her palms.

She hadn't ventured from the estate even once over the past month. Not since Carlo had gotten her with child. Therefore, aside from the family and the servants, no one had witnessed her physical condition. Didn't this man realize it was rude to stare so? Though she knew it was silly, it embarrassed her to think he might be dwelling on the fact that her expanded waistline was the obvious result of copulation with her husband.

Silver eyes lifted at last to meet hers. "My pleasure," he solemnly informed her.

The velvet rumble of his voice drove a shiver of awareness down her spine. She might not have Jane's Fey ability to read strong emotions, but her Human intuition told her she intrigued him more than the others did.

Something brushed her skirts, and she glanced down, relieved to have a reason to look away from Dominic. Lyon's panthers had sidled closer. Lured by the smells of food from her kitchen, they no doubt hoped to sneak into the house while everyone was preoccupied. She stroked their silky heads, and they angled their faces against her hand, marking her with their ownership.

"Wait your turns, you two," she scolded softly. "You'll get leftovers as usual, after we've eaten."

"Out!" Carlo commanded, pushing her aside with a brusque nudge and shooing the animals away with slaps upon their rumps. Liber, the larger of the two, snapped at him with his spiked pearly teeth. Carlo drew back a hand to strike him more fiercely.

Before Emma could raise her own objections, Lyon caught Carlo's arm with stern fingers and glared at him. Like his pets, Lyon had never quite warmed to her husband.

Sensing imminent conflict, Juliette stepped between the two men and took Lyon's arm, urging him toward the interior of the house.

Emma pasted on a smile. "Excellent suggestion, Juliette. Let us all adjourn to the *sala da pranzo*," she told the group at large. "Dinner is prepared and waiting to be served."

Turning, Emma went to the front door and gently coaxed the panthers outside. They went, grumbling in a way that struck her as similar to the behavior of the men she and Juliette had just ushered down the corridor. A small, genuine smile curved her lips at the comparison.

As she began to close the door behind the animals, a hand caught its edge. Dominic's. His powerful warrior's body leaned closer, and he braced his other hand on the doorjamb, caging her in the rectangular opening.

Disconcerted, she flattened a palm to his chest and then yanked it away when she realized what she'd done. "What are you—" she sputtered, recoiling from him and the frightening rush of attraction she'd felt.

His eyes caught hers briefly, and heat flared in them, stealing her breath. He loomed nearer until she felt surrounded by him. She garnered the distinct impression that he was contemplating drawing her with him outside into the shadows.

He reached out, and she parted her lips, intending to call for help. But his outstretched arm only moved beyond her to retrieve Carlo's bag from where he'd left it on the porch.

"*Mi scusi,* signora," he said, straightening as he hoisted it and dropped it just inside the hall.

"Yes. Yes, of course. Thank you." Feeling a bit ridiculous for her wild imaginings, Emma slipped under his arm and rejoined the rest of the family, hearing him shut the door behind her.

As she, Dominic, and Carlo trailed the others, her husband slung a proprietary arm around her in a rare display of possessiveness. He seemed to have picked up on his companion's interest in her, and he didn't like it.

Though curious at Carlo's uncharacteristic desire to claim her, Emma allowed the embrace, glad Dominic bore witness to this reinforcement of the fact that she was linked to another. Held tight to Carlo's side, she turned her face into his uniform jacket and away from the larger man.

Almost absently, he shrugged her away as he instructed a passing male servant to deliver the bag Dominic had left in the entry hall to his bedchamber.

His rejection went unremarked. But she felt Dominic's sharp interest as he took in every nuance of their byplay. Impossible to know what conclusions he drew, for the easily interpreted emotions he'd displayed a moment ago in the doorway had now fled his expression.

"Dominic will be staying with us tonight," Carlo informed her.

"Of course," she replied, mentally sifting through the available quarters.

Though their renovated carriage house was not as luxurious as the *castellos* in which the others dwelled, she was thankful it was large enough to afford privacy. She'd make sure their visitor was stationed as far from their bedchambers as possible. There must be no chance of him overhearing any telltale sounds of concupiscence that might issue from their rooms during the night. Her cheeks pinkened at the thought.

"If you are sure I do not put anyone out," Dominic murmured. She was surprised to note the barest trace of masculine humor in his voice, as if he'd read her mind and been amused by her modesty.

"Any acquaintance of my husband's is most welcome," she replied, relieved when they arrived at their destination at last.

"*Grazie.*" Those sinful lips of his curved upward, sending a fresh jolt of awareness through her.

What was wrong with her? she wondered as she instructed the servants to set an additional place and commence the serving of the meal.

Something about Carlo's friend flustered her, but she shook off the feeling. It wasn't him. It was his type. Charismatic men had always made her uneasy. He was too large. Too confident.

Nicholas, Raine, and Lyon were, as well, but they were an entirely different matter. She'd known them for fifteen years, ever since Jane had married Nicholas and brought her to live on the estate. They were comfortable and familiar, like brothers.

Perhaps her discomfort was simply due to the effects of impending motherhood, she decided as she sat at the opposite end of the table from her husband and his guest.

"Tell me, Dominic, why haven't we encountered you previously?" Nicholas said once they were all seated, launching what she suspected would be a lengthy interrogation.

"Or even heard your name spoken?" added Lyon.

"I have no idea," came the blithe reply. Dominic was toying with his food, and Emma suddenly wondered if it was unfamiliar to him. She motioned to the servants to offer him some of the other platters and dishes.

"You must understand that the nature of our work is sensitive and necessarily clandestine," Carlo hastened to explain. "When the fighting today brought us close to the gate, we were temporarily severed from our regiment. As I'd already planned to come here to Emma, it seemed safest to simply bring Dom with me."

"Only for the night," Dominic remarked. "Tomorrow I go."

"Will trouble follow on your heels?" asked Raine.

"I lagged behind in order to ensure we were not trailed," Dominic assured him.

The soup tureen was offered to him, and he took its handles from the disconcerted servant and then stared at its contents, as though unsure what to do next.

"Cristoforo, do please ladle some soup for the signore," Emma bid the servant, trying to smooth over her guest's faux pas. Fortunately the serving boy was quick-witted. With a small, improvised bow of gratitude to Dominic for holding the tureen, he simply took the ladle from it and filled his bowl with soup before seizing the tureen and resuming his route around the table.

"Your scent," noted Raine, who was gifted with the most acutely sensitive and capable olfactory abilities of the family. "It's nonexistent."

Dominic shrugged, unconcerned. "Excised at a young age in order that I might fulfill the secretive nature of my duties."

"Which are?" Lyon enquired.

Dominic lifted a haughty brow. "Secret."

Lyon leaned forward, scowling. "I ask not out of curiosity but because we have our own secrets and our families to protect here—"

"Cease!" said Carlo, throwing his hand up as if to slice the conversation and render it dead. "Suffice it to say that I've known Dominic for some time. He is what he says and no danger to us."

Lifting his wine, Nicholas stepped in to defuse tempers. "Very well. Tell us, Carlo. What news is there of the war?"

"The peace talks have disbanded," Carlo responded, eagerly latching on to the new topic. "Two of the attorneys involved on our side were severely maimed by our enemies, and the rest have fled the negotiations for fear of similar retaliation."

"Is it known who was responsible?" Jordan asked.

"I'm not privy to the nuances of what transpired. But the war rages on, and I hear no more talk of progress toward peace. Our stronghold in the east fell last week. Even the temple of Bacchus isn't sacred to some. A month ago, it was attacked."

"By whom?" all three lords demanded simultaneously.

"Demons, most likely," Carlo informed them, earning himself a sharp look from Dominic.

Seeing it, Carlo set a hand on his friend's sleeve and ducked his head close to speak in an undertone. "The term doesn't carry the taboo here in this world that it does in the other. You may speak freely."

Emma gaped at that hand, wondering anew at her husband's easy way with this man. When it was withdrawn, she raised curious eyes to Dominic's face.

In the depths of his dark-lashed gaze, she detected a challenge of some sort directed her way. Did he think she would be jealous because Carlo had made a friend? On the contrary, she was glad someone had been watching out for him on the battlefield.

However much emotional and physical distance there might be between them, she would prefer that her child not lose its father before it was even born!

"What of the mirrors?" Raine asked, his intelligent brow creasing.

"Only the statue in the front exterior niche of the temple was destroyed."

"'Only,' you say?" Lyon echoed, sounding flabbergasted. "What of the statue's contents?"

Carlo shrugged. "Dominic has been to the temple in the aftermath. Let him tell you more of it."

"The amulet was stolen," Dominic put forth as he stabbed several slices of venison from the platter a servant offered to him. Though an expectant pause fell, he seemed to think his words sufficed, for he didn't elaborate.

Carlo filled the breach. "The rumor is that although most of the statue was smashed, two pieces of its anatomy were left in pristine condition." He paused for dramatic effect. Once the four women had leaned in, he said, "Its right hand. And its male organ."

Juliette gasped, putting a hand to her throat. Lyon slid a huge paw around her, offering his wife a reassuring smile.

"Each was painstakingly severed from the body," Carlo gleefully continued.

"Carlo! That's hardly conversation fit for the dining table," Emma scolded, but he only shrugged, an unrepentant grin playing on his sulky mouth.

"Grim news," Jane added. "But let us save such talk for tomorrow. When everyone is less ... tense."

An intimate glance heated the air between her and Nicholas. Emma automatically looked away. Having grown up in their home, she'd witnessed thousands of similar private exchanges between them over the years. Even at the age of twelve when she hadn't yet understood the precise nature of what such glances between men and women meant, she had already begun to feel like an intruder when she'd intercepted them.

A desire to avoid making more such intrusions was one reason she'd leaped at the only invitation to marry that had been presented to her. However, the happy state of all three of the Satyr lords' marriages was an all too painful contrast to the sorry state of her own.

For the duration of the meal, Emma said little, and Dominic was equally quiet. Whenever he did speak, she noticed a formality in his way of phrasing things, as though he was uncertain of his Italian.

She was glad when his voice came, for it gave her an excuse to look his way. On each occasion, she drank in the sight of him from a safe distance, fascinated by the strange pull he exerted. It was as if he were a steady, sure planet and she a hapless moon wobbling uncertainly within his orbit.

However, he spoke little, and she wondered if he kept his thoughts to himself fearing a misstep with their language. The idea that there might be a chink in the self-assurance of this rugged male softened her toward him. When he looked up and read the gentle sympathy in her face, his expression lit with a blazing heat that was so quickly snuffed she thought she must've imagined it.

Still, it left her breathlessly wary.

As it often did when the family gathered, dinner conversation eventually turned to the ancient vines that covered the sloping hills at the center of the Satyr compound, and the wine they produced.

But as the daylight further waned, talk dwindled, too, and the atmosphere grew ever more charged.

4

Though it went unspoken, everyone at the table was well aware that once night fell, a carnal ritual peculiar to the Satyr would begin. This knowledge was apparent in small ways. In the manner in which each Satyr husband watched his Fey wife. And in the wanting glances and subtle touches that passed between them.

From the corner of her eye, Emma saw that Nicholas had begun toying with her sister's silky, blond hair. The knuckles of Raine's left hand were surreptitiously dusting Jordan's nape. Lyon's hand had disappeared under the table in Juliette's direction, and although his wife avoided his gaze, her cheeks had suffused with pink. The air around the three couples fairly hummed with their mutual desire.

Heat suffused Emma's cheeks as well when she thought of what would happen between her husband and herself, once they were alone.

She glanced to the far end of the table. Carlo had seated himself next to Dominic and was fawning on him in a manner that was almost flirtatious—actually going so far as to run his fingers along the other man's sleeve or to offer him delicacies from his plate now and then. Carlo had always gravitated toward weaker men he could dominate. Why had he chosen to befriend a man so imposing? On his part, Dominic largely ignored these overtures and ate with the methodical precision of one who took in his food as fuel rather than for any sort of enjoyment.

They made an odd sort of triangle, for while her attention was on Carlo, his was on Dominic, who in turn had for some reason decided to focus on her.

Was he perhaps wondering why Carlo had chosen to marry her? She, who was so different from the rest of them?

She'd wondered that very thing herself often enough. In the beginning she'd thought he loved her, but now she was sure he never had.

And why should he? She wasn't as delicate and beautiful as her sister or her aunts, for they each bore the blood of a Fey king who'd selected their beautiful Human mothers as his mates. Although she was blessed with a keen intelligence and an insatiable greed for the written word, such things didn't attract men.

She possessed no extraordinary abilities. In fact Emma was the only one in the family who was entirely Human.

Everyone else had the blood of either Faerie or Satyr flowing in their veins, mingling there with Human blood. Under the circumstances, she couldn't help but feel like an outsider.

"Is there more of the Sangiovese?" Carlo's voice was beginning to slur from the effects of drink. She frowned at him and gave an imperceptible shake of her head, but he mutinously refilled his goblet.

As usual, wine flowed freely during and after the meal, all of it the best-quality vintage produced by grapes grown in the vineyard on Satyr land. Thick green bottles and amber ones wrapped in raffia, all with the trademark SV molded into their sides, had been brought from the cellar and uncorked to celebrate the occasion of Carlo's return.

The others were more conservative in their consumption, cognizant of the fact that it would soon be Moonful. Emma abstained from taking spirits altogether, for in her current condition they made her ill.

As time passed, she grew more worried at Carlo's continued abandoned imbibing. It was crucial that he have his wits gathered sufficiently tonight. He must not fail to bed her. He of all people should be aware of that.

She caught the concerned question in Jane's eyes but could only raise her brows and shrug in response to indicate that she was confused as well. Impossible to know what impulses might be driving her husband.

Toward the end of the evening, Nicholas drew Carlo aside, speaking in sotto voce. Thereafter, Carlo's glass remained empty. It was obvious he'd been taken to task, and Emma was grateful. These Satyr males were all headstrong, but in the end they always deferred to Nicholas, the eldest of them.

When dusk was imminent, the family made to depart. Soon elixirs of a more supernatural sort would commence to flow. There would be rituals. And then lovemaking in the sacred glen, a verdant place in the center of the estate where magic clung, thick and low to the ground. Ringed with statues of ancient gods, maenads, nymphs, fawns, and other mythical creatures entangled in a lecherous ecstasy, the glen had shocked Emma when she'd first viewed it as a girl. So much so that she'd never been back.

She and Carlo had always observed these rituals here in the privacy of their own home. Primarily because he was reluctant to be observed under a full moon by his brothers, whom he considered superior to him in every way. But most particularly with regard to their sexual prowess.

"I wish you and Carlo well tonight," Jane said, her voice lit with affection. As they said their good-byes, Nicholas awaited her on the front path, conversing with Raine and Jordan. Lyon and Juliette had already gone.

"I'm suddenly nervous," Emma confided, clasping her sister's hands.

Jane gave her fingers an encouraging squeeze. "I'm a mother three times over now, and one of those births triplets," she reassured. "So you may credit what I say on this issue. No matter how vigorous your engagements with your husband tonight, none of it will damage your child. Have no fear on that score. This will be a Moonful Calling like any other between the two of you."

"Except for the birthing at its finish," Emma put in.

"Yes, but any unpleasantness related to that will be brief and won't occur until dawn. Don't waste the hours between now and then with worry. All will be as I've told you previously. Now I must be off." With a final hug, she made to go. "I'll come tomorrow to welcome your newborn child into our family as soon as I can get away."

When her sister rejoined Nicholas, he enfolded her in his protective embrace, and his dark head bent to her blond one. Watching them depart, Emma sighed wistfully.

For though Carlo would certainly bed her tonight, it would not be the true lovemaking her sister would enjoy. And though it was necessary—compulsive, in fact—the act would not bring her the bliss her sister imagined it might. Not the sort of soul-deep rapture she knew Jane would find in the coming hours with her own husband.

Upon her return to the house, Emma entered the green *salotto* where Carlo had retired with his guest. It was his domain when he was in residence, and she rarely ventured inside.

Knocking lightly, she then slipped inside where she found the two men in conversation. Noting that Carlo held another glass of spirits in his hand, she looked askance at it and opened her mouth to scold him.

Preempting her, he defiantly downed the goblet's contents

in one long gulp. Then, straightening one leg, he reached deep into his trouser pocket and withdrew something small from inside.

Tossing the object in the air, he caught it and opened his palm to reveal that it was a large gold coin.

Emma stared, blanching as she recognized what he held.

"Tell me, Dominic," he mused in a wine-slurred voice, studying her instead of his companion as he spoke. "What would you think of a wife who intentionally sought to block her husband's seed from implanting itself within her?"

She felt Dominic's eyes sharpen on her in speculation but didn't look his way.

"Carlo, perhaps you shouldn't—" she began, moving to take his goblet.

When her fingers were within inches of it, he grabbed her wrist and held her in a painful grip. With his other hand, he flipped the coin high again, and once more he caught it. Still restraining her, he began to toy with it, weaving it in and out of his fingers with the skill of a sleight-of-hand trickster.

"Would you call her a murderess?" he went on to his friend. "This woman who condemned her husband's seed to shrivel and die on its journey toward her womb? This woman who knew her husband greatly desired heirs. Yet who intentionally deceived him. For on the rare nights that he was able to come to her bed, doing his best to breed her, she intentionally thwarted his diligent efforts—"

Dominic raised his goblet. Though it was obviously only half empty, he said, "*Permesso*, Carlo, my glass needs attention."

"Oh, of course. See to it, Emma." Her wrist was instantly relinquished, and she took Dominic's drink, giving him a grateful, tremulous smile. However, his expression was lost to her, for her eyes were brimming with tears of pain and humiliation.

Taking his glass to the wine cart, she lifted the carafe and prepared to refill it. Behind her, the coin flipped high, winking in the candlelight, and then landed with a *plunk* in Carlo's hand.

"Last Moonful I came late to her bed and managed to catch her unawares," he went on, refusing to let the matter go. "She was engaged in an evil pastime. Inserting *this* into her cunt."

The carafe Emma held hit the cart with a crack. Though she was frozen in place, she saw from the corner of her eye that he now held the offending coin on edge between his thumb and forefinger, extending it toward Dominic as if submitting it for evidence in a courtroom proceeding.

"Regardless, it appears you succeeded in your pursuit of paternity," Dominic interjected grimly, cutting short the verbal attack. "I suggest you cease belaboring the past."

Soft, dewy brown tangled with hard silver in a quick exchange of glances. Gratitude swelled in her yet again, but it was tempered by the knowledge that what Carlo accused her of was true. Last month, when he'd come to her bed unexpectedly and awakened her from slumber, she had begged for a moment to ready herself and had slipped behind her privacy screen to do so.

She was an informed woman, having thrice read Charles Knowlton's volume, *The Fruits of Philosophy: or The Private Companion of Young Married People*, which offered advice for couples who wished to limit the number of their offspring. Recently published in New York, it had described the use of female preventives, including "womb veils," and she'd secretly been employing them since the beginning of her marriage.

On the night of which he spoke, her husband had emptied his pockets on the bedside table before coming to her bed. Out of desperation, she'd surreptitiously and randomly selected one of the coins from the pile he'd left before retiring behind the screen. Crouching there in an undignified manner, she'd reached a hand under her nightgown, intending to insert the disk high within her feminine channel.

It had been thick and heavy, and she'd feared he might detect it when his organ deeply breeched her. The other type of "veil" she'd previously utilized had been less obvious—a pliable hoop covered with oiled silk that was more suited to such a use and which he hadn't noticed.

As she'd struggled with the insertion of the coin, he'd come behind the screen and caught her at it, forcing from her an admission that she'd been deceiving him in a similar way throughout the past year. Furious, he had flung the coin away and had used her roughly that night. Had hurt her with his hands, his body, and his words.

Leaving Dominic's goblet unfilled on the cart, Emma fled to the door. Without glancing toward either man, she spoke to them in a voice rife with suppressed emotion. "I'll have the guest chamber prepared for you in the west end of the house, Signore Janus. Carlo will show you there when you're ready to retire. Now I'll leave you both to your conversation."

"Await me in my room," Carlo muttered into his glass. "A son should be born in his father's bed."

With a curt nod, she stepped into the hall and shut the paneled door soundlessly, though she wished to slam it. Inside her husband continued on his tirade.

"I'm certain she learned this whore's trick from her books," she heard him say.

Dominic's rumbled reply was indecipherable through the door.

"But some of her reading borders on the heretical," Carlo blustered, "even going so far as to suggest that conception occurs when sperm and egg join! Yet it's a well-known fact that the man's seed is life, and a woman's function is simply to house and birth it! Mark my words—too much reading despoils the brain, especially that of a female."

Emma rolled her eyes.

A small silence fell, and she could almost see the coin flipping into the air again. "I carry this with me to remind myself that the cunts and minds of women are untrustworthy."

Not wishing to hear more, she retreated upstairs where she enjoined the servants to assist her in freshening the guest room. Under her supervision, linens were hung and water poured in the basins. Seeing to the familiar tasks calmed her mind and kept it from wandering to more disturbing venues of thought.

Their visitor had brought no belongings because his sojourn here had apparently been unplanned. Therefore she supplied shaving equipment, soap, and tooth powder. She'd have the servants see to his clothing if he wished such assistance in the morning.

On the way to her own room, she shifted the damask curtain aside at the western window along the corridor and studied the deepening shadows. By her estimate, a full moon would rise in half an hour.

Carlo wouldn't be long.

Her fingers trembled on the drape, and she caught them in her other hand to still them. There was no need to be afraid, she reminded herself as she strode on to her bedchamber. He might not care whether or not he hurt her, but he wouldn't chance injuring the precious heir she incubated.

In her room, a maid awaited, who helped remove her gown and unbind and brush out her hair. Then she was left to her ablutions in solitude, for the "day servants" departed the estate upon sunset, as was the custom at all Satyr domiciles.

Upon their leave-taking, other far more unusual "night servants" would appear to roam the house at will. Distantly related to a clan of the ancients in ElseWorld, these innocuous, servile beings hid away during the day and always kept to themselves at Moonful. On other nights, their time would be spent tirelessly polishing floors, mucking stables, and assuming other unpleasant chores, thus generally making life easier for everyone.

Once she was ready, Emma went through the door that adjoined her bedchamber to Carlo's. There she scurried about, making preparations for his impending visit. Lighting candles, pouring a dish of oil that had been scented with lavender, vanilla, and sandalwood—fragrances said to contain calming properties—and filling five basins, three with cleansing herbs and two with clear rinse water.

And lastly she set a container of cream upon the bedside table. It was a new jar, for she'd dashed last month's against the wall in a fit of temper after Carlo had left her. She glanced across the room. The stain was still there on the wallpaper, a constant reminder of that awful night.

In search of solace while she waited, she went to her room to retrieve the book of poetry she'd been reading earlier that day. Returning to Carlo's chamber, she sat at his dressing table positioned just inside the door to the hall. Then she opened the slender volume to the pressed-violet bookmark Jane had made for her.

Concentrating her thoughts on a page, she Willed it to turn. After several reluctant seconds, it obediently lifted to stand at an angle perpendicular to the book's spine, as if being held there by her fingers instead of her Will.

Scowling, she tried to frighten it into turning. It shuddered as though making the attempt, but then it seemed to give up and only fell back into its original position to rejoin the others like it.

It was a carnival trick. One of the very few she could perform. Compared to the extraordinary abilities of the other members of her family, it fell as flat as the page itself.

When she'd first come here, Lyon had tried to help her increase her talents, but to no avail, and they'd long since given up their extrasensory lessons. Still she occasionally practiced this single trick in secret, always hoping.

Would this minor talent pass from her to her son or daughter? As though to indicate its hopes in that direction, her child chose that moment to kick. Her hand curved atop her belly, and a maternal smile curved her lips.

"Soon," she whispered gently.

Carlo was wrong to think she hadn't desired children. She had. Someday. But she'd chosen her husband too rashly and had been uncertain of him almost from the beginning. When last they were together, he'd proven himself dishonorable by the way in which he'd sired his progeny.

Nevertheless she would love this child they'd created. And she would willingly sacrifice herself in his bed over the next eight hours to bring about its birth.

By morning, she would be a mother. A sweet joy filled her at the prospect, but concern over her husband's mood tamped it down again.

After he departed for ElseWorld tomorrow morning, she would announce her own travel plans to the rest of the family. Within the month, she would take her child and leave the estate.

Footfalls sounded on the carpet out in the corridor. Boots. Carlo.

5

A subtle *whoosh* of air fluttered the hem of Emma's night-clothes as the bedchamber door swung open behind her.

Quickly standing, she slipped her robe from her shoulders, letting it drop to the footstool's needlepoint cushion. She left her nightgown in place, though it, too, would no doubt fall by the wayside sometime in the hours of darkness ahead. It was new and fragile, stitched by a maker of specialty lingerie in Paris.

Would her husband ruin it as he had the one she'd worn a month ago?

Drawing a fortifying breath, she turned toward the door, planning to start matters off on a pleasant footing and hope they didn't deteriorate. "I trust you will be kind for the sake of our child?"

Her determined smile wobbled and withered when she saw her husband was not alone. Two men stood blocking the doorway, both tall and massive. And the larger of them was Dominic.

The shock of encountering those predatory eyes hadn't diminished since she'd first noticed him standing outside on the porch. What was he doing here?

Stunned, she sought her robe. It sprang from the stool to her fingers without her having to bend to it, but she was too rattled to mark this.

"Please, Carlo! I'm not properly dressed," she protested, clasping it to her chest. Belatedly realizing her backside would still be visible to the men through her translucent gown in the looking glass behind her, she shifted a few feet away from the dressing table so her back was to the wall.

"It was my understanding that you were wholly Human," Dominic said, frowning at the robe she'd Willed to lift.

"Both of her parents were," said Carlo, speaking for her. "And she is as well, but she has these confounding bursts of magic. Nicholas has posited that her Human mother retained some residual enchantment due to King Feydon's mating of her—the mating that produced Jane—and that a bit of this supernatural ability was in turn passed on to Emma."

"What does that matter at the moment?" she asked. "Again, I must strongly object to your joint visit. If you have more business to discuss, I ask that you adjourn to Signore Janus's bedchamber. Which is on the west side of the house," she added pointedly.

"Leave off your robe," Carlo said, moving past her. Lifting the large square of linen that hung next to the dressing table, he draped it over the mirror. She watched him do it so that she wouldn't have to further acknowledge his companion.

Mirrors in their bedchambers were always to be covered on Moonful nights when her husband was in residence, and the linen had been hung there on the peg for this specific purpose. It was an odd fetish of his, and one she was accustomed to.

When he'd adjusted the covering to his liking, Carlo set his weapon on the table and began emptying his pockets. He spoke, his back to them. "Dom is of the family."

"I still don't see—" She stopped, uncertain. She'd known Dominic was a creature of ElseWorld. However, many factions dwelled there. His clan could have been one of any number that existed in that other realm.

"I am full-blood Satyr," Dominic informed her in that formal tone of his.

Full blood. Not half blood like her brother-in-law. Not quarter blood or less, like Carlo. He was the first full-blood Else-World creature of any kind she'd ever met. Yet, like the other Satyr lords, he could easily pass for Human. An extraordinarily tall, compellingly masculine Human with broad shoulders and an expansive chest. But Human nevertheless.

"But your name—Janus," she said stupidly. "The god who looks both forward and backward. A protector in wartime. I assumed you were descended from his line."

"My wife is a great reader, brimming with a wealth of such information," Carlo sneered, interrupting her. He picked up her book of poetry from the table, fanned its pages, and then shut it with a disdainful snap. His actions were exaggerated, she noted worriedly, the influence of the excessive wine he'd taken in.

Dominic ignored him, answering her instead. "Janus is an ancestor's surname and one of a half dozen that make up the entirety of my own."

Still, this didn't explain why he was here in Carlo's chamber tonight of all nights. Why wasn't he in his own quarters taking Shimmerskins to his bed? Such insentient females were easily conjured from the ether at a Satyr's whim in order to serve his every carnal need.

"I'm not dressed to receive company of any sort," she persisted, addressing her husband.

Dominic frowned toward Carlo. "In one year of marriage, she still has not grown accustomed to our ways?"

Carlo shrugged.

Emma glanced warily between the two giant males that stood on either side of the room. "What ways?"

"While in her mate's presence, it is customary for an Else-World consort to display her body un—" Dominic searched for the correct word, his expression frustrated for a moment when he couldn't locate it. "Ah," he said at last. "To display herself in a far more un*curtained* state than yours, regardless of who else is in attendance."

"Well, this isn't ElseWorld, is it?" Emma protested. "And here in EarthWorld, we *consorts* wear clothing, not curtains. And we wear them when in every sort of company."

"Emma!" Carlo scolded. "Show some respect. Dominic's of royal blood and has saved my life in battle more than once."

"I'm sorry to be impolite," she said. "It's just that the moon is soon to rise." She hesitated, glancing toward the window.

Dominic's knowing gaze dared her to continue.

Couldn't the man decipher so broad a hint? Save for folding his arms across that formidable chest, he hadn't budged from the doorway. Almost as though he was intentionally blocking any egress. The back of her neck prickled with unease at the realization.

Her husband shot her an unreadable glance and then moved to the window and flung the drape wide with one hand. Beyond him only a glistening edge of orange remained of the daylight to outline the distant indigo hills.

As both men's eyes were drawn to the view of the oncoming twilight, Emma took advantage of their distraction to unobtrusively slip her robe on over her gown.

"There's something I didn't tell the family," Carlo said in a dull monotone as she fumbled to tie its single ribbon at her breast. "Something I don't want them to know."

His face, reflected in the window glass, was unusually solemn. A tremor of fear touched her. "What is it?"

He looked at her over his shoulder. "First I must have your promise that you'll keep my secret."

"Of course," she agreed easily, her curiosity mounting.

He turned back to inspect the evening sky. When he spoke again, his voice was low and tortured. "Something happened to me in ElseWorld. During a mission nearly four weeks ago, I was injured. Just after last Moonful, on the very morning I left your warm bed."

Emma went to his side and lay a tentative, compassionate hand on his sleeve, a reflexive action intended to relieve another's suffering.

"Why didn't you say something earlier, while the others were still here to help? Are you all right?"

"No," he barked. With a hard twist of his body, he shook her off. "As it happens, I'm far from all right."

Emma faltered under his glower and the fumes of alcohol he exhaled. He began stalking her, and she took a backward step for each of his paces forward.

When her spine hit the bedpost, she set her hands against his chest. He towered over her, taking her shoulders in a painful grip. "My injuries were severe. Quite severe. I lay unconscious for days. When I awoke, I was told . . ."

He took an unsteady breath and rammed both hands into his pockets. She wrapped an arm around the voluptuous mahogany bedpost and sank to the mattress, her eyes glued to his.

"I was told that the injury had rendered me impotent." He spat the admission, as if it tasted vile on his tongue.

She surveyed him blankly, trying to understand the ramifications of what he was telling her.

"Well?" he demanded in a belligerent tone.

Emma pushed to her feet. Sidling away from his volatile mood, she inadvertently bumped into Dominic. When had he moved so close?

His broad palm branded the hollow of her lower back, steadying her, and she started in reaction.

"*Mi scusi,* signore." Darting an embarrassed glare at him, she edged around him and toward escape. But somehow he was there at the hallway door before her, shutting it with a deceptively casual air.

She glanced covetously at the doorknob and then up at him. A chill swept her as she gleaned from his expression that he fully entended to ensure she stay.

"Did you understand me, wife?" Carlo had returned to the window where he continued to study the deepening shadows as though waiting for something. The moon.

The fingers of one hand speared into his hair, his elbow bumping the glass so hard she thought it might crack. "Do you comprehend what this means? To me, on a night such as this?"

Emma pressed two fingertips to the pulse at her temple in an attempt to corral her muddled thoughts. She'd once dreamed of creating a family with him. He was telling her that was not to be. But she'd already decided that for herself, though he didn't know it.

"I can imagine, but . . ."

Beside her, the ever-vigilant Dominic shifted, causing the muscles of his shoulders to strain the breadth of his uniform. It was difficult to think, much less speak under the weight of his silent quicksilver study.

"Don't mind Dom," Carlo said. He'd been watching their reflection in the windowpane. "He's all too aware of our situation."

"Situation?" Emma echoed.

With a huff of annoyance, Carlo turned to lean his hips against the windowsill. "Has motherhood rendered you thickheaded? Let me put it to you more plainly, *cara.* I cannot be to you what a husband should. Not ever."

A small, uncharitable spurt of gladness sprouted within her. He was telling her his seed could no longer sire children. From her perspective, this was something of a gift. Never again would he be able to force another babe into her womb without her consent. Relief, immediately chased by a touch of guilt for her selfishness, made it easy to be sympathetic.

"A loss, to be sure, but we must be grateful that your life was not taken, too. After all, it's not necessary that we—" She'd taken a few steps toward him as she spoke, but his next words had her stalling in the middle of the room.

"It damn well *is* necessary—I'm part Satyr, for pity's sake!" he bellowed in outrage. "Dominic understands what this 'loss' means to me even if you do not!"

Still guarding the door, his guest was unabashedly eavesdropping. Was he so obtuse he didn't know when a married couple required privacy? Enough! She rounded on him to request that he leave.

"Signore, perhaps you will allow us to continue our discussion of this matter in seclusion?"

But Dominic's emotionless eyes had left her, and he was now staring fixedly at her husband.

Behind her, Carlo muttered, "He stays."

"But why?"

"Little idiot! Do you care nothing for our unborn child?" he bit out, gesturing toward the swell at her waist. "If I don't fuck you tonight, it will die where it lies within you!"

Scandalized by his crude, hurtful words, she was slow to take in their precise meaning.

"Lust is a vital part of my makeup," he went on, slamming a fist to his chest. "Fucking has been like breathing to me for all my adult life. Tonight I feel sick with the need to mate from dusk to daybreak. The fiendish cruelty of my condition is that though the ability to do so is gone, the drive remains."

Emma paled as the true horror of their situation finally dawned on her. "Do you mean to say you cannot function in that way? At *all*?"

"At last she comprehends!" He flung up his hands, bitter laughter erupting from him. "You know the ways of the Satyr. Children bred at Moonful must be birthed during the following one. A month's gestation. Our offspring must enter this world with tomorrow's sunrise. As the catalyst for a birthing, you must first experience the pleasures of tonight's Calling ritual. However, my cock is sadly incapable of entertaining you in the coming hours. Or ever again."

He palmed himself graphically, cupping and grinding his own genitals through his trousers as if he despised what they contained.

"But there must be some way," she protested, hugging her middle protectively. "That is, could we summon a physician? Or could we—?"

Carlo blasted toward her. She backed away from the fury in his face, but she understood the reason for it now. Grabbing her by the shoulders, he exerted his strength, pressuring her downward until she sank to the floor to kneel between his legs.

"Carlo! Our child! You must take care with me!" she cried, clutching for balance.

Hard fingers dove into her hair to hold her as his other hand wrenched open his trousers.

Lowering her eyes to the shrouded gap at the front of his trousers, she beheld the true extent of the injuries he'd unveiled. Though he hadn't loved her, his body had always been ready to couple with hers under a fully waxed moon. But no more. Now his manhood hung shrunken and defeated.

"Show me how we can make it work," he bit out. His tone was scathing, as though he despised her. "Take me in your mouth, wife. If you can get a rise out of me, I will gladly fuck you."

Emma heard Dominic take a step toward them and then check himself. Apparently he was reluctant to interfere in another man's way of dealing with his dashed dreams.

Her lashes fluttered lower, and shame rouged her cheeks. "Please. Not in front of him," she whispered.

"Do as I say," Carlo instructed. "As an obedient wife should."

"Very well," she agreed, unsure how else to defuse this situation other than to comply. Reaching out, she traced the angry, jagged slashes that diagonally dissected his pelvis to arrow low toward his groin. The surrounding skin was splotched with horrible yellow and purple bruises.

"I'm so sorry," she commiserated, brushing her fingertips over the abrasions.

"Then show me. Lend me comfort." His fingers tightened against her scalp, and she winced as he drew her head forward.

With a garbled sound of protest, she clawed at his offending hands. "Stop! You're hurting!"

A masculine thumb and forefinger dug into the hinges of her jaw, forcing her lips to open and prompting her to action. Only after she lifted his crown and took it and then the rest of him into her mouth did he release his remorseless grip.

It quickly became impossible not to distinguish the horrible difference. On the previous occasions she'd performed this service for him, the thrust of his rod had bruised her throat with its strength and size. But now . . .

She felt Dominic observing them and wanted to rail at him to turn away, but her husband's fuse was short, and she didn't dare release him long enough to do so.

Forcing saliva to pool in her mouth, she bathed Carlo's meager length, earnestly undertaking the challenge he'd set for her. Using the O of her lips, she suckled him strongly, drawing back and attempting to extend him in the way he'd taught her on their wedding night. But when she inadvertently loosened him, his shaft recoiled so unexpectedly that she lost it.

He sucked an angry breath through his teeth and quickly replaced himself in her mouth. Holding her cheeks in his hands, he rocked once, twice, thrice, moving his flaccid cock along her tongue.

She gripped the fabric of his trousers as her cheeks pumped to the lecherous rhythm he'd set. Stroking from his root to the ridge of his crown and back, she diligently tried to bring life to that which was dead.

Try as she might, he didn't stir.

Then came the touch of a foreign hand. The heat of a body— a masculine one looming behind her.

Dominic!

Shocked, she attempted to jerk away from her task. But his broad fingers gently wove through her hair on either side of her skull, easily holding her head and riding its back-and-forth movements as he watched her fellate another man. It was as if he'd been driven to participate with them in some small way, to soothe her with thumbs that stroked the tendons at her nape and hands that massaged in a sensuous caress.

"A dutiful wife, is she not?" Carlo's voice inquired from somewhere above her. "Alas, her ministrations are for naught."

Dominic spoke at last, his voice a low command. "It is you who should be readying her with your mouth." With a slow, lingering reluctance, his touch left her.

At his words, her husband stilled. Then, as though he found it impossible to disobey his companion, his touch on her fell away, too. "Yes. You're right, of course."

When he stepped back, his shriveled penis slipped from her mouth, flopping free to dangle uselessly at his groin. Frustration lent his hands unnecessary force as he shoved her from him and then yanked up his trousers and tucked himself inside.

Chestnut tresses cascaded over Emma's shoulders, trailing on the carpet as she fell awkwardly to her hands and knees. Carlo bent to help her, as though momentarily regretting his actions. But when she only glared up at him, he straightened away and simply finished adjusting his clothing.

Emma attempted to gather herself from the floor on her own, but with a full-term baby housed inside her, this proved impossible.

Strong hands came under her armpits, and she found herself lifted to her feet. Dominic again. Touching her when he had no right.

Whirling away as soon as she'd regained her balance, she pushed the curtain of hair from her face and wiped her lips with the back of one wrist. Embarrassed at what he'd been witness to and by his overly familiar behavior, she scanned his expression.

His face had taken on a grim quality, all planes and angles softened only by the shadowy beginnings of a blue-black evening stubble along his jaw. Those eyes had seen too much, knew too much. They were molten silver, pitiless and flat. She saw her own reflection in them, but nothing of him.

"You have no right to touch another man's wife, signore," she rebuked, angry and confused by the fact that Carlo hadn't bothered to chastise him.

Though his gaze was on her, it was her husband to whom he spoke. "Prepare her, Carlo. My time draws near."

6

With methodical precision, Dominic removed the weapon that hung at his side and positioned it on the mantel with the same care Emma had once seen a concert violinist employ in the handling of his instrument. Would he take such care with a woman? she wondered.

The wayward thought shocked her into speech.

"As you say, it grows late, signore. Why do you linger here?" she demanded, wary now not only of him but of her reaction to him.

His voice when it came was softness threaded with iron. "It is for your husband to explain."

Those long fingers of his found the top button on his uniform and purposefully unfastened it. She took a faltering backward step, her wide eyes riveted to that large, capable hand working at his open collar.

Her incredulous gaze shot up to tangle with his, and what she read there confirmed her shocking deduction. Finally Carlo's full intentions in bringing him here to her sank in.

"Carlo?" she gasped weakly, still unable to believe it could be true.

"Take off that damned robe and gown and let's get on with this." Carlo sighed. Though his tone was weary, the resolve in it shook her.

"No!" She folded the edges of her robe one atop the other, sealing the fabric so tightly at her throat she was nearly choked. Her eyes went to the door, but Dominic was watching her too keenly, and she knew he would prevent her from dashing through it, were she to try.

"Have you listened to nothing I've said?" Carlo asked, his voice full of misery. "I can't fuck you tonight. He can."

Going to him, she latched urgently on to his arm, giving it a hard shake. "No!"

"Yes, darling wife. My illustrious comrade here has graciously agreed to service you tonight in my stead. You shouldn't find him too onerous. His partners in ElseWorld are said to enjoy him."

She darted a mortified glance at Dominic. By now, all nine buttons had been released from their moorings. The vertical split in his tunic hung open to reveal a heavily muscled chest, its sculpted velvet skin crisscrossed with the long-healed scars of vicious wounds.

"Remove your nightclothes, Emma, or I'll do it for you," Carlo threatened. But she didn't hear. Her attention remained fixated on that shadowy, masculine chest. On its well-defined ridges, planes, and valleys. Her skin tingled with awareness of him, a stranger standing half a room away. Her fingernails dug half moons into her husband's skin.

When she didn't immediately comply with his wishes, Carlo turned angry. Ripping her hands away, he raised his arm as if to backhand her.

With a curt shriek, she ducked her head.

For a giant, Dominic moved quickly. Before the blow could fall, he'd blocked it.

Clasping a trembling hand over her lips, Emma eyed the door. Her view of it was framed in the gap between the two men who stood before her, and she watched for an opportunity to bolt past them. She'd never seen her husband so out of control, not even last month.

Carlo hesitated, searching Dominic's expression. Something he read there had him lowering his arm and coming to comfort her.

Taking both of her hands in his, he spoke earnestly. "We must take care to ensure that our child arrives into this world in good health, for I cannot sire another in you, Emma." His face contorted with emotion. "Give me this one gift, *cara*. I beg you. And make it a son."

"Have you sought medical aid outside of the military hospital?" she argued, gripping his sleeve. "Is there truly no source of help for you?"

He shook his head, hopeless. When he spoke again, his tone was leaden. "There's nothing to be done. Enjoy Dominic's fucking of you. It will be the last you'll have for the rest of your days."

For the briefest and longest of moments she stood motionless, quietly panicking as she read the immutable truth of this in his eyes. Instinct pulled her toward escape. She slid her hands from his and sidled along the foot of the bed, this time heading in the direction of the door that adjoined her room, instead of toward the one that led to the hall.

The sudden heat of Dominic's body at her back stopped her. Realizing her mistake, she tried to evade him. But fingers of iron grasped her upper arms, imprisoning her.

Though he still wore his tunic, it hung open now. Locked close, his sleek torso scorched her spine through her nightclothes.

She reached across herself, crumpling the cuff of his sleeve with imploring fingers. "Signore. Dominic. You must help us—"

"That's precisely why he's here," her husband jeered.

"On your knees, Carlo." She felt the words rumble in the chest behind her. Heard them expelled from lips bent close to her ear. "Prepare her with your mouth. Bring her to the edge of pleasure, that she might better accept me."

But for once, Carlo didn't leap to obey his idol. He only watched as, despite her opposition, Dominic easily drew lace and silk over her head and tossed her clothing to the floor.

Emma yelped in alarm and slapped a palm to cover the apex of her thighs. Wrapping a concealing forearm across her breasts, she punished Dominic's midriff with her elbow to try to force him away.

Heedless of her efforts, he snaked a viselike arm around her, securing it just below her own at her breasts. Though he manacled her to him, his embrace was that of elegant strength rather than the crude force her husband had employed.

Jerking his head to indicate the waning light at the window, Dominic again remonstrated with Carlo. "Daylight slips away! Ready your wife for me before it's too late!"

Carlo visibly shook himself from a torpor and then obediently bent to go down on one knee.

"And bring the cream."

At Dominic's low-voiced command, Carlo's face drained of color. His and Emma's eyes flew in tandem to the jar on the night table at the far side of the bed, both gazing at it in mesmerized horror. She had earlier placed it there herself, intending it for Carlo's use. But now it seemed another man would employ it.

A wounded snarl sprang from Emma's throat, and she renewed her struggles. Dominic grunted whenever a sharp elbow dented his stomach, but otherwise he ignored her. She felt him shrug the tunic from his shoulders and then rip it off with his free hand.

Her mind raced down one avenue and then another, anxiously seeking a more palatable solution to their situation. But no other viable option presented itself. She needed more time to think.

Without a word, Carlo secured the jar of cream, opened it, and set it upon a side table, which he brought within Dominic's reach. Knowing exactly what would be required once they began, her husband moved the dish of oil and one of the basins closer as well. Then he came to stand before her at the foot of the bed.

Emma twisted her fingers in the collar of Carlo's tunic, and her frantic eyes tried to catch his. "Summon Jane. And your brothers," she begged. "Ask them for help. Ask them if there's another way."

Averting his gaze, Carlo carefully detached himself from her grip. "No."

"They won't think less of you because you can't perform," she argued, accurately gauging the basis for his refusal. "Your injuries aren't your fault. Nor are they any cause for shame."

Dominic's warm breath stirred the hair at her nape as he spoke. "Do you really think the members of your family will welcome an interruption? Now? Have you forgotten they will be engaged in the same Moonful rituals as we are soon to be?"

He was right. She knew he was, yet—

The wool of his trousers rasped as his thigh split her softer ones, sending a rush of vulnerability through her. Boldly it moved ever higher between hers until her naked, gaping flesh rode the seductive rub of its long–muscled strength. She moaned, helpless under a first, unanticipated brush of pleasure.

Carlo sank to his knees in front of her in much the same way she had earlier knelt before him. His hand ran upward along the length of Dominic's thigh, which retreated to make way for him.

Catching her knees when she made a futile attempt to close them, Carlo held them wide. His thumbs parted her pursed slit, and he leaned close until his hair tickled the underside of her belly. "Resign yourself, Emma. Another course of action could prove disastrous."

His tongue flicked out. She jerked at its first lash, then drew an unsteady breath as it stroked the length of her opening. Once. Twice. And then on its third pass, it snaked inside her and out again, and then again as quickly, mimicking the thrust of a male organ.

He'd only performed this service for her once before, on the evening of their marriage. She'd found it interesting. But it had been a brief exercise between them then, a mere tantalization too quickly withdrawn.

Now his lips and tongue worked their wiles on her far more intently and with obvious skill. Where he had honed such skill, she couldn't help but wonder. He seemed determined to woo her body into submission, but she had a niggling suspicion that his performance was for some reason intended more to impress his comrade than to please her.

Though her channel dutifully moistened, her churning thoughts kept true pleasure at bay. For the moment, it was easy to deny any further stirrings of it.

She felt Dominic's stillness, his keen awareness that another man was working between her legs, servicing her with his mouth. His grip on her arms tensed, and she sensed his covetous desire. Somehow she knew he was imagining himself acting in her husband's stead. Knew she would soon be handed over to him to do just that.

Warm, unfamiliar lips touched the column of her throat and traced it downward, pausing to savor the angled nook where throat eased into shoulder. Lightly he suckled her skin, mimicking Carlo's attentions to her elsewhere. She shifted, stiffening when the soft skin of her bottom encountered the masculine thatch at Dominic's groin. And something else. Something thick and hard that prodded her hip.

He'd unfastened his trousers! This somehow made the ultimate goal of this entire engagement suddenly seem far more shockingly possible.

Gasping, she pulled away and glanced at him, putting a hand over the place on her neck that he'd just marked with his mouth. His head lifted, and silver tangled with brown. Thick, charcoal lashes lowered to half mast as he read the new awareness in her gaze.

Something simmered deep within this man, she realized. Something evil that warred with the good in him.

Her eyes fell to his lips, saw they were wet. The place they'd kissed was wet as well and cool in the night air.

"Please. Summon my family. Or a physician from Florence," she entreated. "I'm Human. Perhaps my child can be born in the usual way of Human children."

Warm, silken breath drifted over her cheek, but Dominic's tone when he spoke was stark and implacable. "Your child bears the blood of the Satyr and must therefore be born by means of the ancient ritual. In the hours that lie ahead, I will service you in your husband's stead. But only so your body can perform the function of giving birth come dawn. Carlo will remain with us throughout the night. If it comforts you, imagine I am he when I come into you—"

His words were abruptly severed as his entire body ripped taut. Ridged abdominal muscles contracted and clenched against her spine, hardening to iron. The arm that manacled her ribs tightened, stealing her breath.

She and Carlo both stilled as a bolt of recognition struck them.

Dominic was beginning to undergo the Change.

Behind her, he bit out a low, gravelled groan that was a blend of both joy and suffering. Then, with a rough, animal snarl, he shoved his trousers lower to sag and bunch haphazardly over the tops of his black boots. He fought the fabric's restraint for a few seconds and then kicked them off.

He was fully naked now except for those boots. A light coat of faun-colored fur was sprouting on his haunches, tickling her bottom and the back of her thighs. It was one of the first of the changes that would come over him on this sacred night.

Unable to help herself, she twisted, peering downward between them. Her breath hitched at the daunting sight that met her eyes. His prick was enormous! Straining high and eager from the coarse, tangled nest at his groin, it was easily as thick as her wrist and as almost as long as her forearm.

She swallowed audibly and looked toward the window as panic rose to a boil within her. The moon had not yet shown itself. But soon.

With its appearance would come another more profound change. One that would gift this untamed male animal with a second rod that was twin to this one. Then he would open her with them and slide those shafts as deep inside her as it was possible for a man to go.

And then he would give her his seed.

It seemed impossible that he would fit. Yet already, high in the waiting aperture between her legs, her tissues were moistening, beginning to ready for him, yearn for him. A long, low growl emanated from his throat as if he knew.

His handling of her changed subtly, becoming more purposeful. His hands were more possessive now and sensuous as his body realigned itself with hers, pressing her right shoulder into the cushioned bone of his pectoral muscle. The plush globes of her buttocks gave against the rock of his thigh.

And all the while, his breath came in steady, deep draughts. Those beautiful lips nuzzled her shoulder, her nape, and her throat. He was locking on her scent. Marking her with his.

Soon, very soon, he would lose his grip on the power of higher reasoning. The primal need percolating in his veins would begin to dictate his every action. Once completely in the throes of the Calling, he would kill in order to mate with her. Not Carlo— not even the Satyr lords themselves—would be able to stop him then. Not without killing him.

Carlo's tongue found her again, more voluptuous in its duties now, as if Dominic's altered physical state had excited him. She glanced toward her husband where he still worked between her thighs. Unlike his friend, he didn't grimace and groan. His cheekbones weren't flushed with desire.

It was true then. There could be no question. Carlo remained unaffected by the moon's pull. He wasn't going to experience the Change.

If she didn't accept this other man—this stranger—into her body tonight, her son or daughter wouldn't emerge at sunrise. It would die inside her, unborn.

Carlo's need to prove himself in ElseWorld's war had exacted far too terrible a price. She felt angry at his sacrifice. And a trifle guilty. For she'd long suspected that the only reason he'd retreated to that other world had been to escape her. To escape the burden of her need for a love he didn't feel for her.

Was this one night too much of a sacrifice for her to make in return so their child could live? So he could become a father and she a mother?

This reasoning calmed her as nothing had before, and she gave in to the inevitable necessity of what must happen in the hours ahead. A naked male stranger was embracing her. Planning to copulate with her. Her husband condoned this. And she would allow it. For tonight. For her child.

Once her struggles ebbed, it became impossible to ignore the potent stimulation her two lovers were providing.

Under Carlo's attention, her feminine flesh had plumped and swollen with the heated rush of lustful blood. Her splayed thighs trembled now, and her hips swayed languidly back and forth, aiding his tongue in its stroke. Her channel had become a slick void, ready to welcome him inside, if only he could oblige.

From the corner of her eye, she saw a masculine hand reach out. Dominic's. Transfixed, she watched him scoop a dollop of cream from the jar on the table.

The muscles of his left arm shifted along her back. She jerked when blunt fingers came between her rear cheeks, daubing her pruney ring with cool cream. Gently he began oiling it.

For a while, his heavy cock set the pace of their ménage, rocking at her hip in time to the languorous stroke it required. Her slit and Carlo's mouth could only haplessly dance to his tune, which determined how often and how deeply the lips of a wife and a husband would marry.

She tried to disassociate her mind from what was happening. To shut out the slick smacking sounds of fingers and tongues and mouths as the two men attended to her.

Dominic's right hand covered her breast, surprising her into overlaying his with her own.

Her free hand fell to the top of Carlo's head, and for a moment, her palms connected her to both men. Absently she smoothed a lock of her husband's fine hair and watched it flop back into place. She no longer loved him, and it was impossible for her to fully understand his physical loss, but she felt regret for the grief it caused him.

The fingers at her breast drew outward to pluck and twist at her sensitive nipple, sending a prurient thrill over her. Dominic's touch on her there almost seemed to hum, alive with some strange, stimulating force. Sparks arrowed directly from this distended peak to throb at the nubbed stem of flesh Carlo now worshipped. An erotic pulse, stronger than any she'd ever felt before, reverberated outward from it along her slit.

It squeezed. Once. Hard.

No! Surely, she wasn't going to embarrass herself in *that* way. Surely she wouldn't attain fulfillment standing here in the middle of the room, where her features would be revealed to anyone who cared to look when *it* happened.

Embarrassed, she pushed Carlo away. And immediately she wished him back. Wished for a finish to the wildfire passion he and Dominic had lit in her. She stroked his hair again, trying to induce him closer without the use of words.

But her husband only pressed his cheek to the sloping underside of her rounded midriff, kissing her there with masculine lips still rouged by her own feminine juices.

Dominic's mischievous palm at her breast began to rove. Like a dark cloud, it stroked stealthily down the landscape of her body, along her breastbone, between ribs, and over her gently rounded belly. There, his strong fingers spread wide, shaping the mound of her child as though he was staking a claim.

Carlo's head yanked back, startled. Off balance, he tottered back on his heels and gaped at the possessive hand that had forced his lips away.

Emma saw how it crushed him to see another man usurp his rights to her, his wife. How, then, was he going to bear watching his friend mate with her throughout the long hours that stretched ahead?

Her husband's eyes rose to hers, and he saw the pity there. He looked beyond her to search Dominic's face, and whatever he read there distorted his features with agony.

Without warning, Dominic's creamy finger prodded the prudish, tight ring of muscle along her rear cleft. It invaded, going deep.

A cry that was a confusion of shock and raw need welled from the depths of her soul. Hurt tinged the pain in Carlo's face, an emotion that quickly flamed into jealous anger.

"What did you expect?" she whispered. Had he intended her to endure his friend's touch, yet somehow inure herself to the pleasure of it?

A second finger joined the first, stretching her. The fans of her lashes drooped to half veil her eyes as her chin lifted on a moan.

With jerky, uncoordinated movements, Carlo stood and began backing away.

"Wait," Emma croaked. She reached her hand toward him, but he ignored it and continued making his way toward the door, his eyes glued to Dominic.

Oblivious to the drama being played out, Dominic nuzzled her nape, shifting her hair aside to make way for the graze of lips and white teeth. The clever fingers at her backside left her, and she heard a splash. He'd plunged that hand in the crystal waters of the basin she'd readied earlier for cleansing.

Abruptly the first strands of moonlight came then, lancing through the window glass to bathe them all in its silver.

Dominic raised his face toward the sacred light, glorying in its cool caress. Along Emma's back, the muscles of his abdomen rippled and yanked taut. A terse, strangled shout broke from him.

Carlo halted, transfixed by the sight of her and Dominic's naked bodies locked in an erotic embrace. He watched with obvious envy as his friend hunched over her, his massive frame cruelly seized by the brutal cramping that heralded the last physical effects of the Calling.

Dominic clutched her to him, and her body bowed willingly within the cavern of his. Ravaged by the onslaught of this new primal pleasure-pain, his lungs sawed with ragged breath. Held this close, she felt the final Change come over him with a zinging sweep of ElseWorld magic.

When he slowly uncoiled behind her, the transformation in him was palpable. His skin was hotter now, his body harder, his demeanor more passionate and determined.

But the greatest difference could be felt pressed high along the hollow of her back. For instead of one male shaft extending from him, there were now two.

There was nothing subtle in the way he handled her now. Nothing subtle in the way his twin cocks angled high, twitching and straining for a taste of her. He was readying for rut. Within minutes, he would make her his.

Carlo stumbled awkwardly backward, tripping over the footstool and then knocking into the dressing table.

His attention riveted on Emma, Dominic didn't acknowledge the disturbance in any way.

Fumbling behind himself, Carlo blindly gathered his belongings from the table where he'd set them. The clink of coins came, and the whoosh of the drape falling from the mirror. The creak of the doorknob. Emma's fingers dug into the muscles of Dominic's arm, trying to dislodge him. Trying to reach the dubious haven that was her husband.

"No! Don't leave us!" she pleaded, realizing he was about to go.

A calloused male hand rose to her breast again, covering it. The pad of a thumb brushed her nipple. She moaned, helpless to deny the pleasure it wrought in her.

Across the room, Carlo's face contorted with despair. His throat worked soundlessly, and he shook his head.

"I'm sorry. I can't."

With that, he swung around and fled, slamming the door behind him.

7

Emma froze in horrified disbelief.

Dominic had promised Carlo would stay. That had been the plan. But in the end it seemed her husband hadn't been willing to watch another man join himself to her, even one he himself had chosen.

Instead he'd deserted her when she needed him more desperately than she'd ever needed anyone before. Instead he had acted the coward and had left her to be mated in solitude by a fellow warrior—a virtual stranger to her—until sunrise.

She heard a dragging sound. Dominic had hooked the tip of his boot under the footstool and yanked it closer to where they stood at the foot of Carlo's bed. As he moved, his groin was briefly reflected in the mirror, and she saw his second shaft—a vestige of his ancient Satyr heritage—which had erupted from his pelvis, just above the original cock that speared from his thatch. Both were corpulent and painted a feverish red, with networks of gnarled, dilated veins rooted along lengths that were crowned with shiny-smooth mushroom caps.

Fresh panic sizzled through her. At the first sign of Moonful, Carlo's body had always changed in this way, too. Before. But he hadn't been this robust in size.

A furred leg intruded between her thighs. Lifting her left knee with his, Dominic swung it wide, planting his booted foot on the low stool to his left. Her thigh rode atop his now, her bare foot dangling alongside his outer calf.

In the mirror, she watched his hand round the side of her belly to thread lower through her nest of curls. Forking his two longest fingers, he parted and pulled back plump, flushed, fleshy outer lips to reveal ruffled inner lips of a much darker rose color. With the fingers of one hand he stretched the outer lips wide, causing her inner petals to bloom until cool air found her core.

She'd never seen herself like this, yet she could not look away. It was obscene. Shocking. Titillating. Carlo had left her wet, florid, and gaping. Ready for the use of this man.

She glanced up to the mirror, saw he was staring at her there, his face raw and hungry. She grabbed his arm convulsively with both hands. Not in an attempt to stop what he would do, but rather from a need to feel that she exerted some measure of control over it.

"Not yet," she whispered. "You must find someone to go after Carlo. In his drunkenness, he might wander too far. It's imperative that he be here with us, especially toward the end of things."

But Dominic only dipped slightly, sending his larger, lower cock pushing between her legs from behind to plow its length along her furrow. There was no indication he'd even heard. Perhaps he hadn't. During the Calling, Satyr men sought fornication with an unswerving single-minded concentration. The beast within him had taken over. The Human in him was for the moment beyond reach. And she was alone with him, bound to him. At his mercy until morning.

Emma sucked in a quick, suspended breath when his smooth crown paused, finding the opening it sought. His damp fingers caught the fat knob, quickly basted it in her juices, and then impelled its slippery smoothness inward.

She watched her inner lips part for it, bestowing upon it a small, moist kiss that was summarily stretched into a gasping, stunned, perfect O. As he worked himself into her, the fleshy part of his hand at the base of his thumb rubbed at the knot of her sex, making it swell and throb. She began to feel faint and realized she'd forgotten to breathe.

Without ceasing this work, his left hand came at her back, leading his other cock along the crease between the plush rounds of her bottom to find the puckered star of her anus. Though he'd oiled her well in preparation for this, his size was shocking, and a harsh puff of air left her at the quick bite of his piercing.

Both of her entrances were dilated uncomfortably wide as they swallowed his crowns—the greatest of his girths. And then her openings were closing around him to hug his plinths. She was given little time to adjust, for without pause, his iron lengths tunneled smoothly onward, opening her throats like clenched, erotic fists gloved in sleek satin.

Emma bumped the back of her arm against the male ribs behind her. "Wait," she said as she began to fear he might not fit inside her. "I'm not sure. . . . You're so . . ."

Dominic only grunted in response, a rough, lecherous, male sound. The musk of heated pheromones filled her nostrils as his corpulent, avid cocks plumbed her in a series of ever-deeper lunges and retreats.

She clutched the bedpost, a maelstrom of pleasure and worry hammering at her ribs as the invasive fullness increased dramatically with each flex of his hips. Reaching for calm, she consoled herself with the knowledge that it was impossible for this joining to harm her. The Satyr possessed the ability to cause any female body to conform to their dual dimensions during copulation. Jane had explained this fact to her upon her engagement to Carlo, and her wedding night with him had confirmed the truth of it.

Nevertheless, for just a moment, hysteria battled reason. Perhaps a full Satyr could not be safely mated to a full Human. Had anyone ever tested it? Though she knew her tension would only make things more difficult, panic made her tighten against him.

Oblivious to her mounting concern, Dominic had begun to murmur his appreciation of her body's acceptance of his, speaking a mix of Latin, Italian, and other more unfamiliar languages. Though she often couldn't understand their meaning, the dark, salacious tenor of his words began to affect her like a warm, stimulating aphrodisiac.

The hot fire of an earlier lust spiraled from embers and sparked back to life in her. And then her cry was mingling with his triumphant growl as he finally slid home, going impossibly, incredibly deep in a . . . Long. Last. Velvet. Glide.

"Gods, Emma . . . Gods." The words were an exhalation, a joyful benediction that sent a shiver of arousal through her. He kicked the stool away, and his arms crossed over her, hugging her to him with a breast reverently cupped in each hand as though savoring the completeness of their cleaving. The sun-warmed rock that was his body surrounded her with unyielding muscle, and his thatch gently cushioned the cheeks of her bottom. He was inside her, as deep as a man could go.

"So full," she whispered, turning her face into his throat. Lips brushed her hair, and then his hands were roving again, exploring the silky terrain of her body, shaping throat, shoulder, breast, rib, belly. With shaking fingers, she tugged the fall of her hair from where it fell between them and brought it over one shoulder to drape her chest. His stroking hands took hers under them, twining their fingers so the silky strands caught among them. Then he taught them to polish the gentle abrasion of her tresses over her nipples, and over and over, until they blushed taut.

A slow retreat began, suctioning both cocks from her. They returned again in a forceful lunge that had her gasping and going on tiptoe. Hands grasped her hips, anchoring her. And then a second retreat and return and a third. . . .

Falteringly at first, and then more surely, her body began to anticipate the actions of his and to sway with his rhythm. Her channels adjusted and conformed to his overwhelming size. She relaxed into him, beginning to tolerate—even to encourage him.

At her ear, Dominic waxed on in a blend of guttural languages, telling her how much she pleased him. "It's good. Fuck. Tight."

Time passed—she knew not how much. Their groans entwined, spicing the air. At her back he was solid and dominating, pumping into her with long, sultry drags. Every fiber of his being seemed focused on her, around her, in her.

That ruthless mouth of his rasped the sensitive skin of her nape, behind her ear, down the slope of her throat. And still he spoke to her, using words she couldn't comprehend, uttered in desperate, needy tones she easily deciphered and echoed.

Her head lolled on the cushion of his shoulder, and her hand caressed his beautiful, scarred, masculine jaw. "Yes," she whispered. "Yes."

The fingers of his gloved hand found the flushed, hardened knot of her sex, setting off more of those odd, warm sparks. Under his leathery stroke, her clit gave a violent wrench. Her knees buckled.

Crumpling forward at the waist, she braced both forearms on the mattress before her. Strong hands came at her hips, supporting her weight and protecting her child as he stood behind her, never pausing in his unrelenting rut.

And she let him do it. Wanted it. Craved it. Spread her legs and offered her ass up, begging for it. Her breath and his came in harsh mutual expulsions as she yielded to his every visit. Her bottom met each rigorous impalement with an eager shudder of welcome. Her passages embraced him, bathed his shafts with frothy, passionate cream and jealously clung to them when they tried to go.

With each withdrawal and thrust, her breasts were dragged

across the mattress in a back-and-forth motion that teased at already tender nipples. It was as if she were a wave and he the ocean tide, dashing her upon the shore only to tug her back and dash her again in an unceasing, erotic rhythm.

Forgotten was the fact that this was meant only to be a ritual that would prepare her body for a birthing. Forgotten were the reasons she was allowing someone other than her husband to mate himself to her.

Her world had shrunk to this one room. To this one glorious male. The entire purpose of her being had crystallized into a single, ardent goal—the quenching of this incredible fever that burned within her.

Then he deliberately withdrew any hope that she might achieve the decadent pleasure she desperately sought, pulling his pricks so far from her that she almost lost him.

"No!" she protested. Her bottom tilted up, seeking, yearning for another visit. He seized her hips, holding her away. Her empty passages were desolate vessels crying for want of him. Her hands reached back and gripped the bunched, heated muscles of his thighs, trying to woo him closer.

But still, his crowns only teased at her entrances, parting her mouths but not fucking them.

"Oh, please . . . *please*," she whimpered softly, agonized by her fervent need for a finish. "Please, Dominic."

At the sound of his name on her tongue, a primitive growl was wrung from him. He rammed deep, so deep inside her that his cock slit pressed an open-mouthed kiss upon the lips of her womb. He fell over her, bracing himself on one forearm and cradling her weight with another arm wrapped low under her belly, careful of her child even in this.

Where his roots stretched her rings, she felt the hard pulse of the thick, veinlike duct that speared each of the undersides. He went completely rigid, every muscle straining as he tautened toward . . .

A harsh, ragged groan came at her ear, an erotic sound low in his throat as hot semen blasted from him. Another pulse came, and with it another more ragged groan and another vigorous spurt of cum. And another, flooding her tissues with his intoxicating passion.

Her hands mangled the bed linens, and her eyes squeezed tight as she sought to find what he had found, sensing it was close. He reached between them and found her defenseless clit, pressing it against his slick rod and rubbing at it with a few curt strokes. The swollen nub twisted, jerking with sparks of sensation.

With a startled cry, she exploded, tumbling with him into the hedonistic ecstasy of orgasm.

Yes! At last! This was what she'd longed for. What her sister regularly enjoyed with Nicholas. The sort of pure, flawless pleasure Jordan found with Raine, and Juliette with Lyon.

Dominic's breath heaved in his lungs in time with hers, and his beautiful, scarred body scalded her back as they swayed to the rhythm of his coming. His balls drew up against her bottom, clenching with each gift of seed and then releasing, only to clench again with the next. Long moments passed, and still her nether throats demanded his cum, milked and sucked it from him in fierce, molten bursts.

And all the while, she prayed this exquisite stretch of time would never end.

But eventually their gasps of exertion slowed and then ceased to stir the silence that fell between them. In the aftermath, Emma drooped, cradling her abdomen with one arm and resting her forehead on her opposite wrist.

She made a desultory protest as Dominic's lesser cock slid from her rear with a squishy, muted pop. Behind her, she felt it retract into the haven of his pelvis. As it was with all the Satyr, this cock which had arrived with the coming of the moon had now been satisfied with the single taking of her it had just accomplished. Having disappeared inside him, it would not hunger again until next Moonful.

His remaining penis still sojourned within the cradle of her feminine passage, thick and heavy and drowned in their mingled cream. Without speaking, he leisurely dislodged from her. At his departure, a thin, viscous trickle of cum trailed along her inner thigh.

His fingers caught it and followed it upward between her legs, finding her gaping, ruffled slit and glossing it with the amalgam of their sluice. His touch ignited echoes of her recent climax, sending them spiraling through her again. Two fingers slipped inside and gently sawed her as if he wanted to feel where he'd been, wanted to feel her coming. She moaned softly against her wrist and pressed her thighs together, holding him, savoring it.

When her pulsing faded, the hand slipped away, and the bed sank as he sat next to her. She heard him remove his boots and then the thud of them hitting the floor.

Her channel still hummed with giddy pleasure. Having sampled what he could provide, it craved more of the same. She'd attained fulfillment through copulation before—twice, to be exact. But this, with him, had been an entirely foreign and delightful experience. The kind of soul-deep completion she had quietly yearned for yet never found with . . .

Carlo! She'd completely forgotten him. She pushed to her elbows and then her hands, combing trembling fingers through her hair and scrambling to reign in her roiling emotions. It was only the effects of the Calling, she reassured herself. Her body had reveled in the necessity of this joining, but her mind had not. She didn't even know this man!

Yet when he half lay beside her and turned her to lie on her back, her heart melted just a bit at the sight of him. Ruddy color now suffused his cheekbones, and a shadow of coal-black bristle dusted his strong jaw. Silver glinted from beneath lowered lashes as he gazed at her belly with brooding intensity.

His palm covered her there, gently burnishing over her skin and exploring her rounded shape. A subtle, almost tender expression stole across his face. The thought struck her that he was somehow attempting to communicate with her child, but she swept this aside as silly.

The texture of his hand was different than it should be, she realized. For some reason, at some point, he'd donned a glove! Only one, on this—his right hand. She brushed the back of it with her fingers, curious.

He stilled at her touch, but the glove itself vibrated slightly in reaction, shooting tiny pinpricks of sensation frissoning over her flesh. Startled, she pushed it away.

His face turned to stone, and he stood, stepping close so his thighs divided hers. Between them his cock speared the air, shiny and fat. If anything, it seemed even more enormous than before, in spite of the satisfaction engendered by their prior coupling. Gloved fingers wrapped themselves high around his shaft, near his crown.

Nervous, she eased higher on the bed. A hand planted itself by her shoulder, among the bed sheets, bracing his body as it loomed over hers. Her palms came up to his ribs, and her eyes shot up to his, saw he'd been watching her face. She felt him tilt the angle of his cock lower. Felt him find her opening. And push.

She pressed her knees into his sides, stalling him. "Carlo . . ."

She'd meant the word as a wedge—a reminder that she was not his and he was not hers. An incantation she hoped would keep either of them from wanting this more than they ought.

For a split second, he hovered there, the muscles of his torso shifting subtly with his breath as he surveyed her. Then, in one arrogant motion, he plunged until bone met bone and his thatch meshed with hers. Slowly and deliberately, he withdrew and then thrust again, just as deep.

Below jutting brows, silver gleamed from coal-black sockets

as he watched their bodies join and release, only to join again. His hand slid up the underside of her thigh to lift her knee high and render her open to the onslaught that commenced as he began to work himself in her with a diligence that sought to overwhelm her senses.

Tendons strained along the strong, thick column of his neck, and muscles knotted and flexed in his arms and shoulders. Flat, taut nipples marked the bronze landscape of his chest, its smoothness marred here and there by battle scars long healed, each one a testament to the dangers he faced in his world. Moonlight played over him, rendering his features pagan and stark. Suddenly she couldn't recall why she'd ever thought him less than handsome.

Her gaze went to his lips. He was speaking again in that mesmerizing voice of his. In that language she couldn't understand. Nicholas and the others could bespell the unsuspecting with their voices when they so chose. Did this man have a similar ability?

The hand at her knee came under her bottom, tilting her to an angle that better suited him—and her, for every movement now dragged his cock against her clit. Within seconds, her passion reignited, intensified. Her breath caught as orgasm began to gather, slow and sweet this time. . . .

Hours later, Dominic lay among the covers, watching her, his legs open, and one slightly drawn up. Sitting next to him, Emma worked briskly, running a damp cloth over his manhood and then rinsing it in one of the bowls of clear, tepid water she'd provided at the bedside. Water she had poured earlier that night when she believed it would be Carlo she'd be cleansing in this way.

Leaving him, she went to wring out the cloth at the basin on the washstand and rinse her own hands. From the corner of her eye, she noticed her gown and robe lying in a heap of silk on the carpet. Shame drifted over her like a transparent garment, the only one she currently wore.

What would the family think if they could see her now? Would they think less of her if they ever found out what she'd done tonight? No, she couldn't bear that. They must never know.

Her hands curved over her abdomen. Was the coupling they'd already done sufficient to initiate the Birthing, come sunrise?

She'd need Carlo with her then, at least for the ritual that would follow. Would he return with the morning light? Should she seek him out? Her troubled thoughts went to him, carrying her away.

"Emma."

Surprised to hear her name, she glanced Dominic's way. Though she hadn't heard him move, he was beside her, strong and masculine.

He held out his gloved hand, and she stared at it, wary. As if surprised to realize that he'd offered that hand, he lowered it and offered his ungloved one instead.

"Come."

He'd already taken her repeatedly, seeming to know precisely where and how to touch her for maximum stimulation in order to reawaken a desire that might otherwise have dwindled over three hours of lovemaking. The seeker, a physical vestige of his Satyr heritage, had tended her intermittently as time went on, healing abraded tissues and seeing to her comfort.

"Perhaps what we've done is enough," she murmured. "A continuation might be unwise. For both of us."

Frowning, he jerked his chin toward the window, indicating the luminous moon that still hung there, unhurriedly making its way across an inky sky.

It would be hours until dawn. Hours before Dominic's passion was slaked. Hours during which he'd fill her time and time again. Give her pleasure unlike any she'd ever known or would likely know again once he left.

Emma placed her hand in his.

And tried to pretend to herself that she wasn't relishing the prospect of what lay ahead.

8

As the first gauzy hint of sunrise filtered through the window glass, Dominic's lust drained away, and he slowly withdrew from Emma and her bed. Lying amid a tangle of bedcovers, she watched an eerie change come over him, visibly transforming him from lusty Satyr to hardened warrior.

Muscles and tendons flexed as he stretched mightily. With both arms overhead, he stood in the center of the room, surveying his surroundings almost as if he were coming out of a trance. In the first blush of morning sunlight, he looked strong and splendid, like some golden god. His body was scarred but still ruggedly handsome. Many women would welcome him in their beds.

How had Carlo convinced him to come here to couple with her? she couldn't help wondering. She was without ElseWorld talent, without any special beauty or impressive ancestry. He couldn't have wanted her. Probably pitied her, in fact.

Two lonely tears of humiliation welled at the thought. They slid unnoticed down her temples, losing themselves in her hair.

Studying her, his brow knit, and he ran a hand over his face as though he was attempting to comprehend his situation. She shuddered to imagine how she must look, with her wild hair and weary face. Satyr males were energized by the Calling ritual. Not so, their mates.

Denied his warmth, her skin prickled under the early spring morning chill. She shivered, rubbing her arms. Seeing this, he gathered her gown and robe from where they had fallen to the floor. He stared at them a moment, remembering.

Then he held them out to her, assisting when he saw she was struggling to sit upright. Gratefully she sat up and took the nightclothes and then stood with her back to him, slipping them on.

"Where's your husband?"

Emma's gaze ricocheted off his. "He left us."

"When?"

"Last night."

"I see." His eyes traveled over her. Then, "Are you . . . Is everything . . . ?"

"Yes." She nodded quickly, unwilling to discuss what had passed between them.

He sighed. One hand rubbed across his chest, drawing her attention to the glove, the only clothing he wore. Mere hours ago, she would have been shocked to stand here in this bedchamber, with him naked and her nearly so. But last night had forever changed things between them.

She gestured toward the glove, as much to change the subject as to elicit a reply. "Why do you wear that?"

An odd tension swept him. His lips parted, but then he frowned, and his gaze dropped to her belly.

"It's time," he announced ominously. Coming to her side, he took her upper arm, holding her. His other hand—the gloved one—cupped her abdomen.

Surprised, she covered it with both of hers and felt the now familiar, sparking warmth his palm imparted.

"The child comes."

Her eyes shot to his. "Wh—?"

Savage pain knifed through her, and with its coming, all else was forgotten. Grimacing, she cried out and groped for support. He was there for her, strong and solid.

Terrible cramps hit anew, tightening her belly in their fiendish grip. Her skin went pallid, and her breath came in pants.

"Damnation. Where is Carlo?"

"Do you think I know?" She gave him a weak push. "Go. Have someone find him. We'll need him soon." Her voice trailed off, becoming a keening wail as agony struck yet again.

But he only lifted her into his arms as though she and her unborn child weighed no more than his boots. "There's no time."

She wrapped her arms around his neck, trying to absorb his strength. "Have you assisted in a Birthing before?"

"Yes."

She scanned his expression, silently questioning.

"A man is called to many duties in time of war."

Setting her on the bed, he shoved the pillows together at its head in one sweeping motion and settled her against them. Then he lay beside her with an arm beneath her shoulders.

"How much do you know of what will happen?" his voice asked close to her ear.

"Jane said there would be pain but that it would not prove as prolonged as that which women in this world endure when bearing a child that is solely Human." She gasped as another robust contraction shimmied over her abdomen.

"I'm here," he reassured. "And your sister did not lie. All of this will be over in less than an hour."

In truth, as matters got underway, her discomfort actually seemed to lessen rather than increase. Still, Emma clung to Dominic through each bout of it, grateful for his comforting words and his physical support. Just when she thought she would scream with the desperate need to dispel the fullness that was her unborn child, the birthing of it finally began.

At another time, she would have been too embarrassed to accept his assistance as her body performed this raw, primitive function. This was woman's work that left Emma helpless and exposed as nothing else could. But he'd been on her and in her for nearly eight hours last night. She smelled of him and he of her. She had nothing left to hide. Not from him.

As time passed, his alert eyes watched her every twitch. Capable hands stroked her hair and soothed the spasms from her lower back. And in the final moments, they came between her legs, bringing her child into the world.

9

"A girl!" Dominic stared at the newborn in his arms, stunned.

"Healthy?" Emma croaked tiredly.

Hardly knowing what he did, he set the child on toweling and began to wash her with fresh water that sat waiting for this purpose.

This tiny female was the Chosen One? Protector of his people? There had never been a female demonhand in all of recorded history.

"Dominic! Is something wrong?"

Finally noticing the fear in her voice, he held the squirming infant high to show her. She had managed the Birthing in less than half an hour and had seen it through bravely. "She's perfect. You've done well."

"Bring her to me," Emma insisted, obviously not believing him.

"A moment longer." He bustled around, his thoughts racing as he competently bathed the child. Until her palm turned silver, there was no way to know if she actually was a Chosen One. Yet the Facilitators had never before been mistaken in these matters. And in his soul he knew there could be little doubt. He gazed into the child's innocent face and wished it were otherwise.

A short while later, he was patting her dry. Then he delivered her into Emma's arms and returned to the basins to hastily wash himself.

Mother and child studied one another solemnly, and then Emma smiled and brushed a fingertip over a soft cheek.

"Gray eyes. Where did you get those, daughter?" she asked drowsily. Her tone and expression were loving and maternal. Fascinated, Dominic tried to commit the look of her, now, at this moment, to memory.

Heretofore, he'd passed every Calling night of his life in the temple, where the effects on his mental faculties were deliberately dulled by an aura of magic that had been woven in ancient times and was still kept intact by those who prayed and dwelled there. Last night had been a thrilling, dangerous exception. He'd lost control of his wits and been at the mercy of his physical desires. What was it about this world—about this woman— that had held him in such thrall?

"You're pleased with her?" he heard himself ask as he took cloth and basin to the bed to cleanse her as well.

"Mmmhmm," she said, her attention all for the bundle in her arms.

Once he'd finished washing her, Dominic glanced toward the window. Night's silver light had given way to the golden light of day. The sun was rising, quickly bathing the landscape. It was time for the Bonding, the sacred ritual that would bind the child with its parents—with its mother and its father. He was neither.

Carlo must know his family needed him now. Where was

he? Out there somewhere, sulking or asleep in a drunken fog? Regardless there was no way to locate him in time. He squared his shoulders to do what must be done.

Carlo's bed was a shambles by now. He went to the door that adjoined this room to another like it. The bedchamber beyond was done in pale colors of yellow and sage.

He cocked his head toward the feminine room. "Yours?" he asked.

Emma's sleepy gaze followed his, and she gave a single, almost imperceptible nod, as if her head were too heavy to move a second time.

But she frowned as he hoisted her and the child as one into his arms, heading for her chamber. "No, Dominic, where are you going? We mustn't."

Standing in the doorway that connected the rooms, he gritted, "Carlo isn't here. Shall I leave you to the Bonding on your own?"

When she made no reply, he let her feet slide to the floor. Her legs were wobbly, and she stood in the circle of his arms, holding her precious bundle and looking forlorn. She could barely stand. Yet he stepped away from her, cruel, leaving her to try.

Almost immediately she slumped forward, her child cradled between them against his chest.

His arms remained at his sides. "Ask me to stay."

He felt her lips move at his breast, and her soft words fell into the morning silence. "Stay. Please. Though it's unwise. You know it is."

"Yes." He swung her into his arms again and carried her to the bed where he lay her and her daughter amid fresh, butter-colored sheets smelling of fragrant soap and tantalizing perfume. He paused there, staring down at the two of them. They were soft, innocent, feminine. The antithesis of everything that was his life.

Her hand brushed his belly, and he took it in his. Her lashes fluttered but didn't open. "Thank you for this," she whispered. "I—we do need you."

As Dominic joined her on the bed, he took stock of his own mood. In spite of her understandable reluctance, he was exhilarated. Foolishly eager.

He rested his dark head on crisp, ruffled pillows and pulled her across his body so her back lay upon his chest and her legs fell between his. A lace-edged handkerchief embroidered with her initials lay on the pillow next to him, and he lifted it, sniffing. It smelled like her.

He was all too aware of how well the room's furnishings suited her and how ill they suited him. Accustomed as he was to the grim realities of war, such frilly linens seemed delicate and foreign. And too easily ruined by men like him.

Tired as she was, Emma was malleable and allowed him to position her as he pleased. He encircled her in his embrace so her buttocks nestled comfortably in the cradle of his thighs. Her head was pillowed on his breast, and she dozed.

His eyes roved her, noting the bruised shadows under the sweep of her lashes, the chafing his beard had left on her pretty neck, the heavy swells of her breasts marked by his mouth.

He smoothed curls of luxuriant hair back from her face and throat and simply lay there a minute, feeling at peace with her lying warm against his nakedness. And then, as was necessary before the Bonding could begin, he slowly let his heart open toward this woman and this girl who were not his.

At his side, the infant was beginning to stir. In moments she would be crying for sustenance.

Gently he cupped Emma's breast. It was heavy with the weight of a mother's milk. He began a slow massage, drawing his hand outward toward its pebbled nipple in a motion designed to bring on lactation. He continued the motion over and over until he felt the first drop seep from her.

She shifted weakly when he placed the child to her nipple and coaxed it to nurse. She murmured in discomfort as small greedy lips latched on to her and commenced suckling.

He winced, imagining how tender her breasts must be this morning after his rough handling of them during the night. But the child was hungry and would no doubt require more breakfast. He began working Emma's other breast, bringing her milk down there as well.

His touch was easy on her, betraying none of his anger and deep concern. She'd been right. Carlo should be here, doing this with her. It was dangerous and forbidden that he performed this function in his stead.

The Bonding time was a crucial finale of every Satyr Birthing ritual. It brought mates closer, binding their hearts and minds. By bonding with Emma and her child as he was now, he did them all irreparable harm. After this, deep in their souls and in the very marrow of their bones, the three of them would forever feel a familial connection. When Carlo returned to take his rightful place as husband to Emma and as father to his own child, he'd find it impossible to negate Dominic's hold on them.

The baby began to fuss, so he repositioned it at Emma's other breast. She didn't wake. She was exhausted, as women always were after a Calling Birth. Most slept through this ritual.

The fierce, insistent pull of the Bonding tugged at him, and he fought the need to run soothing hands over the woman in his arms. But bonds were forming between them nevertheless. Irrevocable ones that would be troublesome in the future. He fisted a hand on his thigh and forced his gaze away from the child nursing at Emma's pale breast. The sounds of exuberant feeding reassured him Carlo's daughter was healthy and that his wife was well able to provide nourishment. That was all that mattered.

He'd heard other men in ElseWorld speak of the joy they felt at the Bonding. After a night of intense physical satiation followed by the thrill of attending to the sunrise Birthing, men played an important role in this final rite. With every fiber of his being, he knew it was wrong that he was attending to Emma now in her husband's place. He would pay for this folly, and so would she.

Then why did it feel so right?

In her sleep, Emma caressed her child with a gentle hand. Dominic's heart twisted. It was an organ that had never before affected him in any remotely similar way, and therefore this was deeply troubling.

Her right hand fell to his thigh, palm up, alongside his own. The twining of delicate blue veins on the underside of her wrist was so feminine, so vulnerable. Without warning, her fingers found and threaded his gloved hand in a gesture that both offered and took comfort.

His eyes flew to hers. She was sleeping, unaware of what she was doing.

But, Gods! The sensation of her touching him there was indescribable. Unexpected emotion choked him. No one had touched that hand since he was a boy. Not willingly.

His fingers folded over hers, and he looked toward the pinkening sky, willing time to slow.

Where was Carlo?

10

Carlo tore through the night. Rushing toward the gate, he fled the horror of what had just been revealed to him in his own bedchamber.

A month! He'd known Dominic an entire month. Ever since he'd come to serve in the regiment. They'd fought side by side. Killed to protect one another. Stitched each other's wounds. And all the while Dominic had somehow hidden the truth of what he was from everyone.

He must've bespelled his hand in order to hide the glove. That was the only explanation.

It still seemed impossible! But there could be no doubt. He'd seen for himself. When the palm of Dominic's right hand had cupped Emma's belly, the spell had faltered. The glove and the glow of the powerful mirror that shimmered beneath it had become visible.

And that's when Carlo had realized the terrible truth—that Dominic was the infamous repository of evil souls.

The demonhand.

"Gods, why him?" he sobbed, his anguished cry ripping the ebony silence.

He lifted his face to the moon overhead, seeking its light. But the bright, luminous face, whose smile had heretofore always been a balm to him, now eyed him without recognition. Without sympathy or interest. His connection to it had been severed, along with his ability to perform the carnal rituals it demanded of the Satyr.

His fingers wove themselves into the hair on both sides of his head, wrenching until his scalp ached. Images of the couple he'd left behind moments ago tortured him, luring him to the brink of madness.

Emma had pitied him. He'd seen it in her eyes. She'd thought him jealous. And he was, but not in the way she assumed.

She would be shocked to know the secrets he'd kept hidden from her and his family.

For in her world, it was a disgrace for any freeborn male to consent to penetration by another male. However, ElseWorld society took a different, more lenient perspective, and he had long ago discovered in himself a craving for such things.

A craving that had recently focused itself on Dominic. From the instant they'd met a few weeks ago, he'd quietly lusted after him. He'd yearned for his touch, basked in his every glance, cherished his every word. And though Dominic hadn't encouraged him, he hadn't spurned him either.

So he'd remained hopeful.

After he was injured, it had seemed natural to turn to Dominic for help in his predicament. And there were those who'd urged him in that direction. When Dom had agreed to come today to save the life of his child, Carlo had taken it as a hopeful sign.

But, just now, his comrade's interest in Emma had been all too blatant. Dominic hadn't been thinking of anyone else tonight. Hadn't wanted anyone else. Only her.

Carlo staggered on, his boots thumping in time with his tormented thoughts.

Dominic. Emma. Entwined. Mating. Bringing forth his child.

Had Dominic even noticed he'd gone? Did he care?

Shards of jealousy pierced his heart, shattering the rosy image he'd envisioned when he'd invited Dominic here. Foolishly he'd imagined that the carnal ritual between his wife and his friend might stretch to include him. At least to the extent he could still participate in it in view of his condition.

He still had fingers, did he not? And a mouth? An asshole? All skilled at providing carnal pleasure.

A downed branch caught his boot and tripped him. He fell to the ground, swearing. Something sharp bruised his thigh. He reached into his pocket and found the coin. The one Emma had employed last month in an attempt block his seed.

Kurr had given it to him, telling him to safeguard it and that it would bring luck. And last Moonful it had. He'd fathered a child in spite of his wife's attempts to deny him. And the following day Dominic had entered his life.

But tonight the luck it had brought had been anything but good.

Kicking the branch away, he got to his feet in a swirl of silvery green olive leaves. With a vicious swing of his arm, he hurled the coin into the distance. It fell silently, he knew not where, for he tromped on, snapping twigs and crushing ivy underfoot.

What would Nicholas and his brothers think of him, once they discovered he'd deserted Emma? Had left her with a fucking *demonhand*.

Would Dominic tell them what else he knew?

What would they think if they learned the true details of the service Carlo performed in the war? For he didn't only carry arms in battle, as they believed. If they found out, the precariously constructed fabric of his life would begin to unravel.

He would never be able to return to this world again. In a

small way this would be a relief, for he'd always felt unworthy of his Satyr brethren. Had never been able to live up to their reputations as notorious lovers. His life must only be in ElseWorld now, though that prospect wasn't without its own difficulties.

He hesitated, standing on the gnarled roots of oak, ash, and hawthorn that grew at the entrance to the cave in which the sacred gate lay, trying to decide what to do.

Kurr would be waiting for him at their home a few miles beyond the other side of the gate. He'd be mightily displeased when he learned that Carlo hadn't kept his bargain.

So great was Carlo's disillusionment that he considered going back to steal the child and kill Emma so he could blame Dominic. It was no more than Dominic deserved for not loving him. And then he could deliver the child to Kurr, as promised.

But, no, he was too much the coward for such an awful task.

Stepping through the gate, he entered the tunnel and followed its gloomy length until it expelled him into daylight. Here in his world, night and day were of shorter duration than in EarthWorld and were more or less reversed.

At the tunnel's end, idling guards sprang to attention. They were of the Feroce faction, currently allies of the Satyr, though that circumstance changed almost daily.

Carlo spread his legs and arms, proffering himself for search. Hands patted him down, rummaging over his shoulders and along his arms, chest, belly, thighs, boots, between his legs.

"Where is your companion?" one of them asked, looking beyond him toward the gate.

"He comes later." His expression crumpled at his own words, for it was a certainty that Dominic was coming inside *his* wife this very moment. A fresh bolt of agony shot through him.

"Your insignia?" one of them demanded, nudging him with the barrel of his weapon. "Where is it?"

Carlo fumbled in his pocket for the small metal rectangle that designated his rank and pinned it to his uniform.

"You're *cinaedi*?" the man asked, noting the symbol on his pin.

He nodded.

Overhearing, another soldier called out to him, "Service!"

Released by the guardsman, Carlo went, wanting to be used. Wanting to feel needed—by someone. Wanting to feel something other than this awful pain of betrayal.

He'd joined the ranks of the *cinaedi* shortly after coming here, and as such, had been trained in the art of sexual submission. It was his duty to bring succor to soldiers of every rank when summoned. Refusing such aid was a punishable offence.

"How may I serve you, Peacekeeper?" he asked. He presented himself before the soldier in the traditional way, head bowed and hands clasped behind his back.

The soldier set his weapon aside but in easy reach. "Submit," he instructed.

Readily acquiescing, Carlo unfastened his trousers and made ready to offer himself as a *homo delicatus*, a receptive bottom.

It was what the troops generally required of him. Most were anxious for the sight of his backside. But they were understandably loath to turn their own backs to him for fear of a swift betrayal and the feel of his knife thrust between their ribs.

"What's wrong with you?" the man inquired, halting him when he noticed Carlo's limp cock and the reddened cuts on his pelvis.

"I was injured in the fighting. I can now enjoy only a receptive role."

The soldier stepped back from him, obviously horrified by his disfigurement. "How can you bear to live like that?"

"It's not my choice, I assure you," said Carlo, terribly hurt by this rejection on top of all he'd already endured tonight. He made to close his trousers again. "Shall I go, then?"

"No," the man grumbled. "Repulsive as you are, you'll have to do. At this hour, few come our way."

"Yes, Peacekeeper," he said, lowering his uniform to his knees. Bracing his hands on his thighs, he tacitly gave consent to let himself be used as wife.

When he felt the nudge of a distended prick, he bore down, opening his puckered ring, and felt the man glide inside him. Hard, masculine fingers grasped his hip bones.

It was a brief exchange, and he was pulling up his trousers minutes later. What he did was respectable work. Considered indispensable to morale.

A year ago when he'd come here, he'd intended only to accompany Nicholas in order to see something of the world he assumed had helped spawn him. But he'd found a home here as he had found none in EarthWorld.

He'd always been a misfit in EarthWorld. First when he lived among Humans, trying to hide his magic. Then among the virile Satyr lords, trying to hide the fact that he didn't lust after women as they did.

The precise nature of his origins was unknown. It had been serendipitous that Nicholas had stumbled upon him on a visit to Rome and had brought him to live on the estate.

There Carlo had discovered others like himself for the first time. Relatives who changed with the effects of the moon as he did. It had been a relief, at least initially.

In an effort to ingratiate himself with his new family, he'd wooed Emma and convinced her to wed him. But then he'd found himself unable to live as expected—regularly mating himself to a woman.

"I'm going to report you," the soldier muttered as he righted his own uniform. "You should be taken out of service. We see enough blood and disfigurement here. We don't need to be ministered to by the likes of you."

"No, Peacekeeper, please. Did I not give you succor in spite of it?" Carlo whispered, reaching toward him.

"Go! Get off with you, freak." The man dislodged a shot

from his weapon near Carlo's boots, making him jump, and then another until he began to move away.

A mile from home, another Peacekeeper hailed him.

With a nod of his head, he wordlessly bade Carlo to kneel at the side of the road and began opening the trousers of his uniform. Obediently Carlo knelt, took the man's length in his mouth and began to fellate him. A wagonful of soldiers went past, calling out ribald encouragements and filling Carlo's lungs with dust kicked up by their wheels.

By the time he reached his destination, a new darkness had fallen, and he was calmer than when he'd first come through the gate. He'd been waylaid by five more Peacekeepers on his journey. As a result, his jaw was sore, and his ass burned, but his step was light.

As he opened the door to his home, he was met with the tip of a sword.

"What brings you back so soon?" Kurr's masculine voice demanded. "And where's the child?"

Carlo pushed the sword away from his stomach as if it were a gate he were swinging open. "Good day to you, too, husband."

"Did things go wrong? Speak, man!" Kurr tossed the sword away. It fell with a clang, and then he grabbed Carlo by the shirtfront and hauled him against his chest. Grimacing, Kurr recoiled, thrusting him away just as abruptly. "You reek of other men. How often must I ask that you cleanse your mouth of cock breath before returning home to me? I suppose I'll find that your asshole has been loosened and seasoned by male leavings as well."

"What you asked of me is done," said Carlo, shaking him off. He went to the table and poured some wine from the bottle there into a goblet.

"Liar!" Kurr scoffed, gesturing toward the heavens. "To arrive this early, you had to have left them while the Moon was high. You left them together, didn't you? You left them before the child came."

Carlo ducked his head. "Jealousy overcame me."

"Fuck. Go back, you bastard!" Kurr grabbed him by the collar and hauled him to his feet. "While there's still time. Before the Bonding begins."

"Stop your ranting and listen to me. You'll not want the child when you hear." Carlo shook free and sat. Ignoring Kurr's impatience, he took a long draught of spirits, bracing himself to make his disclosure. "The man I took there. The one from my regiment—Dominic."

"Yes? The one you for whom you wish to divorce me? Your lover?" he asked snidely.

"He's not my lover," Carlo muttered into his glass.

"Aha! Your little friend wouldn't fuck you. And so you pouted and ruined everything, is that it?"

Carlo hammered his fist on the table, making the dishes jump. A goblet fell and rolled to the floor. "As it turns out, my *little friend* is the demonhand. Do you really want me to bring you a child that his seed helped bring to life?"

A silence fell. He glanced up. Kurr's eyes didn't waver.

"You knew!" Carlo guessed, appalled. "You knew, yet you still offered me a divorce? In exchange for a child tainted by demons? Why?"

"Fool! Where's the amulet?"

Carlo shrugged, not considering it important. "What does that matter?"

"Where is it?" Kurr calmly slapped him full in the face, prompting him into speech.

"On the other side," he said, trying to disentangle himself.

Red rage filled Kurr's face, but he let him sink back into his chair. "You left it in EarthWorld?"

"It was only a simple luck charm, was it not?" Carlo poured another drink, rubbing his bruised cheek.

"It was more than that. Much more. It was stolen from the temple of Bacchus, from the statue."

"Your amulet was *that* amulet? But everyone assumed demons had taken it. Who gave you such an object?" Carlo asked, incredulous.

"I d—d—did."

Carlo's head whipped around, and he gazed into the shadows, suddenly realizing they weren't alone. Eyes glowing white as hot coals and then red as embers gazed back at him.

His husband sank low, genuflecting. Carlo set his glass on the table, placing it so haphazardly that it fell to the floor, where it splintered. Panicking, he stepped toward the door. "I didn't know. I'll return to EarthWorld for it."

But the demon was there before him, moving like a flash of light. Its olive skin glistened as if wet, yet its touch was dry as a lizard's as it stroked a claw down his cheek. "And f—f—for the child as well? Our child?"

Trapped, he swiveled his eyes toward Kurr. "You've become his disciple, haven't you?" he asked, already knowing the answer.

"Oh, it's more than that," Kurr murmured, watching the demon in fascination.

A demon's light faded when it ceased speaking or moving, but this one was constantly twitching, keeping it in almost continuous view.

"How long?" Carlo shouted. The very day he'd arrived here, Kurr had become his first male lover. Had showered him with gifts and affection. Had sucked and fucked him in the initiation of an orgy that had lasted a full week. They'd wed quickly, secretly, in spite of the fact that Carlo had wed himself to Emma only ten days prior.

"Since the beginning."

"Did you ever care for me?" he asked plaintively.

Kurr shrugged.

"He c—c—cares only for me." The demon's breath was so

fetid it nearly felled Carlo, but some unseen power held him there, locked him in place.

"What do you want?" Carlo asked faintly.

"The child, of c—c—course. But it seems I will not have it as easily as I'd hoped, for you f—f—failed me."

The creature rubbed the clawed thumb and forefinger of one hand together as if one were flint and the other tinder, and he were trying to start a fire. A glowing orb appeared between the fingertips. Made of mist, it acted as a crystal ball, displaying the scene Carlo had just witnessed in his bedchamber in Earth-World.

With a toss of demonic fingers, the ball rose and hovered above them in the air, untethered and without support.

Carlo gazed upward. In the orb, he saw the scene he'd fled in EarthWorld. Dominic and Emma.

"In the past, all those of my kind who have gazed upon the demonhand have been destroyed by him, their souls taken. But we know the look of him now. You've shown it to us. He won't be safe hiding behind the spells that disguise him any longer."

Unable to stop himself, Carlo gazed into the orb. Saw Dominic mating himself to Emma. He'd known it would happen between them. But to see it! He jerked his face away, unable to bear any more.

"It's more than just your desire for a child," Carlo guessed frantically. "It's this particular one, isn't it? Why? Emma is not King Feydon's offspring as her sister is. Possession of our child won't afford you entrance into EarthWorld."

"B—b—bah!" The orb dodged the arm that the demon sliced through the air, leaving a trail of mist. "I c—c—care nothing about that other world. I seek power for my kind here in this one."

"And you think to obtain that via *my* child?"

"D—d—did you think you'd created the child all on your own? With this little thing?" The clawed hand ripped through the front of his trousers with a single draw and then lingered, flicking his limp cock. "The amulet is what b—b—brought life into your woman's womb. Not your seed alone."

"But why do you want *this* child in particular? Why not another?"

The demon only smiled secretively. Leaving Carlo frozen in place, he went to Kurr. Cupping Kurr's jaws, the demon pressed their mouths together, and Carlo watched his husband's face slowly fill with evil. As they stood, nose to nose, the demon shuddered now, and its inner light rose and dimmed. Within minutes, man and demon had coalesced, disciple now acting as host.

Kurr came to his side. "Submit to me, wife," he breathed. Though the stutter was gone now, this was the demon's voice, speaking through him now and housed in his body.

Carlo did as instructed without hesitation, having lost any will to resist. Though his mind shrieked in denial, he released the buttons of his uniform jacket and the fastenings of his trousers. Naked, he kneeled upon the couch where Kurr most enjoyed mating him, and he folded his arms over its high back.

The cushions on either side of him depressed, and warmth surrounded him as Kurr mounted him from behind.

Carlo sobbed. "Will you turn me into one such as yourself?"

"I swear to you I will not, my darling." Kurr was speaking, yet his voice was now shaded by that of the demon that possessed him. It sounded as if two voices spoke identical words in tandem.

Claws pricked his back and then drew down toward his buttocks, painting stripes of blood. And depositing poison.

Carlo moaned as a rigid cock that was both husband and demon filled him in stuttering fits and starts. His vision swam. His throat closed. "What's happening to me?"

A rough hand grabbed his hair, pulling his head high and arching his throat. The ball of mist floated just in front of him.

"Watch. A Chosen One is about to be born," twin voices whispered.

He wailed, a wounded animal sound, as he realized why they wanted his child. It was cursed, destined to become a monster like Dominic. He gazed into the orb and saw Emma. Her face was wreathed in pain, the birth obviously imminent.

"The next step in your life must be your death. When the child draws its first breath, you will breathe your last. For that's the property of the amulet. As it gives one life, it takes another. Balance must be maintained."

"What of the child? What will happen to it?"

"Once the current demonhand succumbs to death, the Chosen One will assume his duties. Duties it will be unable to fulfill once we take it captive. Our numbers will grow unchecked."

In the convex orb, Carlo watched the child emerge. Saw Dominic's gloved hand reach for it.

A gloved hand that held unimaginable evil within its palm, holding a child that could bring down this world.

As he felt himself dying, he felt the hot pump in his ass grow fierce.

His blood, which only moments ago had pounded in fear in his veins, now began turning to a powdery red dust that drifted from the wounds at his back.

Oh, Hells, the rumors were true. The demons were necrophile.

It was the last thought he would ever have.

11

"Are you . . . all right?" Dominic asked Emma later that morning. His voice was graveled, hoarse as a result of their long dark hours of debauchery. His heart was lighter than he could ever recall.

"Quite, thank you." Behind her spectacles, eyes that were the shy brown of a faun darted to his and then away. She looked soft, sleepy.

The skin of her throat was blotchy, and her lips were red from his mouth. He'd been greedy with her, rough. His body still remembered hers. Remembered kissing her, fucking her. It clamored to press itself to her warmth again, to inhale her sweet innocence.

After the Bonding, he'd fallen asleep in her bed, his nose buried in her hair, his arms encircling her and her daughter. He was accustomed to sleeping by day, but never before had he slept in a bed other than his own. It had the most peaceful slumber he'd ever enjoyed.

She'd awakened before him and was fully dressed when he

joined her downstairs. Once again she was shrouded in another long gown that covered her from throat to wrist to ankle, like feminine armor. Her face was pale and her cheeks flushed, her throat long and white.

His lips curved. How could he have ever thought her plain?

He took a step toward her, gently brushing his knuckles along the new, pink skin of her daughter's arm. "There are things you should know," he began.

"What things?" she said sharply, drawing herself and her child away.

He straightened, abruptly realizing her mood. Had he really imagined that one night with him would have her forgetting her husband?

He hardened himself against the surprising dart of hurt that pierced him at the fear he saw in her eyes. After all, he reminded himself, he was a demonhand and was accustomed to inspiring such an emotion in others.

She eased closer to the front door, fidgeting. She wanted him to go. For long seconds, they stood like strangers in the front hall, the same place where he'd first glimpsed her in the flesh last evening.

"You want the child?"

Her brows shot up, and her arms tightened around the bundle she held. "Want her? Of course I want her."

"Yet you took precautions to prevent her conception."

"I want her," she insisted.

The girl stirred, punching the air with a fist, and Emma swayed gently to comfort her. Her hold was gentle, natural. Loving. The child calmed, and her fingers began to fiddle with the lace edging of her mother's bodice, drawing Dominic's gaze there and lower.

Her waist was slender again. Women recovered from a Satyr birthing within hours. In the very next Calling a month from now, it would be physically possible to plant another child in her. Satyr men could father six children a year, were they so careless. Sowing, reaping, sowing, reaping in an endless cycle.

Gods! He'd like to be the one to do the planting the next time. There, he'd admitted it to himself. He wanted to stay here with her. Usurp another man's rights. Fool that he was.

She launched into conversation. "I don't wish to be ungrateful. And I'm not. But as you can imagine, last night was difficult. For Carlo. And me. It will be best for everyone if you are gone when he returns."

Dominic rubbed his right hand with his left. The demons within his palm had been unnaturally silent since he'd crossed the gate, a fact for which he could only be grateful.

They would kill him one day, and immediately upon his last breath his power would pass on to the tiny being swathed in this woman's arms. How could an untutored girl be expected to bear such a crushing burden?

He glanced back at Emma. How much should he tell her?

Parents were never informed until necessary, and the Facilitator had warned him not to speak of such matters to her.

None could cross into this world from his without an invitation. It seemed certain she and the child would remain safe here, happy in their ignorance. Until his death.

Then Emma would learn to hate him. When she discovered what her child was, had become with the help of his mating.

"Look at me," he commanded.

Her defiant gaze found his. For a moment, her spectacles caught the light and turned her eyes bleak, like twin reflecting glasses.

"What happened between us . . . it was not wrong," he said quietly, trying to convince them both.

"Please," she whispered. "It's over. Let's not speak of it." The light changed, and her eyes were revealed again. They were shadowed and hollow. Vulnerable.

But he would not take pity on her. Not he, for all knew him to be pitiless. "You're angry and embarrassed. But you *will* listen." He gripped her shoulders and felt the tension in them. "If anything happens to me, your child will feel the effects in ways you can't imagine."

She shook from his hold and stepped back. "Is that meant to be a threat of some kind?"

Hands on his hips, he glowered at her. "Only a fact."

She shrugged, not comprehending. "Then I bid you keep yourself well so that nothing ill befalls my daughter."

"Emma," he said, pointing up the stairs toward her bedchamber, "like it or not, a part of me passed to you and your child last night. The three of us are bound. It's now my obligation to watch over you both."

"That's the duty of a husband and father," she whispered. "Just go. Please."

He stood irresolute for a few minutes. Then he turned away.

She followed him to the door, obviously anxious to see him gone. His every instinct urged him to take her in his arms. To stay and protect her and the child. But others needed him as well.

He opened the door. Stepping outside, he glanced back to her, speaking more gruffly than he'd intended. "Tell Carlo to contact me if I'm needed."

"You won't be."

With that, she shut the door quietly but firmly, leaving him standing in the desolate chill of the morning.

The gate that would allow him passage to ElseWorld lay hidden in the forest at the center of the Satyr estate. He departed for it on foot, his steps leaden. He tried to banish the niggling feeling that his business here was unfinished. It was only a delusion, a symptom of the Bonding.

Forcing himself to put one foot in front of the other, he trudged on toward the gates that would deliver him home. His life and duties in ElseWorld awaited.

He soon found himself cresting a rise, and he paused there, soaking in the beauty around him. Verdant hillsides covered with new life stretched out on all sides in every direction. Ancient vines sprawled up stakes, along with newly grafted ones. In a few months, they would bear fruit—the wine grapes that gave life to the Satyr lords who dwelled here.

This world wasn't the anathema he'd expected. It wasn't like his own. Days here would be passed tilling the soil. Bringing forth life instead of destroying it. An existence here wouldn't reek of treachery and war, as it did in his world.

He was weary of killing. Perhaps this was the only reason the idyllic picture of a life with Emma and her child had appealed to him so.

His boots ate up the distance to the gate within minutes. Once he passed through it, he would never see her again.

Still the Bond dragged at his senses, urging him to go back. Urging him to nurture the child he had helped bring into the world. Urging him to love and protect the mother.

She would be difficult to forget. But forget her he would. He'd been only a tool last night, a body used to bring forth a Chosen One. It was what he'd agreed to.

Carlo would have enough difficulty breaking the Bond that had been forged tonight without further interference from Dominic. His daughter would grow up with some kind of normal existence here. At least until Dominic died.

"Emma." The name on his lips was an imperceptible sigh. It was the last time he would say it. She could not be his in any meaningful way. It would only bring her harm.

With enough time and distance, he would forget her. He would lose himself in other females.

Yes, it was best for all of them that he left. And stayed gone. This longing for her would fade in time. This episode in his life was over. Finished.

Yet the almost weightless bit of cloth resting in his pocket put the lie to this. A stolen handkerchief monogrammed with Emma's initials. It was too slight to be felt, yet he felt it there, curving his hip like a living presence. A part of her.

It was a talisman. A reminder that because of tonight, the necessity of remaining alive had taken on new meaning for him.

For if he died, Emma's daughter would quickly discover what hell was.

12

Dominic stepped into the silence of the cave. Its walls were a glorious amalgamation of granite striated with gold and other metals encrusted with precious and semiprecious stones.

His steps were silenced by the springy moss underfoot as he crossed the short distance to the gate. He passed through it easily, for travel in the direction he went did not require an invitation as it did in the opposite one. He could not have gone to Emma last night without Carlo to accompany him.

Carlo's scent was fresh in the tunnel. He'd recently been this way. Their paths would likely cross again, but not soon. Dominic would not be rejoining the regiment. The usefulness of that ruse had ended.

On the ElseWorld side of the gate, the walls of the tunnel gave way to other rock and alloys unknown in EarthWorld, metals that flickered and flashed with magnetic properties designed to keep evil at bay—at least within the tunnel closest to the gate. Medallions placed by his superstitious ancestors in hopes of warding off invasion from another world they'd never visited were lodged here and there in mica and hematite.

Magic was thick on the ground along this length of the channel, swirling as high as his waist at times. His black boots cut through it as he stalked homeward, sending it scurrying as if it, too, feared him in the same way his own people did.

The mist dwindled toward the end of the umbilical cord that connected the two disparate realms. Ahead, his world waited to swallow him in its open, black maw.

He'd almost forgotten that all would be in darkness here at home, for day and night were reversed in the two adjacent worlds. And on Moonful, the nights here lasted for very nearly a day and two nights, spanning a thirty-two-hour period.

Before he'd gone with Carlo to EarthWorld, he had already passed one Moonful here in ElseWorld in the company of female Shimmerskins. Then, scant hours later, he'd crossed through the gate to pass a second Moonful with . . . Emma. A thrill ran through him at the thought of her.

Even after last night's long hours of fucking, his cock twitched at the prospect of taking her to bed again. Emma, of the long and lovely throat, soft skin, and guileless, doelike gaze.

Suddenly he was disgorged into a world dipped in moonlight. The inky darkness momentarily disoriented him.

The first blow came from out of nowhere, blasting his shoulder and bringing him to his knees. Foolishly mooning over a woman he could not have, he had let his guard down. Hadn't been expecting it.

A second strike fell. Pain seared his right wrist. This dagger had been purposefully aimed, meant to sever his gloved hand from his arm.

Leaping to his feet, he stood half crouched with his arms tense at his side. Sensing their own kind nearby, the unnatural souls he housed beneath the glove shrieked for a release he would not allow.

Demons. Four males and one female. All naked, with olive complexions, muscled arms and legs, and tufts of greasy hair atop their heads and crotches.

Assuming a fighting stance, he faced all five of them.

"Fools! Do you still believe chopping off my hand will free those I keep in thrall?" he taunted, trying to force them into action. They were visible only when they moved, so it was best to wait for them to attack.

Even without his sight to guide him, he sensed their locations from their body heat and their stench. Knew they were more or less arranged in a semicircle before him.

Like him, they existed only to kill. Unlike him, they were stupid. Too stupid to understand that if they succeeded at felling him, the souls of their kind that he held captive in his palm would not go free. They would simply rise up in the palm of another— his successor, Emma's daughter.

The thought lent him new strength and a determination to defeat them.

Another lunge came at him. Two of the males at once. He feinted back and then drew his weapon from his boot and slipped it into the closest one's gut, twisting it in his entrails. Its face came close for just a moment, and he glimpsed himself in its savage red eyes.

His free hand grabbed and rotated the other's wrist so the point of its own dagger struck it high between its ribs. With a savage downward thrust, Dominic nailed the demon to the earth with its own weapon.

Something sliced his side, and agony seared him. More attacks were delivered in rapid-fire flashes of multihued light. He ducked from the next blow and the next and then lashed out, mortally wounding two more of them in a single strike.

They'd left themselves open. Demons were lethal, but they were driven by bloodlust and rarely took time to think before pouncing. They overcame their victims only by attacking in sheer numbers.

He pivoted toward the last remaining one, but only an occasional hint of its flash was visible now and then as it retreated in the distance. The female. They were always the quickest, the smartest. When he'd skewered the last of her companions, she had departed, living to fight another day.

He straightened, his lungs heaving. Blood and breath still pumped wildly in him, primed for battle.

Four bodies littered the ground at his feet, silver fluid seeping out of them to soak the surrounding vegetation. Stalking to the first of them, he kneeled alongside it in the dirt. It stirred, fluttering in alarm at his approach.

Though he'd fatally wounded these four, he'd left them alive. It was best not to kill completely before the extraction took place.

Removing his glove, he drew out a hand that was pale compared to the rest of his body, for it was rarely exposed to sunlight. He turned it upward toward the moon, revealing a silvered palm as reflective as any mirror. It caught the lunar light. Captured and amplified its strength until it blazed with a luminescence as brilliant as the sun.

The skin of this hand was sensitive. Even the soft drift of the surrounding air over its nerve endings was disturbing as he reached out toward his victim. He took the base of the creature's silver-green throat in a choke hold.

The demon hissed at him, trying to scuttle away, but the dagger that had felled him held him pinned to the ground like an insect.

"How did you know I would be here?" Dominic demanded. "I'll make this quick if you answer. If not . . ."

A furious string of curses and denials spewed from his victim's lips.

Flattening his palm at the scaly neck, Dominic located the sluggish pulse in the hollow at the base of the demon's throat. For that was where the soul reposed. His hand warmed, heated, throbbed. Seethed with the insistent, furious clamor of souls he and his predecessors had already imprisoned there.

The creature's eyes widened, its slitted pupils swelling. Its body bucked and shivered. Its silver tongue flailed as it cursed him with its last breath.

An excruciating pain like the sting of a hundred wasps encompassed his palm. He groaned as yet another soul slipped inside him. Within his uniform, his cock was tumid, but he hardly noticed, long since inured to the shameful sexual thrill that coursed through him with the taking of each soul. The mirrored light of his palm burned bright for a few seconds and then dimmed.

With the flash of a blade in his left hand, he hacked off the demon's head directly under the jaw, severing mind from body. Leaving it lifeless. Soulless.

He stood, grimacing.

Then he moved on to the other three that remained.

Moments later, he slipped his right hand back into the glove. None had confessed any information regarding how they'd known to find him here.

But somehow they had.

13

ElseWorld

Getting to his feet, Dominic staggered, nearly pitching over atop the last of the demons he'd just killed. He was losing blood. Pressing his left hand against his side, he felt a sanguine stickiness seep between his fingers.

He stepped over one of the decapitated bodies and turned to make his way toward the temple. Toward home, where it would be safe to recuperate. With plodding, determined steps, he forced himself to keep going, but all the while his mind raced.

No matter how many demons he killed, more came. Always more. He carried with him a constant sense of frustration and failure because he could not eradicate them. Could not even locate the source that spawned them. There were no eggs, and the females' innards of the species were identical to the males'. No one knew how they duplicated.

They couldn't simply spring from nothing. For centuries something had brought them to life and drawn them here to attack him and his people. What was it?

When he woke later, he was lying on his monastic pallet in his solitary alcove. Judging by the light streaming in from the aperture overhead in the temple, it was noon. He'd somehow made it here last night. A few hours of rest had restored his health far more quickly than it would have the average Satyr.

His stomach rumbled. He was hungry.

He reached across his chest and ran his gloved hand along his damaged ribs. Within his palm, he felt the malevolent hum that informed him he still held his captives. He only vaguely recalled cleansing his wounds when he'd arrived here last night.

He'd obviously staunched the flow of blood and sewn himself shut, for the jagged tear in his side felt largely healed and was now only a jagged pink line. Another set of scars was the least of his concerns.

Footsteps clattered beyond his chamber, crossing the temple floor. Someone was approaching. Judging by her scent, it was a woman. One he knew. She entered, and he sat up, causing his head to swim and his side to throb.

His eyes traveled over her with jaded suspicion. Like all females in ElseWorld, she wore clothing made of a translucent fabric that left her body largely visible for the pleasure of males. Her breasts were firm and high, her legs slim.

She removed her hood, revealing her face. Her skin was unlined, unwrinkled. Although she was considerably older than he, she appeared to be his equal in age. She was still the beautiful woman he remembered from that day fifteen years ago. A day that had irrevocably changed both their lives.

For it was then that the Facilitator had come to their home bearing the stunning news that Dominic was a Chosen One—the successor to the previous demonhand, who'd died only an hour earlier. Until that moment, no one in his family had known.

At ten years old he'd been taken to his predecessor's deathbed, where he'd dutifully accepted the burden of the souls into his right palm. In exchange for giving him over to the temple, this woman had been gifted with riches. With a title. Lifelong youth.

He rubbed the bristle on his jaw, annoyed. "Go away, Mother."

Her hand tightened on the hood she held, and she wrinkled her nose. "You stink of death. And sex."

"And you of wealth."

She traced a manicured fingertip along the bumpy line of semi-precious jewels that edged the neckline of her saffron gown. Still more studded its hem. "I paid for what I have."

"How exactly?" He pushed to his feet, his face impassive as he awaited an answer that wasn't forthcoming. Standing unabashedly naked before her, he stretched his arms overhead, wincing.

She nodded toward his sliced ribs. "You're wounded?"

"Spare me any false concern," he gritted. "Say whatever you came to say and then go."

"Did you rape her?"

In a flash, he had her backed against the wall, his forearm hard against her throat. "What do you know of that business?"

He'd used his right arm, and the wrist of his glove pressed at the underside of her jaw. She gazed toward it from the corner of wild, frightened eyes that were remarkably similar to his own.

"Yes, you should fear me, Mother. I've learned much of destruction and death since you last saw me. Now speak."

Choked words tumbled from her lips. "I know you crossed over last night at the behest of the Facilitator. I know that a Chosen One was brought forth. I only wondered if its mother was raped. As I was by your predecessor in order to bring you into the world twenty-five years ago."

His eyes searched hers, and then he slowly relaxed his hold. He hadn't known. Had never considered things from her point of view. Perhaps they *had* both paid for what he was.

Going to the corner of his room, he turned a lever positioned over the basalt slab that had been hollowed to form a sink. The spigot high above it trickled merrily into the rock basin. He leaned from the waist and dunked his head, enjoying the bracing chill of its waters. Straightening, he reached for toweling and then briskly rubbed the moisture from his face and hair.

"How is it you come by this knowledge of my whereabouts?" he asked with his back to her.

"From me."

He turned to see the Facilitator standing in the doorway of his alcove. His mother scooted toward the relative safety the elder afforded.

Dominic threw the crumpled towel to his pallet. "You summoned her here? Why, after all this time?"

"It's my place to deliver today's news to you," his mother informed him, brave now that she stood in the Facilitator's shadow.

"What news?"

"The glad tidings that you're soon to be wed."

Dominic laughed, a grating, skeptical sound. It died away as he realized she was serious. His hard eyes shot to the man beside her.

"Come with me," the Facilitator instructed.

Scowling dangerously, he made to follow, but the older man stopped him with a glance that encompassed the entirety of his person in one blink. "Clothe yourself first. Your betrothed awaits."

He ground his teeth. What new misery was this?

Throwing on leather trousers and boots, he followed the pair to the central temple. It was the first time in a month he hadn't donned the disguise of the regiment's uniform.

The two Acolytes awaited them there alongside the large obsidian disk in which he'd first observed Emma a month ago. Its inky surface had already been awakened, and the illusion of a flat, gold disk the size of his head rotated endlessly upon it, displaying the ornate decorative carving on each of its sides.

"The missing amulet," the Facilitator explained, gesturing toward it. "We broadcast its image continuously to the other temples and outposts so that others may be on the watch for it, should it come their way."

Upon his command, the Acolytes softly clapped their pale hands. In response, the amulet disappeared to be replaced by the image of a stunning young woman with two long blond plaits. The lower half of her face was veiled, and her nubile body was draped in a traditional virgin's gown.

Glistening white fabric sheathed her arms from wrist to shoulder and fell from there to her sandaled feet. The gown drew together at her waist, where it was secured with what appeared to be a diamond closure. Above and below it, her breasts and genitals were on display beneath a scant covering of gossamer fabric. At the back of the gown, a froth of opaque pink trailed off in a meticulously arranged train that meandered several yards behind her.

Eyes modestly downcast, she stood prepared to meet her fate.

A gaggle of what he assumed to be her relatives loitered in the background, obviously having gathered to witness the occasion of their meeting. Murmurs and whispers floated amongst them. He could well imagine what they made of his bloody, largely unwashed appearance.

"My betrothed?" he queried in a mocking tone.

"The offspring of King Feydon and one of his concubines here in ElseWorld," he was informed.

The Facilitator flicked his hand, and the girl's veil drifted away as if by magic. "This marriage will bind the Satyr and the Fey more closely. It's wise to secure allies in this time of war. Her family does you a great honor in offering her."

"Cey!" one of the relatives in the background scolded. At

that, the girl's frightened eyes darted up to catch Dominic's and then as quickly dropped.

"She doesn't appear especially eager to have me," he commented dispassionately. An understatement, for his trembling betrothed was terrified of him. An unwilling pawn in this, as he was.

"Can you present us with any suitable female who *would* be eager?" his mother inquired.

His mind leaped to a remembrance of Emma. Of how she'd kissed him last night. How she'd covered the evil in him with her own hand. Emma, who was already wed. His fists clenched.

"No." He shrugged. "Making such a presentation to me is folly, for I'm not in need of a wife."

At his words, more whispers and agitation ensued from the virgin's relatives.

The Facilitator eyed him; then, bowing to the image in the mirror, he bid a lengthy and courteous farewell to the woman and her family. While Dominic looked on, appearing anything but cooperative, the Facilitator calmly assured them that he would cooperate in their wedding plans.

Once the last bow and scrape had been executed, the two Acolytes clapped their hands in unison, and the image faded away.

"Why this sudden herding of me toward marriage?" Dominic challenged.

"There has never been a female demonhand," said the Facilitator. "It concerns us."

Dominic's tensed. "How did you know?"

"The new Chosen One is *female*?" his mother gasped at the same time.

The Facilitator nodded, ignoring his mother's outburst. "I observed her Birthing. Last night, through the conduit of the mirror."

Dominic's heart began to pound. "How? The mirror in

Carlo's bedchamber was shielded. I saw him cover it, as is traditional during Moonful."

"See for yourself." The Facilitator gestured toward the obsidian mirror. Taking their cue, the Acolytes brought it to life again.

Rustling noises emitted from it, but its surface remained dark for a long, potent moment. Then, as if a curtain had been ripped open, two figures came into view, replacing the blackness.

A man and a woman. Him. And Emma. They were in a bedchamber, standing with their naked bodies pressed together. He was behind her, one hand at her hip and the other cupping her swollen belly. His lips were tracing her shoulder.

She seemed to be gazing at them, an audience she could not see. Her hand was reaching toward something that was out of the mirror's range. She was attempting to struggle away from him, even as she extended a hand toward the real him, now, without knowing she did so.

Masculine fingers came into view at the side of the mirror, moving toward the dressing table. There was a clinking sound as Carlo collected his belongings.

"No! Don't leave us!" Emma's voice pleaded.

At that, his own reflection roused, and he watched his hand lift from her hip to her breast. His thumb strummed her nipple.

Carlo's anguished, disembodied voice answered her. "I'm sorry. I can't." A door opened and then slammed. The sound of him quitting the room.

"Did you notice?" The Facilitator's voice broke in. "The mirror in that room was obviously covered when you began. Then its cover was removed. Purposely, by an unseen hand. It was done only after you'd fallen under the moon's spell and could be caught unaware."

Upon his desertion, Emma's hand faltered and dropped. Her expression filled with a poignant mixture of rejection and fear—the two sides of the carnal coin she'd been offered last night—for one man had rejected her, and she'd feared his replacement.

Oblivious, Dominic's reflection held her fast against him, wrapping her in his arms, his body focused only on its zealous need to mate itself to hers.

Beside him, his mother whimpered. "Look at you. Forcing the poor girl like some heathen." The men ignored her, but they'd all heard.

Dominic cheeks slowly stained with red as he watched himself play the role of stud. He'd never seen himself display so much passion. Once, during Moonful, he'd chanced to see his reflection in a pond as he'd mated a Shimmerskin. He'd been startled at how little emotion his face had betrayed, even in the heat of orgasm.

"Your glove," the Facilitator accused softly. "Why didn't you bespell it?"

Dominic's eyes flew to his hand where it embraced Emma's abdomen. "It's visible?"

"Of course, fool!" his mother blurted.

"But I *did* bespell it, as always," he admitted, mystified.

"Perhaps not well enough to counteract the strong emotions that were engendered that night," the Facilitator murmured with his usual tact.

"Not yet." It was Emma's voice. In the mirror, his hand slipped between her legs, opening her for his impalement. She sucked in a quick breath. The look on her face indicated the instant he breached her.

The Facilitator and Acolytes evinced no reaction at this, but Dominic felt his mother's repugnance as she beheld him in the throes of rut. Her horror was no greater than his own at this public reprising of last night's events.

"Turn it off!" he ordered. A muscle in his jaw jumped, the only sign of anger.

Instead, the Facilitator forwarded from this scene to later events, eventually pausing on a clear view of him holding the child Emma had just birthed for her inspection.

"A female Chosen One?" his mother bemoaned, finding a chair and falling into it. "We're doomed! What use is a female against the likes of demons?"

"You have little faith in your own gender," Dominic chided, ignoring her hysterics. "I would concern yourself more with her age. A babe, whether male or female, cannot possibly take my place. It's crucial that she have time to mature before I'm destroyed."

"True enough," said the Facilitator. "And therein lies the crux of my worry and the reason for this hasty betrothal. Until now, you've been of great service to the citizens in ElseWorld. But with the unfortunate exposure of your identity and that of the Chosen One as well—"

"How many saw this?" Dominic asked.

"Anyone who possesses a scrying mirror."

"Hells." He traced the scar along his jaw with calloused fingertips. "All is ruined."

"My status as Honored Mother will not be taken from me, will it?" his mother worried anxiously. "I've done nothing wrong! My son's the one who's brought ruin on all our heads."

"You're both overstating matters," the Facilitator placidly argued. Then to Dominic, he continued. "More to the point—your life will now be at even greater risk and could be lost to us at any moment. The Chosen One is far from ready to defend us in such an eventuality. The family of your betrothed can offer us much in the way of weaponry and troops."

"Of what use are those?" Dominic countered. "Neither can cage the evil of demon souls."

"Times grow more desperate. What could it hurt to wed the girl!" his mother persisted. "There is talk that some of the demons are evolving, taking disciples as hosts. Soon they may walk undetected among us."

The Facilitator shushed her. "Those are rumors, best ig-nored."

Gods. Dominic turned away, frustrated. Things were mov-ing so fast. In the span of twenty-four hours, all seemed to be precipitously teetering on the verge of utter chaos.

From the corner of his eye, he watched himself lift Emma's nipple to her daughter's ravenous pink lips. His expression as he gazed at them was besotted.

"Cease this display if you don't wish to see it splintered into pieces!" he roared, slapping the side of the mirror so hard that the scene upon it sputtered and jumped.

With the wave of a hand, the Facilitator obliterated the image.

Another took its place—the gold disk. It pivoted there in the mirror's center once again, endlessly exhibiting its alternating sides. The figure of Bacchus was etched in low relief upon its front, and the grapevines of the ancient Satyr on the reverse.

"It's larger than I expected," his mother commented after a bit. She was studying the amulet, obviously uncomfortable with the taut silence that had fallen in the room.

"It's been enlarged so its engravings are more easily discern-able," she was informed. "We're hoping someone will report having seen it. But thus far, nothing."

Dominic stared at the screen, his mind elsewhere. His stom-ach growled, reminding him he hadn't eaten.

"I need food," he grunted irritably.

The Facilitator snapped his fingers. One of his minions in-stantly arrived, and he began requesting Dominic's usual morn-ing repast of fruit, vegetables, meat, bread, and goat's milk. It was an unvaried menu that had been delivered to him here twice a day for the past fifteen years. He didn't question it, for the notion had been instilled in him long ago that he was a weapon, and that food was therefore to be taken in for the sole purpose of maintaining his powerful physique.

Dominic only half listened to the request for sustenance, the remainder of his attention on the mirror. He watched the image of the disk flip over and over with mesmerizing slowness.

Bacchus. Vines. Bacchus. Vines. Gold glinted each time it flipped as if tossed by an invisible hand. . . .

"Bacchus!" he muttered as realization struck. Without turning his head, he spoke, "Mother, go to the kitchens and oversee the preparation of my meal." When she didn't move, he rounded on her, his expression fierce. "Go!"

At that, she stepped back so quickly she dropped her hood.

He retrieved it with his gloved hand and held it out to her.

She glanced at it, backing away. "Never mind. I have others like it."

He captured her wrist, slapped the piece of fabric into her palm, and closed her fist on it.

She let out an involuntary sound of distress and shrank from him, snatching her hand away. "Why must you be so offensive?"

"It's my nature. Now go, Mother, and leave us."

She went, grumbling. "I'll go, all right. I'm leaving. I won't stay to dine with the likes of you."

Dominic spoke to the Acolytes once she'd gone, pointing toward the mirror. "Go back to the image you showed me of last night in EarthWorld. To the moment before Emma's husband departed his bedchamber."

Gazing at him curiously, they nevertheless complied, and the scene sprang into view again. Carlo's hand reached into view at the side of the mirror, moving toward the dressing table. There was a clinking sound.

"There. Stop!" Dominic instructed. "Enlarge and look closely at the object he is about to pick up."

When they obeyed, he saw it was as he'd thought. There, lying on the table, was a gold coin. On the displayed side was the figure of Bacchus, an engraving identical to that on the disk that had been a revolving exhibit on this mirror just moments ago.

"The amulet!" the Facilitator said, dumbfounded. Beside him, the Acolytes murmured in gentle excitement.

"Continue watching," Dominic told them. After an interval, the table once more came into view. The gold disk was gone.

"Where is it now?" The Facilitator's eyes searched him. "Do you have it?"

Dominic shook his head. "Carlo must."

He'd said he kept it close to remind him of how he'd been duped when Emma had attempted to utilize it as a contraceptive. She'd done that a month ago, immediately after the temple had been vandalized.

"But how did he come by it to begin with? Do you believe he and his wife were in league with the demons responsible for its theft? It would explain how she came to bear the Chosen One—the amulet's magic. Perhaps the two of them uncovered the mirror intentionally to expose you and make the location of your successor known to all."

The notion filled Dominic with a shocking sense of betrayal. He could readily believe Carlo might act so deviously. But not her. Please, not her.

At his bleak expression, the Facilitator hedged. "Forgive me. This is all conjecture. We needn't assume—"

"Last night when I came out of the tunnel, five of our enemies were waiting," Dominic informed him.

"You were attacked?"

In reply, he gestured to his fresh wound. "They were expecting me. They knew I'd be returning through the gate."

The Facilitator and the others shook their heads, tsking. "It was strangely quiet here last night. We'd begun to hope they might've gone underground."

"They'll go underground only once we've buried them all." Dominic pivoted on his heel.

"What of your breakfast? Where are you going?" the Facilitator called after him.

"To locate Carlo. I suspect he'll have the amulet or know its whereabouts."

"I must have your agreement first. On the marriage."

"You have it. When?" Dominic asked, not faltering in his departure.

"At next Moonful."

He was to wed in one month. With a brusque nod, Dominic assented. Striding through a series of arches, he located his jacket and a shirt. Then he was through the nave and beyond, outside the temple. Passing the empty pedestal upon which the statue of Bacchus had once stood, he hurried down the nine marble steps.

At the base of the staircase, something caught his eye. His mother's gem-studded hood lay discarded on the dirt. She'd lost no time in ridding herself of something he'd touched. Something he'd tainted.

He crushed it underfoot and walked on.

14

Seven days later, Dominic knelt on one knee alongside Carlo's decomposing body. A dozen soldiers stood guard nearby just outside the gully, darting sidelong glances at him.

Two hours after leaving the temple, he'd located the regiment in which he'd served with Carlo only to learn that his comrade hadn't reported in upon his return from EarthWorld.

From there, his search had taken him to Carlo's unoccupied home, where a neighbor had disclosed the news that he didn't live there alone. It seemed that Emma's husband had also wed himself to an ElseWorld husband in secret. That he served with the *cinaedi* and had a calling toward men had been well known. Most of the *cinaedi* bound themselves to an assortment of wives, husbands, and concubines. There was nothing scandalous about this in ElseWorld. Why had Carlo kept the relationship hidden?

A series of leads had brought Dominic here to this gully. And this body.

Taking the point of Carlo's chin in his fingers, he rotated the lifeless head, noting the telltale gouges at the throat. A puff of rust-colored powder escaped them, pressured by the motion. The blood in his veins had turned to dust.

His suspicions were confirmed. Demons had done this. He nudged the naked body, flipping it to lie facedown. As he expected, it had been brutally sodomized.

And it had been discarded here a week ago, if he was any judge. Yet vultures and insects hadn't yet begun to feast. Another indication that demons were responsible, for their peculiar stench kept predators away.

"The work of demons. Probably a lord," he announced loudly enough for the ranking officer to hear. A few gawkers had gathered beyond the gully where the soldiers kept them at bay. Everywhere he went now, he was recognized. Because it was too draining to keep himself constantly disguised with a bespelling, the Facilitator had insisted that he travel with this entourage of two-legged watchdogs.

He thrust his left hand inside the gaping wounds on the body. The soldiers paled and looked away as he methodically searched cavities and innards for the amulet.

"Nothing," he announced at last.

Standing, he went to the stream running in the lower part of the gully, cleansing himself of offal. "Cordon off the area and search the surrounding grounds!" he ordered.

"What are we looking for?" asked the Peacekeeper who led the guards.

"The amulet that was stolen from the Temple of Bacchus."

Every eye widened, flying to Carlo's body in surprise. "He was involved?" one of the soldiers ventured.

"Move it!" he barked, and the contingent immediately ceased their questions and scurried to do his bidding.

An exhaustive search commenced that continued far into the following day, but the amulet remained elusive.

"Stop. It's not here," Dominic said at last. "The demons have it."

They'd drawn a crowd by now—peasants, farmers, three goats, a pair of milkmaids. Even the well-to-do occupants of a passing carriage had paused to watch from their windows. Well aware that he was the focus of their furtive stares and whispers, he ignored them.

He'd kept his dual identity secret from everyone outside his sect for a quarter of a century. But judging by the ripple of excitement he caused whenever he ventured near to the onlookers, everyone here was aware of the spectacle he'd made of himself that night he'd spent in EarthWorld.

It had endangered his people. Exposed his fleshly weakness for a woman who didn't want him. He didn't know which disturbed him more.

"Where are his remains to go?" one of the soldiers asked him, nodding toward Carlo. His body had been wrapped but not yet removed for cremation.

"To the family. In EarthWorld. Send his ashes to Nicholas, the eldest of the Satyr lords who dwell there. Include a request that I be invited through the gate for a meeting with him as soon as possible."

Dominic straightened to his full height, only then allowing himself to consider the full ramifications of Carlo's demise.

Emma.

His heart skipped a beat.

She was a widow.

15

Satyr Estate in Tuscany, Italy
EarthWorld

"I'm leaving the estate," Emma announced. How good it felt to say it aloud.

However, no one remarked on her startling statement, and no arguments ensued—simply because there was no one in the immediate vicinity to hear her, save butterflies, birds, two svelte gazelles, and her three-week-old daughter, Rosetta.

Other than their company, Emma sat alone on the lush, blue-green lawn at the rear of the carriage house that had been her home for just over one year. Though all here was rendered cheerful by dappled sunlight, she felt anything but cheery.

Upon the lap of her dark bombazine gown lay a letter she'd already read a dozen times. It had been written in a careful hand, each word precise and well selected by an elderly, verbose British gentleman of means.

Its contents offered a singular opportunity.

She sighed and rocked her daughter's crib with fingers

stained with intermingled shades of purple, yellow, carmine, cobalt, and jade. "What do you think, Rosie? Shall we hie off to London? Will it be the same place I left fifteen years ago?"

A circular flower bed, divided into twelve equal segments, ringed them. Once carefully tended, the bouquets it grew had been shredded and now littered the courtyard like brightly colored confetti. Her culpability in this destruction was painted on both hands.

As a girl, she'd designed an horologium florae—a clock based on Carl Linnaeus's description in his seminal botanical work, *Philosophia Botanica*. It had enabled her to tell the time simply through observation of the blooming and fading cycles of a variety of wildflower blossoms.

She had created this more elaborate garden a year ago. On the day following her wedding to Carlo. On the day he'd gone to ElseWorld, to war.

It had served as a calendar of months rather than days. The flowers that grew in each planter had been carefully selected to follow the pattern of his monthly comings and goings. Blooming at Moonfuls and fading in the interims. It had been a wife's gift to her husband, this physical display of her anticipation of his rare sojourns in her bed.

The cycle had been completed only once since their marriage. He'd been a husband to her only twelve times in one year.

Just moments ago, the fading primroses of February, the violets of March, and a few early daisies of April had all been wrenched from their moorings and now lay strewn about her. After all, there was no need to mark the passing of time any longer.

Carlo was dead.

Her soiled hands left fingerprints on the letter as she unfolded it a third time.

Salutations, Madame,

*It is with utmost pleasure that I summon you to Lon-
don to assist me in my illustrious endeavors. Your love of
the printed word being as sincerely and clearly evident as
my own, and your knowledge of Latin, combined with
your experience assisting in the organization of Lord
Nicholas Satyr's libraries, recommend yourself to me. The
library I have recently inherited remains in complete dis-
array, and your offer of services is most welcome and for-
tuitous.*

The letter rambled on for several more paragraphs, and
then . . .

*The position I humbly extend to you is for a period of
one year as I have previously explained. If that is agree-
able, you may present yourself at my offices at 12 White-
hall Street, London, as soon as might prove convenient.*

*Please accept my wishes for your safe travel and good
health in the coming weeks until we meet.*

Lord Anthony George Randolph Stanton

Would her employer prove this long-winded in person? His
letter had come from London yesterday, having been penned
by him three weeks earlier—the very date Rose had been born.
It had come in response to her query regarding employment,
which she'd posted well before her daughter had been conceived.

She should inform Lord Stanton of the birth before she embarked on her journey, but that exchange of letters might take
weeks. He seemed an enlightened sort, to have accepted a
woman as his assistant. So she'd decided to proceed with her
plans in the hopes that he would accept her child as well. If that

proved not to be the case, she would look for another position in London and return here only if none presented itself.

Tonight she would tell the family of her decision. She was determined not to stay here, not to become an idle burden on them. She wanted to be truly useful, to indulge her passion for books.

The family would be surprised at her resolve to depart them and would expect her to alter her plans upon their objections. After all, she'd always been untroublesome. Obedient.

Spying a fire lily in the grass, she picked it up, stroking a fingertip along a delicate filament to dust the pollen from an anther at its tip. The stamens—male sex organs.

Dominic.

A cloud passed over the sun, and she shivered. Just over a week after he'd gone, he'd sent Carlo's remains through the gate. A rolled sheet of parchment addressed to Nicholas had accompanied them, explaining that the circumstances of his death were unknown. There had been no message for her.

Realizing she was stroking the lily's smooth, black petals along her collarbone—where Dominic's lips had traveled—she flung the flower away. Flushing, she brushed at the trail of pollen dust it had left at her throat.

The marks on her skin made by his hands and mouth had faded, but memories of her night with Dominic remained fresh. Though she'd grown adept at pushing them away, they sometimes crept up on her unexpectedly.

Especially at night when all was quiet and lonely. Then they mercilessly haunted her dreams, making her body quake with a confusing, shameful desire. It was another reason she wanted to put some distance between her and this place that held remembrances of him. Just for a while.

She stood abruptly and shook out her skirt. It was unadorned black, a dress of full mourning, edged in crepe. A dress appropriate for a new widow.

"Come along, *cara mia*." She lifted Rosetta's crib and made her way toward the house.

Gazing toward the patchworked hills in the distance, she felt a pang. It was a joyous time for the Satyr. The grapevines were bursting with an energy waiting to be unleashed in the form of buds.

By leaving now, she would miss that and the harvest next fall. Miss the fruition of vines over which she had toiled. In years past, the credit for her work had always gone to Carlo. All of Italy considered him the vintner rather than she. None knew the truth—that while she was left in charge of their small section of the vineyard, he had left the estate for a war that raged in another world.

She hadn't resented it. It had kept her occupied and had been another thing tying him to her. If she offered him this bounty to call his own, she'd reasoned, he would want her. Want to come back. But now he couldn't come back.

He was dead, his ashes interred in the family columbarium.

A gardener tipped his hat to her as she passed, his eyes full of sympathy. She nodded and hurried on, feeling the usual spurt of guilt.

Every kind word that came her way made her feel more of a sham, for she didn't feel a widow's grief. Instead she was consumed with regret for her behavior last Moonful. Even though Carlo had initiated the events that had transpired, he hadn't expected her to find pleasure with Dominic. She might not have wanted her husband in her bed, but she'd had no right to desire another in his place.

Sometimes she yearned to confess the secrets of that night. To lance the wound they'd left, allowing shameful memories to purge themselves, flowing forth. Escaping her forever.

Instead she kept her secrets locked inside and waited for their wounding presence to heal, turn to scar, and then fade.

As part of her penance, she accepted others' condolences

and kindnesses with stoic grace. And she devoted herself to her child and the vineyard. Life went on.

Emma paused, setting Rose's basket upon the stack-stone wall that enclosed the garden. She took off her spectacles, fogged them with her breath, and then polished the lenses with a corner of her daughter's blanket. Replacing them on her nose, she considered the shortening, early afternoon shadows.

It would soon be time to depart for Jane's. She gathered the arm of the basket again and headed inside. At dinner tonight, she would tell them.

16

"Everyone, we have a visitor!" Jane announced.

Emma half rose from her station at her sister's piano and then sank back onto the long, lacquered bench seat with an uncertain *plunk*. Her cheeks blanched and then as quickly reddened again as the new guest was ceremoniously shown into the salon.

Dominic.

She drank him in with a hungry sweep of her eyes. Noted the solid strength of him, the watchful silver gaze, the midnight blue highlights in his dark hair. He wore black leather now instead of the gray wool uniform. He looked self-assured, dangerously attractive.

It had been three weeks since she'd seen him. Three long, arid weeks since they'd been as intimate as a man and woman could be.

Now, impossibly, he was here. In her sister's home. In the same *salotto* as she. Sitting on Nicholas's least comfortable medieval-era chair. The fact that Jane had shown him to that particular seat was an indication she wasn't as delighted at his visit as she'd sounded.

What did he want?

Jordan and Juliette had gone to Florence that morning and weren't to return until tomorrow night. During their absence, only Jane, the three Satyr lords, and she had gathered here at the *castello* for dinner and conversation.

"Will you take some of the Sangiovese?" she heard Nicholas inquire.

"*Grazie.*" Dominic's rumbled assent sent prickles of sensation along Emma's nape. Where he'd kissed her. Their eyes caught. His dropped to her throat, and the faintest of smiles twisted his lips.

Without realizing it, she'd begun stroking the very place on her skin that his mouth had marked. Snatching her hand away, she needlessly adjusted the spectacles she'd just donned in preparation for playing a selection from one of Giovanni Paisiello's operas. Then she lifted the music from the stand onto her lap, rummaging through it with shaking fingers.

In the general hubbub of greetings, no one noticed her withdrawal at the sight of the new arrival. For all they knew, he was merely a passing acquaintance of hers, introduced to her only briefly on one previous occasion. The night Rose had been born.

"Emma was just about to make some sort of announcement before she plays for us." At the sound of Nicholas's voice, her unseeing eyes froze on the row of ivory keys before her. Her fingers fiddled with the pages in her lap.

"Emma?" Jane prompted.

Emma straightened her spine. She was being ridiculous. Of course she wouldn't postpone her plans simply because Dominic had arrived. He was nothing to do with her. She was to leave soon, and arrangements must be made.

She stacked the sheets of music on the piano stand with a crisp *thwack*.

"I have decided to leave the estate. To go to London," she heard herself say.

Air was abruptly sucked from the room—drawn into every pair of lungs as objections swelled in those around her, bursting to be voiced.

"I depart next week," she rushed on. "I have entered into an agreement of employment—"

"What the devil—?" Lyon protested.

"Emma! Why?" Jane put in at the same time.

"Let her finish," said Nicholas, shushing them.

"My employment is to be at a gentleman's library for a period of one year." Quickly Emma provided them with a smattering of other details, and then, "I know you will think it a poor idea, but I am determined. I don't wish to be a burden any longer."

"You're not a burden!" Jane exclaimed.

"You're an innocent widow with a child." Lyon scowled. "Easy prey."

A single, sharp crack rent the air, sending all eyes whipping to Dominic. His right hand had fisted on the stem of his goblet, its grip so vicious it had snapped an inch-thick column of solid crystal!

"He's right," Dominic muttered, oblivious of the servants who scurried to repair the damage he'd wrought.

Emma frowned at his hand as the remnants of the goblet were removed and the wine he'd spilled mopped up. Tonight it wasn't protected by that strange glove. Yet the glass shards didn't appear to have cut him. "This is none of your affair, signore. I'm a grown woman capable of making my own decisions."

"Who is this employer?" Raine demanded, drawing her attention.

"He could be a lecher, for all she knows," Lyon scoffed before she could speak.

"He's not! He's a gentleman!" Emma leaped from the bench. "I will not argue the matter with you further. The work in his library interests me, and I plan to follow through with my decision."

Fortunately Rose chose that moment to fuss in an adjacent room, giving Emma a pretext to escape their harangue.

"Excuse me, please." With a whoosh of her inky skirts, she slipped down the short hallway to the room where her daughter slept.

Two pink fists and two white, beribboned booties waved in the air above a crib that had once held Jane's son Vincent, who was now nearly grown. Rose was generally a calm sleeper, but it appeared she'd kicked off her blanket and was wide awake. Gently Emma tucked the lightweight wool around her. Rose kicked it off again.

"Determined tonight, are we?" she asked softly.

"Hers seems to be the prevailing attitude."

She straightened at the sound of Dominic's voice, seeing that he'd come alone. "What do you want?"

"A private conversation with you," he murmured, his voice pitched low so the others wouldn't hear.

"Regarding my decision to go to London?"

"And other matters." His eyes went to the crib.

"You've nothing to do with my decision to leave." Emma gave her daughter a final pat and turned so she blocked his view of her child. "Or with Rose."

"Rose." He echoed the name softly, as if growing used to its flavor.

"Rosetta." She came toward him, maneuvered him into the hall, and pulled the door with her, leaving it slightly ajar so she would hear if her daughter stirred again. When she stepped out of the room into the corridor, Dominic was waiting for her.

His hand fell to her waist, and they stood in the doorway, frozen. This close to him, her perfidious flesh tingled with fond remembrance of his. Though their bodies had communicated for over eight hours, they'd spoken no more than a handful of words to one another.

"Just because of . . . what happened, don't believe you have any say in our lives," she said.

"I'm afraid I must."

Her hand came over his, intending to pull it away. She felt that strange, familiar hum she recalled from that night three weeks ago. Confused, she looked down and saw that he had donned the silver glove before coming to her. She plucked at it with her fingers. "Why do you wear this?"

He snatched his hand back, and his gaze ricocheted off the glove to meet hers.

"Wear what?"

"The glove. You didn't have it on earlier."

"You can see it?" He sounded astonished.

Shooting him a quizzical look, she only shrugged and hurried off. He caught her just outside the *salotto* mere yards from the safety of the others. His ungloved hand manacled her arm. She yanked once, trying to wrest away.

"Let go."

"You may choose to have our conversation alone or within your family's hearing," he said. "It matters not to me."

She firmed her sealed lips, mutinous.

With a brief incline of his head, he let her go. "So be it."

They returned to the room, and Emma had just reached Jane's side when he calmly made his announcement. "I have come here tonight to claim the right to rehusband Emma."

Every face filled with varying degrees of shock.

Emma gaped at him, speechless.

"By what right?" Lyon demanded, bolting up from his chair.

Raine stood as well, looking prepared to defend her.

Only Nicholas remained calm, watchful. "Let him speak."

"Surely you aren't considering his suggestion?" said Lyon.

Nicholas held up a hand for silence, and though Lyon scowled, he folded his arms and glowered expectantly in Dominic's direction.

"A joining between our families has obvious advantages," Dominic said smoothly. "I am full Satyr, a desirable candidate to bring new blood to your line. And a wedding will serve to calm tensions between our worlds and keep those who seek to harm your family at bay."

Jane slipped a comforting arm around Emma's waist. "I'll not have my sister used as a political tool."

"Emma?" Nicholas asked. "What have you to say?"

"I don't want to marry him," she said quickly.

"There," said Jane. "You have her answer."

"I cannot accept it," said Dominic with a slow shake of his head. His calm perseverance threatened her more than any show of force might have.

Lyon made a move in his direction, and Raine appeared ready to do the same.

Dominic raised a hand to forestall any attempt to thrash him. "There is a reason I have specifically chosen Emma."

Guessing what he might reveal next, Emma took a step forward to stop him. "Don't!" she choked out.

But he went on, his words driving into her heart like spikes of shame. "When last I visited your compound, I participated in the Calling." She gave him a tiny, beseeching shake of her head, which he ignored. "With Carlo and Emma."

Gasps rent the silence, and five pairs of eyes focused on her.

"Emma?" Nicholas prodded.

"It isn't true. None of what he's saying." Never a good liar, she colored at her own falsehood.

"Carlo was a jealous man. He wouldn't have allowed it," said Lyon.

But she heard the twin threads of doubt and disappointment in Lyon's voice and cringed from them. Emma and Lyon been friends since she'd first come here as a girl. It pained her that he would think ill of her, even for a moment. Around her, she read concern and growing suspicion on every face.

She glared at Dominic, the cause of her embarrassment and her family's disillusionment.

"There are ways of proving the truth of what I say," he warned gently.

"Your suggestion is ridiculous. It's far too soon to even consider another marriage." She swept a hand to indicate the somber widow's weeds she wore. "It's been less than a month since Carlo's death!"

"Yet you are prepared to leave for another city," Dominic noted. "Despite your grief."

She flushed, knowing he'd guessed how little she would miss her marriage. "I need to make my own way. The opportunity in London will allow me to work among books. I've made plans for my life and my daughter's. Please let the matter rest."

His pale eyes were steady on hers as he shook his head, resolute. "I cannot."

Nicholas ran a hand over his face. "If Emma says no—"

"Carlo was impotent." Dominic's quiet words split the atmosphere like a crack of thunder.

Emma stepped back as if he'd slapped her.

"He was rendered impotent from an injury in the war in ElseWorld. Stabbed in the chest and pelvis. It occurred only days after he'd gotten Emma with child."

"Traitor!" The angry words burst from her. "You've betrayed a confidence."

His brow lifted. "*You* assured Carlo you would not tell his secret. I made no such promise."

"But Emma's child. The Birthing," said Raine, looking perplexed.

"Knowing he couldn't bring it about last Moonful due to his condition, Carlo invited me here that night for a specific purpose," Dominic calmly informed his fascinated listeners. "I was to stand in for him as a sexual surrogate with Emma. Which I did."

Emma recoiled from the weight of the gazes directed her way and turned her back on them.

"Is this true?" Jane murmured quietly at her ear. Emma gripped her hand, unspeaking.

"And what part did Carlo play that night?" asked Nicholas.

"Little enough," came Dominic's reply.

"What does that mean?" Lyon blasted.

"He left us soon after the Calling began. I facilitated the Birthing and participated in the family Bonding afterward. Alone, with Emma."

"It must have been difficult for you to stay away from her all this time." Raine sounded impressed. "The Bonding exerts a strong pull."

Emma whirled toward Dominic, seething. "Why did you come here? What purpose has it served to besmirch Carlo's memory?"

"I summoned him," said Nicholas.

At that, everyone began to speak at once, and Emma struggled to be heard.

"But why?" she asked.

"He'd requested admittance through the gate along with Carlo's remains, but I refused him. However, in your husband's last bequest written the day of Moonful, he gave care of you and the child to a male descendant of ElseWorld's royal line if anything should happen to him. The man's name was Dominic Satyr."

A ripple swept the group at the mention of his surname.

"It took me some time to make sufficient inquiries to determine that it was Dominic Janus Satyr he intended to name."

"That's you?" Raine inquired.

Dominic gave a regal nod.

"Under the circumstances, I must sanction this marriage if Dominic requests it," said Nicholas.

"I do," said Dominic.

"No!" cried Emma. "I release you from any duty Carlo imposed upon you."

"You can't force her," said Jane, glaring at Dominic. Then she looked at her husband. "Can he?"

"I have claimed the right to rehusband," Dominic reminded her.

"This isn't your world," Jane insisted. "Things are done differently here."

"Jane . . ." Nicholas began.

Emma exploded in a rare display of anger, cutting him off. "I contest!"

The three lords stilled, surprised to see her customary calm so severely shattered.

However, Dominic only nodded, as if he'd expected her words. "Then come."

Emma regarded the gloved hand he extended to her like it was a viper. An odd, disappointed expression crossed his face. Curling his fingers, he withdrew the hand and gestured toward the door with a brusque nod of his head instead, indicating that she should precede him.

On every side of her, her family's silence supported his demand.

"Use the library," Nicholas suggested, officially endorsing the plan.

Seeing little alternative, Emma swept from the room, leaving Dominic to follow her down the corridor. The library was a good choice. Adjacent to the salon, it would keep them from the prying eyes of her family yet was within earshot.

Lyon's warning floated after them, meant for Dominic. "You're allotted exactly fifteen minutes for the ritual. Then we come."

17

Dominic shut the library doors and leaned against them, examining Emma like a prize exhibit set among the priceless objects in Nicholas's extensive collection.

"Shall we begin?" he asked.

"You'll be disappointed," she told him, standing uncertainly in the center of a room filled with books, parchments, urns, and other antiquities relating to the Satyr family's heritage. "I'm not of ElseWorld blood. Your rituals won't work with me."

Those beautiful, wicked lips of his curved in a smile of masculine optimism. "You've lain with me. Perhaps I've tainted you."

"What is it you're really after by coming here?" she snapped.

His eyes narrowed, cooling. Leaving the doors, he stalked her down a narrow aisle between two massive bookcases. At the far end, her back was pressed to the wall. Slapping a palm to the plaster on either side of her head, he leaned close, a breath away.

"You know what I want."

"No." Steadfastly she trained her eyes on the three gleaming suits of medieval armor that stood along the far wall opposite her and told herself to make her own skin as impervious to his wiles as the armor was to jousting poles. She and Jane had relocated the knights here last month, dubbing them the "triplets" in honor of her sister's youngest children, a trio of ten-year-old sons.

As a collector, Nicholas's interests were eclectic and expensive, but the ancient artifacts he'd painstakingly acquired had once been displayed in his rambling *castello* in a shockingly haphazard manner. Under her and Jane's direction, everything in this room had been organized. Everything in this museum of a house had been as well. No small task, it had taken them a decade. But now all was done, and she would go to London to meet a new challenge. This man would not stop her.

"Look at me."

Her eyes flashed to his. "Do you imagine I'm so foolish as to believe you truly came here for *me*? That you want me?"

"Why wouldn't I?" he asked, sounding genuinely taken aback.

She made a skeptical sound and began counting the reasons on her fingers. "Because I'm twenty-seven! And plain! I have no talent for magic as my sister does. Is it that you wish for something else? Riches? Asylum here in EarthWorld? Whatever it is, speak to Nicholas. Do not use me to gain it."

"Very well. I'll tell you what it is I want." His lips lowered to nuzzle in her hair. His knuckles brushed the side of her throat. "The amulet."

She blinked. "Hmm?" When she realized what he'd said, her heart sank. The very last thing she'd wished for was a second troublesome husband. But for a few seconds, she'd hoped . . . that he would say something altogether different. *Fool!*

She pushed at his chin and felt a soft stubble. "Stop that. What amulet?"

"The one stolen from the temple of Bacchus. Carlo spoke of it at dinner on the night we met."

"Ah! At last we have the truth," she interrupted with a caustic laugh. "But I know nothing of that. Are we finished?"

His teeth punished the side of her neck. She let out an embarrassing squeak and went up on tiptoe, pulling back from him until her spine was in danger of melding with the wall. "You're not allowed to touch."

He cocked his head slightly and considered her, two fingers toying with a tendril of hair that had escaped to curl on her cheek.

"How is it you are familiar with this ritual?" he asked, though she had a feeling he'd originally intended to ask something else.

She nodded toward a nearby shelf. "I've read most of the books in the *castello* libraries. The ancient ones contain a profuse, detailed mention of the various rituals of your kind. And there are references to numerous amulets as well, none of which I have in my possession."

"You understand I refer to the golden coin Carlo had when I visited? The one you'd utilized to—"

"I haven't seen it since that night. Nor do I wish to ever see it again."

Silver eyes bored into hers. Then, seeming to be satisfied at the candor he read there, he murmured, "Well, disappointing as that is, I'll still wed you."

"No. You won't." She glanced past his shoulder toward the gold filigree and enamel pendulum clock that hung just above the triplets. "Nicholas is quite proud of that timepiece on the far wall," she said. "It's accurate to within a fraction of a second, even after one century of keeping time. And it informs me you've already wasted seven minutes of your allotted quarter hour with me."

"I will need far less than the eight that remain. And as your family will undoubtedly barge in upon us and you will dash away the instant we are done here, I plan to dawdle with you a while before getting on with . . . things."

"I'm hardly the type to inspire dawdling." She nudged her spectacles higher on her nose, a barrier between them. "How old are you?"

"Twenty-five."

"There. I'm older than you, and for that reason alone we wouldn't suit. Men don't wed older women. Unless the women are wealthy, which I'm not."

A hint of a smile touched his lips. "Two years is nothing. I assure you I'm centuries older than you in experience. And I've wealth enough for both of us. My people tithe a portion of their incomes to me for certain duties I perform on their behalf, and I've used little enough of it."

The reminder of duty seemed to strengthen his determination to persuade her. His forearms flattened on either side of her, and he crowded her, surrounding her with his masculine body and scent. Yet, keeping to the rules now, he was not touching.

Without warning, he plucked her spectacles away, blindly setting them on a high shelf to his right, out of her reach. She raised her hands to stop him but then thought better of it. Touching him would only make her want him, thus aiding his cause. Any outward sign of physical awareness in her would bolster his right to rehusband in the eyes of the others.

"Six minutes," she informed him in a thin voice.

His mouth hovered over her skin, and his breath came, fresh and warm against her throat, her jaw, her cheek, her lips. She quivered, and a small, betraying moan escaped her. Did his breath count as touching? It should.

"Your words reject me. But your flesh remembers mine," he whispered close to her ear as if he had all the time in the world.

She concentrated on the ticking of the clock.

"It remembers our night together like it was yesterday. It remembers the feel of my cock slipping between your legs, invading you. You could have that again, Emma. Every night. The slide and thrust. The delicious fullness of me inside you."

Her feminine void throbbed dully, craving what he offered. Another moan welled up in her, but she quelled it.

"Not so full as you'd obviously like to think," she fibbed. Was that besotted voice really hers? Her eyes flicked to the clock, desperate. "Four and a half minutes."

He only smiled, supremely confident, but his voice when it came was solemn. "Let me have you, Emma. Do you not wish to lie with me? To feel your softness open, yielding to my hardness? To feel the hot, wet pump of my seed greeting your womb? To feel your flesh gasp and weep and pulse with the coming of ultimate release?"

Under her skirts, her nether mouth gulped, hard, parched for a taste of what he described. She pressed her eyes and lips firmly closed, trying to shut him out. Only three minutes left.

But already she knew it was too late. For she'd felt the flush of blood rush to heat her chest. Inside their confinement, her breasts swelled above her corset, their nipples hardening to points that were visible through her bodice. They poked the cool leather of his jacket, and he slowly rocked his chest side to side, grazing them and sending shivers over her flesh. She couldn't argue that he'd cheated, for her traitorous body had touched *him* in this, not the other way around.

Her hands rose, grasping the rocklike, mounded muscles that were his upper arms. He stilled, waiting until she opened her eyes. Then, deliberately, his knowing gaze dropped to her bosom.

She flattened one hand over her bodice, and when she pushed him away with the other, he allowed it. Bursting past him, she stood with her back to him and tugged the neckline of her dress outward. And saw ...

Gods! Her body had betrayed her as she hadn't believed it capable of doing. For beneath her black mourning, her nipples had taken on a barely discernable, peach-hued glow. She'd read about this phenomenon in the ancient texts. The breasts of ElseWorld females luminesced like this, but only when a male partner with extraordinary pull had aroused them. Dominic had scarcely touched her!

Behind her, he stood with one shoulder braced on the wall where she'd been, his arms folded. Smug. The bulge at his crotch was tremendous. She moaned, cupping her hands over her pink cheeks. What would her family think when they saw?

"But I'm Human!" she whispered. "How can this be happening?"

He shrugged. "Your mother lay with King Feydon. I lay with you. A potent blend of our Fey and Satyr seed is part of your makeup now."

She straightened, pleading. "You cannot truly wish to shackle yourself to an unwilling wife? For both our good, can't you just go?"

Silver eyes flickered over her. "I Bonded with you and your child."

"Carlo's child."

He nodded. "Yet I have a claim, too. As a result of that night, I feel a pull to be with you. To protect your daughter. It was strong in my world, but now that I am here, what's between us is even more overwhelming. Don't you feel it?"

"No," she lied. Then, more honestly, "I don't want to."

He chuckled, his face softening for an instant and offering her a glimpse of the man he must have once been. "It gladdens me that you are a poor liar."

She glared at him.

"Marriage to me will not be so horrible. I'll visit you often enough to remind you that you're a wife and to remind your land it has a keeper. Your share of the vines will wither and die without one of Satyr heritage to occasionally tend them."

"Nicholas and the others can—"

"They have their own vines. Yours will be a burden."

She shrank from the words fearing they were true. "They don't consider me or my vines a burden. We're a family."

"Still, your refusal could cause strife among them. Could mean an escalation in the war in my world."

"So much hinges on me?" she scoffed. "And yet it would all go away if you would take yourself off."

His expression hardened. "I cannot. There's more at stake than you realize. More than I've told—"

A sharp rap sounded on the door. Nicholas entered, immediately followed by his brothers and Jane.

"Well?" he asked.

"Well?" Dominic asked her, his voice low. His eyes hadn't left her despite the intrusion.

"I'll not have another absentee husband, and I won't entrust Rose to an absentee father of whom I know so little," she said only for his ears.

Though he didn't move, his body seemed to loom larger and closer, intending to hold her. She sidled past him, seeking the safety of the others, and he let her go. "No matter what the ritual's outcome, I'm Human and not bound by your ancient rules. I won't wed him," she announced.

"There. You have her answer," said Lyon.

"We'll escort you to the gate," Raine added.

"Wait," Dominic said quietly.

"She has said no." Standing back from the door, Lyon swept his arm wide, indicating that Dominic should precede them from the room and then the *castello*.

"There's another reason this wedding must take place," Dominic went on, not budging despite Lyon's threatening tone. "Tonight."

A new tension permeated the air. Dominic lifted his right hand, immediately drawing every gaze to it. Before their eyes, it shimmered briefly. A silver-threaded glove swam into view, one that had not been discernable before, at least not to eyes other than his own and Emma's.

Emma and Jane glanced at each other, understanding that some momentous ElseWorld force was at work here, but not knowing what it all meant.

"Remove it," said Nicholas, nodding toward the glove. His face was grimmer than she'd ever seen it.

Dominic tugged off the glove and then slowly opened his fingers, displaying his palm. Its concave center was slick and silver. A mirror that flexed with his hand's every movement. He purposely caught the candlelight in it, blinding them all for just a moment. Then he replaced the glove, and his hand fell to his side.

"I don't understand," said Emma.

"Rosetta is a Chosen One," Dominic informed her somberly. "It matters little who fathers such a child. But it's imperative that the existing Chosen One bring him, or *her*, in Rose's case, into the world a month later during Moonful. It's why I came here with Carlo that night. Why I was sent here. To help birth my successor."

As if they were a sharp rocks thrown upon an icy pond, his words broke the atmosphere and cracked through the superficial calm around them.

"Fucking hells!" said Lyon. "We can't wed Emma to a demon-hand."

"A what?" asked Jane.

"I've read about them in the ancient books in your library," said Emma in swiftly dawning horror. "They're protectors of some sort. Apprehenders of ElseWorld creatures called demons."

Dominic inclined his head and regarded her with flat, stoic eyes. "When I die, your child will assume my duties." He held up his right hand again. "She'll wear a glove like this one. And imprison the evil souls of demons in her own mirrored palm."

Emma backed away. "No! She doesn't have a such mirror."

"It will come. In time."

"There's some mistake. You can't have her!" Feeling a sudden need to be certain her child was well, Emma fled the room. Shooting Dominic a hard glare, Jane went after her.

"A female demonhand?" Nicholas asked once they'd gone.

All three brothers were glowering at him as though they would happily see him disappear. But he was accustomed to animosity, and theirs didn't wound him.

So he only nodded. "A first. It has been decided that it's best to keep her here in this world where none from mine can penetrate without your invitation. She must be safeguarded by every possible means. Wedding her mother to me will bolster that protection. I believe you wed your own wives at King Feydon's behest for similar reasons, did you not? To protect them from forces that would do them harm?"

18

A clergyman in Florence was rousted from his bed and brought to the *castello* to preside over what was likely the briefest and most hostile nuptial ceremony of his career.

Thus it was that seven hours after Dominic had arrived in her sister's salon, Emma found herself wed to him. A short time beyond that, the pair stood together under the candlelit portico, and she was bidding her new husband farewell.

"Night comes soon in my world," he said into the near darkness that preceded another dawn in hers. "The demons will begin to stir. I must go but will return if I'm needed. You have only to let me know."

"I won't be here," she said quickly. "I intend to depart this estate as I'd planned and make for London."

In the flickering light from a dozen or more candles set in elaborate sconces, his silver eyes turned implacable. Far different from those of the man who'd earlier flattered and wooed her in the library.

"That I must forbid. You cannot go. Nor the child."

"Then my daughter and I are to be prisoners here?" She twisted the ruby-and-diamond-encrusted ring on her finger, donated for the ceremony from Nicholas's gem collection. It had once belonged to Cleopatra VII of Egypt, a pawn of powerful men. Fitting, she thought.

"You are not the only one whose plans have been disrupted. In ElseWorld, I was betrothed to another," he informed her.

Her heart jolted. He was in love with another woman?

"It was to be an arranged marriage between two strangers," he said, reading her thoughts. "Before I journeyed here, I reneged."

"You're quite the martyr where I'm concerned. First you do Carlo a favor by bedding me. And now you've done your world another by wedding me." She spread her hands in pique. "How do you imagine all this is to work between us? It's assumed that I cannot cross into your world without injury, but I won't send Rose there without me. Ever. Even if she's called by your people."

"As long as I am alive, she won't be called."

"Then I wish your death to be a long time in coming."

"As do I," he said with a rare trace of humor that was quickly gone. "As for how our marriage will work, I will visit your bed when I'm allowed passage into your world, but we will live apart as did you and Carlo."

So she was to be trapped in another loveless marriage. To a man who considered her an obligation and an occasional vessel for his seed. A sob escaped her, and she crossed her arms over her middle, trying to rein in her emotions.

"Emma." His voice softened, and he stepped nearer as though to touch her.

"Don't," she spat, pulling back. "Just tell me one thing and then go—why Rose? Why choose her for this horrible duty?"

He froze. Though her animosity appeared to wound him as her family's had not, he only said, "Remember the amulet I spoke of—the one you used as a contraceptive? It was from the

Temple of Bacchus and had special properties. I think they may have somehow contributed to her selection."

"So I'm to blame?" she challenged, her voice rising.

He shook his head. "No, but neither am I. It's impossible to know all the factors that went into her choosing, just as it was impossible to know why I was elected to wear the glove fifteen years ago. Since that day, each sunrise has been a victory for me because I've survived one more night of battle. I live to fight evil so that good people may go on about their lives."

"I don't want that life for my daughter."

"It's her destiny. I can't change it."

"She didn't ask for it."

"No demonhand does. But I can teach her how to survive it. Prepare her. If I'm allowed to come."

"You don't want this for yourself either," she guessed in slow surprise. "I assumed you'd sought this life out, but . . ."

His shoulders shifted, as though he was uncomfortable that she'd found a chink in his armor, and he sought to rebuild his defenses. "I'm a weapon, Emma. That's all I am. Don't let your imagination gift me with any finer qualities."

The morning song of a lark split the sudden tension between them. The sky had begun to lighten.

"I must go." He glanced at her and ran a frustrated hand through his blue-black hair. "I cannot return to you without an invitation that will allow me passage through the gate."

He waited a beat. No such invitation came his way.

"Maybe when Rose is older," she said. "If it seems she needs you."

"So be it," he said, gruff and distant. "But when you're lying alone in your bed, wife, remember this. Toward the end of that night, you wanted me. I can make you want me again. You need only ask."

With that, he turned and departed for the gate, treading the same path he'd taken just shy of four weeks earlier. He was gone within minutes. Back to his world—the world where she could not trespass.

And that night and every night thereafter, in her solitary bed, she did think of him.

19

Else World
Moonful

Severing himself from the black of night, Dominic entered the temple, reeking of blood and destruction. Around him, the atmosphere was hushed and stagnant as if the air itself were leery of drawing his notice and temper.

The stars overhead were already blazing with light, harbingers of the full moon to come. Soon the Calling would beckon and the Change in him would begin. Then this wrath of his would rechannel itself into a mindless, driving lust.

His boots stomped across the marble tiles. Tomorrow the votives would clean the muddy tracks he'd left, wiping away all trace of him as best they could so that everyone could happily pretend he didn't exist.

After all, weapons were meant to kill, not to intrude on the everyday lives of those they protected.

Having just returned from battle, he was smeared with the

evidence of his exertions. His jacket and shirt had been slashed. At some point he'd discarded them in the dirt and left them behind. Both arms were bloodied, and his body was hot and humid with sweat.

But his wounds were minor and would heal. His opponents had not been so fortunate.

He'd taken down a dozen demons tonight and was tormented with the remembered pain of accepting their souls into his flesh, one by one. To hold them in his possession fouled him, sickened him. This never-ending despicable duty was slowly destroying him. Changing him.

For trouble hadn't found him tonight. No, he had searched it out. When he'd come upon a nest of demons he'd taken delight in slaughtering them. More and more he was coming to wonder who was the more evil of them? Demons existed only to kill. Was he any better?

When he reached the center of the temple, the Facilitator and his two Acolytes were in their usual places. Hovering near the obsidian mirror, they gazed intently into it as though expecting it to impart some mysterious wisdom to them at any moment.

A dozen or so females had gathered as well. They were going through the motions required of them before the celebration of Moonful commenced—diligently cleansing the statues that ringed the enormous chamber and polishing the smaller reflecting mirrors.

Upon his entrance, the Facilitator took one look at him and made an assumption regarding what he required. Waving a gnarled hand toward the women, he beckoned them to abandon their tasks and see to him.

Those who drew near him at the Facilitator's command were plainly terrified yet obedient. None of them had come to this temple out of desire but rather out of obligation. Fresh ones were summoned here regularly each Moonful to attend Do-

minic as he wished. And they came, prepared to sacrifice themselves to the wicked desires of the demonhand.

Were he to bury himself in their bodies, they would be
cleansed of his seed come dawn, and the cloths used to soak it
up would be burned, for his people believed it carried the same
taint as did he. The women would then be sequestered high in
the temple's loge and ultimately released only once they'd bled
again—proof they had not conceived.

Afterward, they would whisper of what had befallen them at
his hands. There would be talk in the streets, fashionable sa-
lons, and harems. By now, tales of his sexual prowess were
widespread and had grown to mythical proportions.

"May I be of service to you, Savior?" one of the females
asked in a voice that shook.

Blood still thundered in his veins, a holdover from his recent
fight to the death. In spite of his rage, he only stared at her, as
stone-faced as the ancient statues that silently observed him
from their shadowy alcoves.

Her hair was blond, not a lustrous ash brown. Her eyes were
emerald, not warm chestnut. She wasn't the one he wanted.
Nor were any of the others who'd come.

"Leave me," he growled. The woman only blinked at him,
incredulous that he was refusing her. "All of you!"

Executing only the most perfunctory of curtsies, she went,
taking her companions with her. All fled him and the temple,
openly gleeful at their good fortune in escaping unscathed by
his legendary lust.

The Facilitator started to speak, but Dominic cut him off.
"You as well," he ordered.

Unperturbed by his foul mood, the elder merely executed
his usual formal bow in response. Then he motioned toward
the Acolytes, making to depart.

"Not them," Dominic said, indicating the Acolytes, who
had also turned to go.

The Facilitator looked as though he wanted to object, but another glance at his scowl had him continuing on his way and leaving them behind.

Dominic approached the mirror. The Acolytes shifted closer to one another, nervous at being alone with him.

"Turn it on," he said, jerking his head toward the reflective disk. "I wish to view the location from EarthWorld that you last showed me. But as it is now, at this very moment."

They eyed him curiously for a few seconds; then, with a simultaneous clap of their long-fingered white hands, they obeyed. The image he sought floated into view, wispy at first and obscured by an ethereal murk.

Gradually shapes and shadows began to clarify themselves.

His body tightened expectantly as a familiar room swam into sight. The bedchamber where he'd mated Emma. Dusky blue linens draped the bed where he'd lain with her. The bed where he'd plunged his cock between her legs. Into her mouth.

The same bed where she'd kissed him. Held him. Begged him.

Carlo's bed.

"No," he murmured. "Show me the other room. The adjoining one where the Birthing of the Chosen One took place."

Another clap, and the image shifted to Emma's bedchamber. It was empty.

Almost immediately, a woman appeared. His entire being surged with expectation and then as quickly deflated.

Not Emma. A servant. One with ElseWorld blood in her veins.

As he watched, she went behind the lacquered changing screen that stood in the corner of the room. The one where Emma had attempted to hide herself from Carlo while employing the amulet as a contraceptive. The large window next to it stood half open, its glass pitch black and opaque. This was one of only three Moonfuls each year in which nighttime in the two worlds coincided.

The servant stepped from the other side of the screen again and came back into the room. He heard splashing sounds. Someone was behind the screen, bathing. His eyes burned over its slick, painted surface, willing it to disappear and reveal whom it hid.

But it held, thwarting him. And a world away, he could only wait. Eventually his fierce patience was rewarded. A figure emerged.

Emma.

At the sight of her, something inside him relaxed. Untwisted. Calmed.

Swathed in toweling, she approached the mirror and gazed into it, unaware he played voyeur.

Tendrils of hair curled at her temples and nape, damp from her bath. Her skin would be warm and feminine. Clean.

By now, her touch on his flesh was but a receding, beguiling memory. But her scent was still caught in his throat. His desire for her was fresh.

It was dangerous to want something—someone—this desperately. Beside him, the Acolytes took careful note of his hungry expression, and he heard the hum of their concerned thoughts passing between them.

"You may go," he muttered. Even before he'd finished the statement, they'd already begun their departure, having anticipated his wishes before he'd given voice to them.

They would tell the Facilitator what he'd asked to view in the mirror. Somewhere in the bowels of the temple, the three of them would huddle together and worry the night away over what it meant, over the possible consequences of his strange attraction to the mother of the Chosen One. There had been consternation enough when he'd wed her a week ago, for he'd gone against duty—a first for him.

The thick bronze doors at the entrance to the temple's enormous nave boomed shut behind the Acolytes. He heard the heavy scrape of metal upon metal as the doors were sealed against invasion for the duration of Moonful.

He was virtually alone here now. Only the statues, a wealth of riches and artifacts, and a few guards and servants remained sequestered inside with him. None would dare disturb him unless he summoned them.

Unlike in EarthWorld, this special night would span nearly thirty-two hours, though the moon would show itself only for the next eight of those. The twelve hours of utter blackness that fell before and after the moon were the most dangerous of the month, for demons were especially active then.

In the mirror, Emma had picked up a tortoiseshell comb and was strumming it through her hair. The servant in the room with her fidgeted and cast a furtive glance toward the mirror. She was a hamadryad, a night creature gifted with unusual perception. Did she sense him watching?

As if taking her cue from his unspoken desire, the servant commenced assisting Emma in the removal of her wrap. His fingers twitched as his eyes found the soft, enticing nest at the apex of her thighs. It was visible for only the merest of seconds before she was enfolded in a concealing gown.

He let out a low growl of protest but could only look on in frustration as the gown slid over her. Its neckline was prim, its drape opaque, and its design even more conservative than that of the one she'd worn last Moonful when he'd bedded her. When the servant added a robe to the ensemble, his ripe curses colored the air. He'd forgotten she wore so many damned garments. He wanted her naked.

Emma moved to the right of the mirror and out of its range, disappearing briefly. When she returned into view, she held a bundle of pale yellow blankets in her arms. A small fist popped from among them. Rose.

She carried her precious bundle to a fragile-looking chair and sat. Dipping one shoulder, she brushed her robe from it.

The front of her gown drooped to bare the upper swell of a breast. She was preparing to feed her child.

A gentle smile curved her lips as the infant latched on to her nipple. The peaceful, loving scene was a balm to his wounds, an antidote to the bite of misery in his silvered palm.

He pressed that gloved hand over his naked heart, willing it to push away the desire for anything more than the duty life had dealt him. The evil it held bussed his skin like muted charges of furious lightning.

From nearby, something unwanted and unfamiliar suddenly intruded on his contemplation of Emma. A promiscuous, cloying scent teased at his nostrils. His hand lashed out blindly to his right, and his fingers closed around an arm. A feminine one.

20

He yanked the woman into the circle of artificial light cast by the mirror. Manacling her shoulders in both hands, he lifted her so she dangled before him.

Silver locked with pewter as each examined the other. She was one of his own sect, one of the females who'd been here when he'd arrived. Apparently she'd stayed behind.

Numerous braids of pitch-black hair snaked to the middle of her slim back where they were caught in a clasp that matched her eyes. Dressed in the traditional flowing garments that revealed more than they concealed, she was voluptuous and beautiful. But she'd been a witness to his weakness and as such was a good target for his wrath.

"Spying on a demonhand is punishable by death," he gritted with silky menace.

She leaned forward and kissed the center of his chest, surprising him. Nibbling her way to a flat nipple, she nursed at him. Her lips were softer than they looked.

Air sucked between his clenched teeth, and he was lulled into allowing her free rein for a moment. No one ever touched him except under duress. He'd expected her to struggle and flee like the others.

"I am Itala," she murmured in a breathy voice when he set her on her feet. "I wish to be of service. The whole moon is coming. You'll need someone." Her eyes went to Emma's image in the mirror and then found his again. "Someone real."

"Get out," he muttered.

"Don't turn me away." She took his fingers and pressed them to her full breasts, squeezing her hands over his to help him massage her through the translucent silk. "I am flesh. Better than any Shimmerskins you'll conjure if I go. Let me tend you."

He eyed her, weighing her motives.

Quickly she knelt at his feet, her upturned eyes tempting him. Her covetous fingers groped him through black leather.

His cock swelled as she began to unfasten the ties at the groin of his pants, and he allowed her to undress him. No longer in the uniform that he'd donned to fool Carlo, he wore only his customary leather leggings and boots. She removed both, and in the end, he helped her.

Sensing his capitulation, she eagerly wrapped his freed root and balls in an avaricious hold. Then she tilted his cock down to her mouth and took him inside in one smooth, wet glide. Lips and tongue fondled and coddled him, making his swollen length throb. Her chin lifted, and her throat muscles relaxed, coaxing his crown ever deeper.

Gods! He braced his legs wider, cradling her head with both hands and watching her suck him off. She was talented. Experienced at pleasing a man. Still, even as she ministered to him, his thoughts were on another.

His gaze rose to find Emma. Her head had lolled back on the chair now, and she was looking directly at him, as if she could actually see him. Shadowed by dark lashes, her eyes were lazy, contented, sweet. Her hair was tousled and would be soft in his hands.

Hands that even now were absently smoothing the darker hair of this other, lesser woman.

As a daughter's innocent mouth worked busily at a mother's plump breast, so the nimble mouth of a stranger worked at his thick, ruddy cock.

After several moments, Itala's lips released him, and her head turned. Unexpectedly her hand covered the back of his where it rested on her hair, and she drew his palm to her mouth. A tongue flicked out and, like a snake, she licked his glove.

Stunned, he shook her off. The sight of her depraved desire for the most heinous part of him filled him with disgust.

She scrambled to her feet, undaunted. "The others are afraid, but I am not like them," she said, a fanatical light in her eyes. "I have prepared myself for you. Made my body as you need. Two openings for your cocks, and . . ."

She reached for his gloved hand again, but he held it high and away. Undeterred, she captured his other in its stead and drew it beneath the loose skirt that lightly draped her from the waist down. Under the translucent fabric, she helped his fingers trace over her belly.

Pressing, she pushed them into a moist, unnatural opening there, just above her pubis.

". . . and one for your hand," she whispered, confirming his worst suspicions.

She'd gone to one of the parlors and had herself mutilated in a way she believed would make her more appealing. Her pelvis had been pierced, and an additional nether throat constructed inside her beyond it, so that as many as three men could fuck her lower body.

Or a man with two cocks and a gloved fist.

He knew her kind. There were others like her on the battlefield, always lurking about the amputee wards, their eyes covetous on the stumps of the maimed.

He recoiled in distaste. She whimpered as he pulled his fingers from her, but she remained fixed on her goal.

"Later, then, when you have more need of it," she cooed. "For now, perhaps a more traditional joining?"

Insinuating herself closer, she led his shaft between her thighs and attempted to manipulate it inside her. The traitorous appendage bobbed with enthusiasm, wanting to be housed in female flesh. Not this particular female's flesh, but he must make do with someone, and she was willing. . . .

A dozen stone-cold faces watched from the alcoves, effigies of ancient, lustful deities, all silently urging him to take what was on offer. Sorely tempted, he reached for her.

As if in reaction, a single moonbeam abruptly infiltrated the surrounding dusk. Then another and another, until all nine smaller mirrors in the circle around him had become cups brimming with light.

In a glory of illumination, the moon burst into full bloom. Its radiant face filled the aperture overhead and, finding him, it demanded that he undergo the Change.

Arms outthrust, Dominic arched his spine, and his face rose to the heavens, accepting its salacious command. Muscles rippled and bunched along his shoulders and torso, and a downy fur sprouted to dust tree-trunk thighs.

Itala avidly monitored these changes. But he'd forgotten her. Forgotten everything. His entire being was now focused only on a lecherous anticipation of what was to come.

His ridged abdomen spasmed as if an invisible hand plucked at its muscles, playing a cruel, carnal melody to which he must dance in the forthcoming hours. A strangled groan of pleasure-pain tore from his lungs as a second cock ripped itself from his belly. Its distended length speared the air to stand just above the cock that already angled from his masculine thatch.

Hands came, uninvited, caressing his genitals. Itala. "At last, you're ready for me, lover," she whispered at his ear. "Come. Come fill me."

His eyes opened to the barest slits. Her breath wasn't sweet. Her hair was wrong. *She* was wrong.

Beyond her, he glimpsed the mirror. Emma still reposed there, an angel with a child at her breast. Her face glowed with a quiet, maternal love. She was his wife, but he could not go to her. Not without that damned invitation.

Still, he would not be reduced to this.

His hand wrapped itself around Itala's throat, squeezing. "Have you a soul to give me?" he taunted ominously.

She closed her eyes and turned her palms to the skies, euphoric. "Yes, Savior! Take it as you fuck me. Take my soul!"

Though he was sick with libidinous need, he nevertheless shoved her away, thoroughly revolted. She clung, her fingernails striping his skin.

She had no concept of what she asked for. He could demolish her with a single touch of his ungloved, mirrored hand if he so chose.

"Go from me. Now!" he snarled.

When she didn't obey, he took her by the arms and half dragged her across the room, where he flung her toward its arched exit. Then he staggered back to the obsidian disk, every step away from her an agony of physical denial. Although the temple's protective aura diminished the Calling's effect on his wits, its physical impact on him was every bit as overwhelming as it had been in EarthWorld a month ago.

Taking a cock in each hand, he drew from roots to crowns and back, masturbating himself. Behind him, her voice rose, castigating him. "Fool! Do you truly think the prim woman you watch so hungrily would willingly take your loathsome flesh into her straight-laced body?"

He took one menacing stomp in her direction. She leaped back and scurried the rest of the way to the portal.

"I trust you will enjoy your own evil hand on your cock," she spat, "whilst I find others more willing to take pleasure in what I can provide. There will be many who want me, I assure you." With that, she flounced from the room.

Her smug steps faded down the corridor as he watched her walk. Almost immediately he heard eager voices—male ones. She was speaking to the two guards posted halfway down the corridor at the entrance to the nave. Offering herself to them. Hoping he would see and hear and become jealous.

He angled his jaw, observing the transaction through cynical eyes. The men she solicited were of the Satyr. They set down their weapons, quickly agreeing to her lascivious proposal.

One positioned himself before her and one behind, both enthusiastically fumbling at their trousers. The moon had affected them as well, he saw when buttons and ties released. A set of two cocks extended from the gap each opened in his uniform.

There were no preliminaries in negotiations such as the one Itala conducted. As soon as their pelvic shafts sprang free, one guard stabbed himself into her anus and the other took the gash she'd had drilled in her abdomen.

Sandwiched between them, she shot an angry dart of pewter in his direction, wanting to know if he watched. He did, still massaging himself with both hands. When pre-cum welled in his cockslits, he siphoned himself in firm strokes from balls to tip, bringing more. Fat droplets beaded, quivered, and then fell to soak linens that had been laid upon the floor for him.

Tomorrow votives would burn these cloths on sacred pyres while humming ancient incantations. Any inadvertent spill of his seed not expelled into the safe haven of a Shimmerskin would be summarily destroyed as tradition dictated.

As matters in the hallway progressed, Itala let out a joyful shriek. The cock rooted low at each of the guard's groins were piercing her now—two squeezing together as one to invade her vaginal channel and stretch her as a child never would. By defiling herself in the parlors, she'd ruined any chance she could ever conceive.

Regardless they would likely take care to withhold their childseed from her. With anyone but a Shimmerskin, it was the safest course. The hours of Moonful were the single span of time during which a Satyr male could sire offspring, and even then it was possible to choose whether or not one's seed would be fertile. Tonight some would breed sons and daughters on their concubines and wives.

However, were Dominic to defy law and do the same, the demons would inevitably learn of it. And they wouldn't rest until they'd crushed what he loved.

No, he would sire no children tonight. Nor any other night.

Yet he *would* fuck.

21

With the ease of long practice, Dominic gathered his Will, concentrating it on an empty space just in front of the mirror. From the unearthly ether that eddied thick along the ground on nights such as this, he summoned forth a female Shimmerskin. One whose cheek had the same gentle curve, whose back had the same slope, and whose eyes and hair were the same winsome brown color as she for whom he pined. A virtual twin to Emma.

An insentient being, she stood before him, docile, sensual, unashamed of her nudity, and eager to please him in all things. He curved a hand at her breast, and her fingers combed down his thatch to find and cup his balls. At her touch, his shafts surged in unison, bumping her belly.

Sex with her would be a meaningless exercise, like that which took place even now in the corridor where the guards bucked themselves into Itala. As they ruthlessly rutted her, she goaded them on with coarse words and greedy hands, jouncing like a rag doll between them.

He could've told them to go, to continue on in another place where he wouldn't bear witness to their fornication. But the crude, passionate violence of the act they performed fueled something dark in him. Sent his unrequited lust soaring. Made him reckless.

Hungry, silver eyes flashed to the mirror. To Emma.

Her child was gone again, presumably to its crib, and she'd wandered to stand at the window of her room. The leftmost of its two expansive glass panels had been unlatched and swung open. Resting a hand on the edge of the one that remained fixed in place, she leaned out and lifted the point of her chin, breathing in the night air. The breeze hugged her figure, gently tailoring fabric to outline her curves.

In her chaste gown, she looked beautiful, endearing, bereft.

Fuckable.

Heat churned through him, and with it came a fierce longing, stronger even than the one he'd felt when he'd first seen her in this mirror weeks ago. A longing to hold her. To ease her loneliness and his. To feel her come.

But she was not here, and the Calling ritual beckoned him into its furious maelstrom. At his unspoken command, the Shimmerskin turned, presenting him with her smooth back. She lolled her head on his chest, and her arm rose, her palm coming over her shoulder to wrap the side of his neck. Though his own hands boldly traced her curves, his eyes were on Emma. Though he would join himself to the replica in his arms, he would pretend that she and the original in the mirror were one in the same.

"Dominic."

He froze at the sound of the voice. *Her* voice.

"Emma." Without thinking, he extended a gloved hand . . . and did what was forbidden. Touched the obsidian disk. Touched *her*.

Looking startled, Emma's reflection clamped a hand to lips his fingers had just brushed.

His pulse stalled, then raced. She'd felt him!

He tapped the edge of the mirror, this time purposely honing its focus so that she and the Shimmerskin's visages and figures became a similar size. Emma hadn't moved, and for a moment he feared the mirror might punish him for his transgression by fading to black. Affecting an offworld being via the obsidian disk went against the primary laws of the ancients. It was an act punishable by death. But he was fearless, for he existed outside these laws. A weapon such as he was simply too valuable to be done away with.

Emma's hand dropped to the window ledge, and relief filled him as he determined her temporary stillness hadn't meant that she was to be summarily removed from view. Wearing a dreamy expression now, she swayed, beginning to fall under the supernatural spell of the disk. Gazing into the night, she spoke again.

"Dominic." His name on her lips was a gentle prayer. A wish. A yearning sigh.

A month ago, there had been two men attending her in this ritual. This month there would be none. But she'd called for him. *She wanted him.*

By the Gods, he wanted her as well. His entire being was quaking with need for her, his every muscle tense, his cocks straining with a lecherous desire to have her. And he *would* have her—in the only way open to him tonight—by means of the surrogate he embraced.

The staunch grip of his fingers tightened, dimpling lush hips. Leaning forward, his body pressed the Shimmerskin's to the mirror until her breasts gave against it.

In her room, Emma's body pressed itself against the windowpane as if held there by an unseen force. As he'd expected, when he relayed an instruction to the Shimmerskin or physically adjusted her, her human twin dutifully mimicked the action.

Emma's profile turned his way and a look of wary anticipation colored her expression. "Is that . . . ? Are you . . . ?"

"I'm here, *cara*," he murmured. "Are you ready for me?"

The Shimmerskin's hands flattened on the mirror at either

side of her head. Emma's crept up the window to brace themselves in a similar position, where they remained as his own hands smoothed down long, sloping, womanly curves, gentling his intended victim to his touch.

The body he held undulated like a cat being stroked, and in the mirror, Emma echoed the movement. His chest would be hot at her back, and the glass cold at her cheek and breast and belly, even through the gown.

He brushed aside a long fall of chestnut hair, kissing a nape, catching and locking on a bewitching scent. The bit of linen peeking from the wrist of his glove snagged his eye and he faltered briefly. Emma's handkerchief. The one he'd stolen from her bedchamber.

It had become his habit to keep it with him when he went into battle, as a reminder that he must not fail her or her child. After a month of fighting, it had become almost as scarred and repulsive as he was.

It was a timely reinforcement of the fact that it was best that he and this woman were separated by worlds, for if she were near, he would no doubt eventually ruin her as he had this square of linen embroidered so neatly with her swirling initials.

He should desist in this.

But malevolence hummed and sparked within the glove where the pulse of demons beat at him, fevered and wanting. Urging him on.

He hoisted the body he held to her toes and shoved her knees apart, inserting his own between them. Emma's legs separated as well. His hands slid up the back of her counterpart's thighs, and Emma's gown rucked upward in response, until the fabric bunched in silky folds at her lower back. His hands roved the delectable peach of her naked bottom, massaging, remembering.

The Shimmerskin's hips tilted up for him and Emma's followed suit. Framed high between her thighs, nether lips parted and plumped. Her feminine slit was prim and pink. Glistening wet.

Waiting for him. He traced a finger along its length, testing its slick, delicate clasp.

In another world, quick snatches of breath fogged window glass.

"That's it," he coaxed, his voice dark and low. "Offer your pristine body to me, wife."

Swollen, ruddy pricks nudged into position at two nether openings. His growl colored the air, harsh and possessive, as he claimed female flesh in a dual glide that pierced and took and gave.

Two female voices moaned in avid harmony.

He withdrew, only to plow again, so vigorously this time that both mirror and window glass shuddered. And then again and again, and with each ardent impact, he watched the mirror, relishing the visceral evidence that his push-pull was affecting Emma. Saw glossy, puckered lips fold inward with his ingress and pout at the threat of each subsequent departure.

Emma's eyes darted toward him over her shoulder, then away.

"Yes, it's me. You know it's me fucking you, don't you?" Would she remember this tomorrow or was her mind too clouded by the disk's bespelling?

"Yes. *Yes.*" Entwined, breathless murmurs marked his every stroke. When the Shimmerskin shivered, Emma shivered. When the Shimmerskin swayed, she swayed. Theirs was a driving, carnal symphony. He, the conductor. And they, the instruments his cock played upon. Three bodies, acting in concert. Two souls, mating.

Behind him, the grunts and groans of those who still fornicated nearby in the corridor, echoed dully off the temple walls, spurring him on toward his own inevitable conclusion.

He shoved deep. "Gods." His mouth seared over the tempting angle where throat met shoulder, branding it.

His hand clutched a feminine belly, anchoring the groins of Emma and her effigy's to his own. His balls were quivering and heavy with unspent cum. His cocks twitched and jerked with the need to feel it pump through them.

A strangled shout left him to join twin dulcet gasps as torrid semen blasted from the depths of his very core, coming in spasmodic, viscous spurts. His massive frame shuddered with each giving of it. The woman he held wrenched tight with impending release, and when she ultimately came, he saw Emma's slit pulse for him, clenching and unclenching in time to the milking he felt at his cock.

Three bodies strained together. Three faces, three cheeks, three sets of lips came close, almost touching, almost kissing. In a bedchamber a world away, a windowpane that was misted by their humid lust grew streaked by the fingers Emma curled into fists of ecstasy.

For a suspended moment, he saw his own reflection in the mirror alongside hers. Saw his satisfaction and his anguish at this heady joy, a joy rendered imperfect by their separation.

"Emma." His breath mingled with hers. His need to be with her was a living torment inside him. He could almost smell her skin, taste it. Though only an inch thickness of mirror separated them, an entire world stood between them.

As their coming eventually ebbed, his pelvic cock retracted from the rear cleft it had so enjoyed. Sufficiently sated, it was efficiently returned into his own flesh until the next Calling night. The woman before him and the one in the mirror both sagged in his embrace. Though the former only feigned satisfaction, as did all of her ilk, the latter slumped at her window, her breath ragged, her face replete. Affected. By him.

As it always was in the Calling, one taking soon segued into the next, and orgasms swelled and broke, tumbling upon one another so often and regularly that they almost became a constant state of being. Womanly passages wept with his leavings, one spill of seed easing the way for more and still more.

And so the delicious hours passed, and he rutted them away, willing time to slow.

But in due course, as the weary moon sought the far horizon, things came down to one final joining. In her world, Emma lay on her back upon her bed now, arms stretched overheard on the pillow, wrist upon wrist as if tethered there by the clasp of a spectral hand. Her long, ivory throat was arched, her naked breasts high and quivering, her eyes screwed tight as she concentrated on the sensation of his prick moving inside her.

Watching her, Dominic drove deep, encasing himself within the Shimmerskin who lay under him on linen-covered stone. Only to suction from her and slam home again. His grip manacled her wrists . . . his thatch rasped hers upon each rut . . . his balls thudded against her, sending a fervid thrill through him. . . .

I'm going to come. Deep inside her, deep. Any minute. . . .

The cruel horizon snuffed another ray of moonlight, attempting to sever the connection between worlds.

No! Not yet. Not yet.

With an agonized groan, he spilled his gift . . . one . . . last . . . time.

In the mirror, he saw rapture shade Emma's face and saw her call out a jubilant cry he could no longer hear. Upon each subsequent loss of moonlight, he would lose more of her. Deprived of her voice and flesh, he would be as a vine without water or sunshine or air.

Beneath him, the Shimmerskin faded into the nothingness from which he'd summoned her. Under the temporary carpet of linen, the stone floor was hard and unforgiving against his bruised knees.

Out in the corridor, three depleted bodies fell together in a heap. Itala and the guards had borne witness to his entire night, as he had to theirs. Word of him fucking the mother of the Chosen One via the sacred mirror would soon filter throughout society, lending new spice to the tales of wickedness that already circulated about him.

Utter darkness consumed him, body and soul. The moon's departure signaled the end of the Calling and the beginning of the black hours that would precede dawn. He had to rally himself. This was the time when the demons were at their most dangerous.

Wearily Dominic rose and went to cleanse himself. Locating a washing cloth, he dipped it in the basin and made to bathe his chest and arms. His eyes returned to the mirror, drawn there by the magnet that was Emma. Oblivious to him now, she still lay sprawled on her back among the pale yellow sheets of her bed. She was nude, save for a strip of blanket artistically draped across her belly.

He tore his gaze from her. Duty called to him. Cloth in hand, he ran it over his genitals, lifting his cock. And then it was that he realized there was *no seed*. None. Anywhere. Not on his prick, his thighs, or his belly. He checked the linens covering the floor and found only a smattering of droplets here and there. Yet he'd ejaculated countless times into the Shimmerskin. Into . . .

The bronze doors that protected the inner nave of the temple shrieked with annoyance as they were abruptly thrown open.

"Savior!"

Dominic swung around at the sound of the ravaged voice just in time to see the Facilitator collapse at his feet. Blood pooled around the elderly man's frail, wounded body, soaking into the linen carpet.

Seeing no one in pursuit, Dominic knelt beside him. "What's happened? Who did this?"

The Facilitator clutched at him with wizened fingers, his face contorted with panic. "The evil. It comes because of you. I didn't know. Gods help me. All this time, I didn't know."

Was the man delirious?

"Stay with him. I'll summon a physician!" Dominic called to the guards who'd gathered with Itala. He made to rise, but the Facilitator held him in a death grip and rushed desperately on.

"Twice now you've crossed the gate into EarthWorld. For the duration of your sojourns there, the evil didn't visit us with the darkness. I've only just now tonight realized . . . Don't you understand?" A froth of blood gurgled from his lips, and he began wheezing, fighting for every breath. "All along, it's been the presence of a demonhand here in this world that brought evil to life. . . . Without you here, they cannot exist. You must go from this world. Go!"

Stunned at the magnitude of what he'd revealed, Dominic could only watch the life in him begin to fade. "The demons," the Facilitator moaned as his eyes rolled back in their sockets. "*You* create them."

As though the Facilitator and the Acolytes had been right all along in their assumption that invoking the name of the demons would summon them, lights began flashing on all sides of him.

Demons were invading the temple, dozens upon dozens of them. More than he'd ever seen at once. As the Facilitator went limp in his arms, they surged near, immediately slaughtering Itala and the guards and knocking Dominic to the ground. Surrounded by more of them than he could possibly prevail against, he nevertheless leaped to his feet and began to fight.

Minutes later—naked, bloodied, and barely conscious—he was being dragged from the nave by clawed hands. His gaze lit one last time on the vision in the mirror that was fading with the end of Moonful.

Blithely unaware of what went on in his world, Emma rolled onto her side with a sigh of contentment he couldn't hear. The bed linens shifted with her. One leg drew up slightly.

A thin rivulet of cum trickled from her, shiny silver on her inner thigh. His seed. It had been potent. There had been no need for him to show restraint with a Shimmerskin. For they could not bear children.

But Emma could.

22

EarthWorld
Moonful

Emma surveyed the milky-colored smears on her bedsheets with horror. She knew exactly what they meant, for she'd found similar stains on these linens on mornings after Carlo had bedded her. And on the morning after Dominic had, one month ago today.

Dominic.

She moaned deep in her throat, a wail of amatory memory and incredulity. Her sheets smelled of *him*. Of sex. And they were strewn with male seed. How was that possible? Ripping them off the bed in a sudden frenzy of denial, she balled them in her arms.

Heading for the corridor, she passed Lord Stanton's letter, which lay open on her writing desk. Growing ever more stale by the day, his invitation offered a perpetual opportunity to escape. One she'd decided to accept.

Tomorrow she would take Rose and leave for London. Not wishing to hear more of her family's arguments against her plan, she had told no one as yet.

She refused to pine here alone in a house that was empty of yet another husband who didn't love her. And she would not let that same husband's world steal Rose from this one if he was destroyed.

Carrying the sheets downstairs, she deposited them in the laundry, raising the brows of the servants for this break in routine. Ignoring their questioning glances, she retraced her steps, rushing up the staircase as if fleeing the stains and what they could mean.

What she was imagining was impossible!

But no more impossible than the fact that her body displayed every sign it had been plowed long and hard last night. The private female flesh secreted high beneath her skirts was unusually slick. And it ached pleasantly with each step she took as if . . . as if last night's dreams had been *real*.

As if Dominic had come to her in the darkness and had lain with her. As if he'd mounted her countless times and found his fulfillment deep within her, even as she'd reached her own. Her dreams of him had been erotic, the stuff of fantasy.

She shut her eyes tight, but still she saw the shine of the quicksilver gaze that had held hers as the fullness of his male organ had come into her. Still she felt the rasp of his evening beard on her throat, at her breast, between her legs. Her hand rose to her bosom and squeezed gently and surreptitiously, trying to relieve the untoward sensation that memories of him had rekindled. It didn't help.

Though she hurried to her bath, she couldn't seem to wash away thoughts of him. They continued to haunt her throughout the day as she packed her belongings and made preparations to close the small house for the coming year.

As the afternoon lengthened, her pace slowed. Her travel arrangements were nearly complete by the time she climbed the narrow staircase that led to the attic to see to one final task.

Ancient floorboards creaked as she made her way across the musty attic, batting at cobwebs. Kneeling, she opened her leather trunk and rummaged through the woolens and fleece she'd brought with her from England fifteen years ago.

It quickly became apparent that none of the girlish clothing here would fit her any longer except a satin-lined muff and a woolen scarf or two. The early spring climate in England would be far cooler than here in Italy. She would have to purchase warmer clothing for Rose and herself immediately upon her arrival in London.

Sighing, she closed the trunk and made to stand. But she immediately sank to her knees again when her head spun. She put a hand to her belly, feeling queasy.

Her heart thumped with panic. She'd felt this way before. The morning after Rose had been conceived. A Satyr child's development in utero was swift, and its effects on a mother were quickly felt.

No! She could *not* be with child. Not again. She hadn't even been intimate with a man!

Pushing a wisp of her hair behind an ear, she cocked her head, listening. For a moment, she thought she'd heard her daughter cry in her crib one floor below.

But all was silent.

Rose had been strangely fitful all day. Usually an easy sleeper, she had woken at dawn and had seemed to grow more distressed by the hour.

It was far too early for teething, and Emma was at a loss to know what else might be troubling her. She'd considered taking her to Jane this morning for advice, but when Rose had quieted later in the afternoon, she had not done so after all.

Exhausted, Emma slumped again, relieved that Rose seemed to have settled down, for she felt ill equipped to deal with a fussy child today. The two of them made quite a pair. She could only hope they were more themselves tomorrow, or her trip would have to be postponed yet again.

Last night's sleepless hours still haunted her. Her nocturnal fantasies were likely the very sort her sister and aunts would soon enjoy in the sacred glen with their Satyr husbands, for tonight was to be a Moonful Calling in this world. It would be the first such night in a year's time during which she would not participate in the ritual. Perhaps that was why she had dreamed of it last night.

Folding her arms atop the trunk, she rested her forehead on them. She yawned once and closed her eyes, just for a minute.

A cool hand touched her cheek, startling her. She glanced up to see one of the night servants. She'd come silently, as they always did. And she'd come with the dark. Twilight had fallen.

Emma blinked at her, trying to come fully awake. "It grows late. I guess I dozed off."

Unlike the rest of the family, she was rarely able to see these creatures unless they specifically wished to reveal themselves to her. Distantly related to the ancient inhabitants of ElseWorld, these innocuous, servile hamadryads hid away during the daylight hours but roamed the Satyr households at will after the Human servants left the estate at dusk.

Emma stood carefully. Encouraged when she didn't grow faint this time, she began briskly dusting her skirt. The creature's touch came again at her elbow, more urgently this time.

Her face was ethereally beautiful with red lips and eyes the color of cedar boughs. Normally the features of the night servants were placid. But this one's expression had knit itself into something resembling fear.

"What is it?" Emma said, straightening. Tucking the muff

and scarf under one arm, she allowed herself to be led down the stairs. Icicles shivered her spine when she realized where the hamadryad was directing her. *Toward the nursery.*

The clothing she held fell to the floor unnoticed, and she began to run, terrified. Was something wrong with Rose? Dire fairy-tale stories of banshees and changelings raced through her mind.

Scurrying ahead of her escort, she dashed inside the nursery. Three sylvan night servants were clustered around the flounced crib.

They stood back, making room for her as she approached. At the sight that met her eyes, Emma put a hand to her chest to slow its pounding. To her immense relief, Rose still lay there amid her blankets, safe.

"Why did you frighten me like that?" she asked, running a gentle hand over her daughter's small frame. "She appears to be fine."

Rose's delicate fists were clutched tight at her chest. The hamadryad who'd found Emma in the attic seized one of them and tucked her finger within the child's grip. Carefully she pried it open, forcing the tiny pink fingers to uncurl.

When the small hand opened fully, Emma could see that something shimmered within its keeping. Frowning, she took the hand in hers and turned its palm more fully to the candle-light. It was silver!

She rubbed her thumb over its glistening surface. "What's this? Her hand seems to have been painted!"

The night servants all appeared concerned and guileless. They adored Rose and wouldn't have done this. But who would have?

Rushing to the basin, she dipped one corner of a linen cloth into the cool water. Dampening it, she then took it to the crib and rubbed at Rose's palm. If anything, the shine of silver in-creased, as if it had been polished.

Emma tried again, rubbing harder. But the luster remained.

Then she took note of something odd. Her daughter wasn't objecting to this treatment.

"Rose?"

No reaction.

Emma took the girl's chubby cheeks between both hands, shouting now. "Rosetta!"

Rose's lashes fluttered tiredly. When they reluctantly opened, Emma gasped. Her daughter's irises, normally a muted gray color, had turned the identical color of her palm.

Silver.

Like Dominic's.

These changes—this illness in her child—had something to do with him. With their time together the night Rose was born. Or perhaps her erotic dreams of him last night had brought this on. She neither knew nor cared what the cause might be. She only wanted her daughter made well again.

Scooping Rose and her blanket in her arms, she made for the door.

"Signora?" one of the servants queried softly.

"I'm going for help," Emma threw over her shoulder. "To my sister and her husband. If any of my family come here for any reason while I'm gone, tell them what has happened and where to find me."

Without waiting for a reply, she dashed downstairs and threw open the carriage-house door. Flying through the courtyard, she took the moonlit path that led to Nicholas's and Jane's *castello*.

Though the full moon would probably have had them convening in the glen as soon as dusk fell, they sometimes conducted the Calling ritual in their home instead. Because it was closer, she tried there first.

Ten minutes later, she burst into their home, her lungs heaving. Running past the surprised majordomo, she flew through the expansive marble-floored entry hall and called to them from the bottom of the stairs.

"Jane! Nicholas!" Her shouts reverberated through the *castello*. Darting from *salotto* to study to library, she found no one. Hearing her, several more night servants gathered in the front hall.

"Are they here?" she demanded.

As one, the hamadryads solemnly shook their heads.

"Where, then? The glen?" They calmly nodded in tandem, but Emma was already heading for the back entrance. "If they return, tell them my daughter is ill. Tell them to find me in the glen!"

She exited by the kitchen door and slipped across the mosaic tile courtyard in the rear garden, locating the footpath she hoped would take her to Jane and Nicholas. Ahead the forest seemed closed to her, a dark, forbidding wall of fir, cedar, and oak.

Picking her way through it, she went at a more leisurely pace than she wished to for fear that she might drop her daughter. The unsympathetic moon refused to permeate the forest's umbrella, so her path grew ever darker and more uncertain.

Long arms of foliage fought her every step of the way, snatching at her hair and skirt. It had rained earlier, and she found herself slipping and nearly losing her footing several times. Eventually she halted in the middle of the trail, thoroughly exhausted and confused.

The glen. Where was it? She'd been there only once with Jane, years ago as a girl. Peculiar forces protected it, just as they protected the gate. Were they purposely leading her astray?

"Jane! Jane! Nicholas!" She stood there in eerie semidarkness, calling desperately but receiving no response in return. The moon would hold the three Satyr lords in thrall, and they in turn would bind their women to them until sunrise. The Calling ritual had likely rendered them all deaf to her pleas.

A cedar bough shifted fleetingly so that a moonbeam caught Rose's face. Her complexion had taken on a pasty hue. Her movements were uncoordinated and abrupt. Convulsions. Emma's heart lurched and began trying to pound its way out of her chest.

When she looked up again, the way ahead had become impenetrable. But a new avenue through the woods seemed to have somehow opened to her left. It was as if the forest were intentionally trying to usher her in that direction.

The ancient gate lay that way. And beyond it, another world. And Dominic.

Hope blossomed. Was she being guided toward him because he'd know how to mend this child he'd helped birth?

Pivoting, she let the forest lead her where it would. It was a desperate move, for she'd been sternly and repeatedly warned away from the gate ever since she'd first come to the estate.

Within minutes she reached the grotto that housed the sacred entrance to ElseWorld. She slipped between a framework formed by a triad of ancient trees—oak, ash, and hawthorn. Their thick, craggy trunks bowed toward one another to form a live, arched entryway, and their branches fingered skyward, tangling to obscure the moon's unblinking eye.

Stepping along gnarled roots that intertwined to form a set of braided stairs, she found her way inside the cavern beyond. There, all smelled of flowers, herbs, grapemust, and enchantment. Made momentarily light-headed by it, she sank onto a low limestone altar set in the moss that covered the floor.

As her eyes grew accustomed to the absence of moonlight, she noticed the strange markings that glittered on the walls on every side of her. The path continued some distance ahead, ending in a void from which a strong aura of powerful magic emanated.

So this was the gate.

The strange humming sound that issued from it had intensified since she'd arrived, making the arms that held Rose tremble. Though ElseWorld creatures couldn't breach it from their side without an invitation, the Satyr could easily traverse the gate from this direction if they so chose. However, she was entirely Human and had long been cautioned by her family that the act of passing through it would likely harm her. Dominic had intimated that his seed had somehow changed her—made her infinitesimally less than Human—but the gate nevertheless sounded most definitely unwelcoming. Was he wrong?

On her lap, her daughter was quiet save for the frail breath rattling in her small, defenseless chest. "Rosie! Darling," she whispered.

No sweet smile came in response. No happy wave of arms and legs. Nothing.

Rose was Carlo's daughter, too, and therefore had Satyr blood in her veins. Would it be enough to keep her alive, or would the crossing-over kill them both? Hardly knowing what she did, Emma stood and moved toward the gate. There seemed little alternative but to risk it.

The humming drone rose to a deafening level in reaction to her approach. At the brink of the portal, she halted, suddenly realizing she couldn't expect Dominic to be waiting for them immediately upon their arrival in his world. If passage through the gate rendered her incapacitated or dead, who, then, would speak for Rose? Whoever found them would require instructions regarding what was to be done with her.

Turning back to the cavern, she scrabbled along its wall, searching for a writing instrument. A piece of rock broke off. It was chalky, like charcoal.

Setting her daughter on the altar, she smoothed the front of her small blanket flat. Forcing her hand to stop shaking so her words would be legible, she scrawled the briefest of instructions upon the soft wool: *To Dominic Janus Satyr*

The last few letters barely fit and were smaller than the others.

"Oh, Gods! Why does his name have to be so damnably long!" she wailed, hoping it would be easily read in spite of this.

When she swaddled her again, Rose didn't react. She had curled into a tight ball, still as death.

A dozen feet away, the gate buzzed in rejection like a furious hive of bees that had been disturbed. What would await them on the other side, she knew not. But there was no time for second-guessing this decision. Somehow she knew that Dominic would protect Rose with his life. If he found her. If he knew how to save her.

She had to try. Even if it meant she herself must die in the crossover.

With a kiss upon Rose's pale face, she took twelve steps. The thirteenth saw her through the gate.

23

ElseWorld

Pinpricks of agony stung every inch of Emma's flesh during the instant it took her to cross the gate. It felt as if there really were insects swarming in its magic, all of which had decided to punish her at once, simply for being Human.

On the other side of the gate, she stumbled and fell to her knees. Her stomach clenched, and her throat closed. Hugging Rose protectively, she slumped onto her side. The gravelly floor scraped her elbow, and the smell of loam was thick in her lungs. Cold earth pillowed her cheek.

She was alive.

Moaning, she drew herself into a fetal position and ducked her head to peek at Rose. Was it her imagination, or had she already begun to look healthier?

"Please, please let it be so," she whispered, gently rocking her.

An unfamiliar, suffocating mist surrounded them, but it seemed to bother only her, not her child. Disoriented, she analyzed it and found it tinged with that metallic scent Carlo had brought with him each time he'd returned from the war.

ElseWorld. She'd made it. Just barely.

With dreamlike lethargy, she shifted Rose to the crook of one arm and attempted to stand on legs made of wet pasta. But she quickly wilted, crumpling back to the hard-packed ground.

"Dominic," she whispered.

Sometime later, a flash of red woke her. Then another. There were creatures gathered close around her in the dark tunnel, all with eyes the color of rubies. One leaned close, and she slapped at him, thinking he would kiss her. Instead he only sniffed at her neck.

"Stop that!" She pushed him away, but several others were sniffing along her body now, their noses like the pokes of fingers.

Rose began to cry, drawing their notice. Ghoulish, clawed hands took the girl and lifted her for inspection. Excited, grotesque sounds unlike any speech Emma had ever heard rustled from their lips when they observed her silvered palm.

Emma protested, reaching for her daughter and calling for Dominic again, hardly knowing what she said. But when she tried to move, her innards rebelled, and then all went black.

Eventually she woke again. Rose was calm and cuddled next to her, nursing, her small body warm and alive. Someone had uncovered her breast, she realized, helping her daughter to suckle.

The earth under them shook rhythmically, and Emma's stomach and head ached in time with each jolt. Footsteps. She and Rose were on a litter being carried somewhere by someone. But who?

A light blanket covered them from head to toe. She lay there, staring at its stifling closeness, desperately wanting to see beyond it but unable to muster the wherewithal to lift it. After an interlude, and to her surprise, an edge of it rose on its own as if by magic, just enough so that she could see something of her surroundings.

One corner of the litter rested upon a mottled, olive-skinned shoulder and was held there by the same macabre fingers she remembered from the tunnel. Testing the air outside, she found it more breathable than that she'd inhaled near the gate. Still, ingesting it caused an irksome sort of tickle in her lungs. She stifled the urge to cough, not wanting to attract attention.

Where were they being taken? It appeared to be early morning here. How much time had passed since she'd come through the gate?

She heard a commotion, and the simple conveyance that bore her paused. Raising the blanket a bit higher via her whim proved as easily and miraculously done as before. Peering out, she saw they were in an expansive, tiled courtyard populated with twenty or so beings going about various commonplace tasks. Ahead stood a gleaming temple with bronze doors, an edifice even more massive and ornate than Nicholas's *castello*.

Two olive-skinned male creatures dressed only in loincloths were arguing several yards away beside a wagon hitched to twin four-legged beasts of a kind Emma had never before seen. Nearby a woman dressed in saffron knelt and shot them worried glances as she plucked surreal, bright-colored grapes from a row of vines.

The litter bearers began conversing among themselves in that strange, discordant language they'd spoken in the tunnel. Yet none of the inhabitants of the rectangular plaza took more than casual note of them. It was as if she and her entourage were a perfectly normal sight. Or as if they could not be seen at all!

The older of the males across the courtyard beckoned the kneeling woman closer, and she went reluctantly. She was skimpily clothed as well, for her long, flowing garments were translucent.

When she reached his side, the man indicated with the spin of a finger that she should turn. Once she had, he flipped up the veil that covered her backside. Then he looked on as, without preliminaries, the younger male loosened his loincloth and thrust into her from behind.

Emma gasped.

A garish face filled the opening of the drape, cutting off her view. Her mind let the blanket go, and it dropped back into place. But before she could scream, something touched her forehead through the coverlet, and she knew no more.

24

Dominic devoured the sight of Emma's peaceful countenance as she lay sleeping on the raised pallet in his chamber within the temple. He'd never been happier to see anyone, or more appalled.

Without warning, she opened her eyes to find him looming over her. A shy delight colored her features at the sight of him.

"You shouldn't have come," he gritted. Her face fell, and he saw he'd hurt her. "Emma. I—"

"Rose?" she croaked, cutting him off. She attempted to rise and failed. Her weakness worried him. She would need her strength if they were to escape their captors.

With a clank of the long chains that bound him to the stone wall behind him, his arm came around her, helping her to sit upright in the corner of his sleeping alcove. "She's here."

He lowered the child he held in the angle of his other arm, letting her take Rose from him. Relief flooded her face at the sight of her sleeping daughter's healthy skin and pink cheeks. "How well she looks! You won't believe it, but the reason I brought her through the gate was because she was ill. Dying."

"From what ailment?" he asked quickly.

"I'm not certain." Pulling Rose's right arm from the blanket, she opened her tiny fist with a forefinger, taking care not to wake her. "But I see that one symptom remains."

Emma turned the small palm his way, showing him. Something flashed there within it—a small mirror like his own.

"Nine hundred thousand Hells!" he snarled. "The mirror shouldn't have come to her until her predecessor died."

Was this a sign that his own demise was imminent?

"You look well enough." Emma searched over him with worried eyes, obviously having a similar concern. Before he could reply, a sudden fit of coughing racked her, and she held her charge out to him, wordlessly requesting assistance. By the time he'd resettled the girl comfortably at the far side of the pallet, Emma had calmed.

"You're ill," he said grimly.

"The air here," she said in a thin voice. "It's unbreathable."

His frown worsened as the probable reason for her and Rose's illnesses came to him. "You and the child are having some sort of opposite reactions to our atmosphere here. Though she may dwell in your world, her health will require that she visit this one on occasion. Whereas you—"

He stopped, seeing that Emma had paled even further as his words. His world was an anathema to her. How long would she last here?

Cursing, he eyed the doorless entrance to his cell as he began to pace like a caged animal. With the Facilitator's deathbed revelation, all had been changed. The notion that he and every other demonhand before him had been not only the slayers of demons but also their unwitting benefactors tortured him.

In the hours he'd been held captive here, he had considered every possible solution to the dilemma that had been presented to him. Even suicide, for the elder had specifically told him that it was his presence in this world that brought the demons.

However, because none but he knew this, he'd worried that Rose would be brought here to assume the glove were he to die in this cell.

But now that she had so unexpectedly arrived, all was again changed. If he died, she would be fitted for a glove. And after her, another Chosen One would spring up to receive a glove, and on and on. The demons would continue to thrive.

At the clanking sound that dogged his every step, Emma seemed to take note of his restraints for the first time. Long, heavy chains attached them from the wall to his wrists, dragging the floor behind him as he walked. It was fortunate that the demons hadn't also shackled his legs, for this oversight had enabled him to don pants and boots once he'd been brought here from the nave.

"Why are you in irons?" she asked, blinking at her surroundings as though trying to shake off the effects of the atmosphere sufficiently to take stock of their situation. "Who were those creatures that brought me here? And where exactly *is* here?"

"It's a temple devoted to the worship of Bacchus. Demons invaded it last night."

"Demons?" she echoed in alarm.

"They brought you and Rose here to my chamber several hours ago."

Her gaze scanned the room, and he wondered what she made of his austere cell with its few creature comforts save a pallet, a clothing shelf, and a basin. It was far from what she was accustomed to in her world.

He had to get her back there, but how? Feeling the need for action, he yanked at his chains for the hundredth time, bruising his wrists.

"Stop—you're hurting yourself to little avail." Sitting forward, Emma gestured him closer, examining his cuts and abrasions. Though her touch was meant only as a kindness, his cock hardly cared, for it tautened, wanting her even at this inopportune time. "Why didn't they simply kill us and be done with their greatest enemies? It doesn't make sense."

He stared down at her, falling into her earnest brown eyes, wanting desperately to protect her and knowing that what he would tell her would only terrify her. "Because—"

"Because we have discovered other uses for you."

Dominic whirled to see the demon who'd spoken standing just inside his cell. He was naked, save for the numerous leather thongs dripping with charms—bits of shaped metal, dried flesh, and other obscene talismans—slung loosely around his waist, neck, ankles, and wrists. The first visitor to speak to Dominic since he'd been brought here, the creature scrupulously remained just out of reach, as though he knew exactly how far Dominic's tethers would stretch.

"I am Lord Kurr."

A small patch of sunlight fell on the creature, sending a cold chill arrowing down Dominic's spine. Stunned, he looked to the small, high window of his cell. As he'd expected, the blackness had gone. Outside, all was daylight—a time when demons could not rise. Yet one stood before him!

Reading his thoughts, the demon gave him a smug nod. "Yes, I live in the day as well as the night, courtesy of my host. Soon more of us will assume the flesh of your sect and live as you do. In time, your world will become ours."

The rumors Dominic's mother had heard of demons taking hosts appeared to be true, for this was a demon the likes of which he'd never seen before. Though patches of his mottled olive skin still luminesced randomly here and there, the overall look of him was undeniably Satyr. Unfortunately this demon didn't appear to be the sole aberration. Behind him were others of his ilk who hadn't fully melded with their hosts yet and so came into view and faded intermittently, their inner lights flashing in time with their movements.

Kurr spoke in a dialect Dominic understood but which Emma would likely have difficulty interpreting. However she obviously comprehended the threat he represented, for she skittered across the pallet, trying to hide her daughter among the blankets and simultaneously blend into the stone wall.

The demon's nostrils flared with interest, and a clawed finger whipped out in her direction. "This one stinks of the amulet," he announced. His eyes roved her, covetous. "Where is it?"

Dominic moved in front of mother and child, a six-and-a-half-foot brawny buffer between them and destruction.

"What is he saying?" Emma asked, kneeling up and laying a hand on his shoulder. His thoughts racing, he covered her hand with his own silently hushing her.

Hoping this demon would prove as stupid as all the others he'd encountered, he smoothly tried to bluff. "She has hidden it in EarthWorld. If you want it, I suggest you let her and the child fetch it back to us."

Kurr's suspicious eyes flicked silver and then red again. His claws retracted with an audible click. "Yet you bear the scent of the amulet as well."

"Due only to my association with her," Dominic countered quickly.

The demon's olive-colored hand fell to idly fondle his own genitals, as though the action helped him to think. Eventually a grotesque smile split his face as he came upon an explanation that pleased him. "You lie in order to see her set free. Because you lust for her. Yes. Good. Good. You will mate with her. As she mated my husband, but with better results. You will produce a male."

"Your husband?" New dread crept over Dominic as he guessed what the demon might mean.

"Carlo, he was named. I spilled my seed in his body only hours before he created the Chosen One. You must have known he hungered for you. An interesting trio we made, no?"

Dominic swore inwardly. This demon had fucked Carlo the very same night he'd gotten Emma with child? That meant the seed of *three* males, all of different origins, had gone into the brew that had made her daughter what she'd become. Unpalatable news he planned to forever keep from the woman behind him.

The demon pointed toward the heap of blankets that was Rose. "Fool that he was, he gave her that. Of what use is a female child? Has she semen to spawn more of her kind? No!" He slapped himself in the head at the duplicity of his previous husband, not seeming to realize Carlo couldn't control such things as his offspring's gender.

An understanding of precisely what the demons intended dawned. They believed that as long as they controlled him, they were safe. Now that they'd rendered him harmless, they would no longer seek to kill him.

Instead they would keep Emma, Rose, and him locked away here and attempt all manner of possible reproductive combinations over time, hoping to achieve the production of another Chosen One they could command. A process that would no doubt be unpleasant for the three of them but which would not achieve the results the demons desired.

Dominic arched a brow, concealing his thoughts. "And if I refuse?"

A sharp claw flicked in Emma's direction. "I'll try her on, then, and we'll see if my seed will grow the child you will not sow."

Dominic lunged toward the demon, snarling furiously, but the chains he wore yanked him back. Emma let out a sharp shriek that devolved into more coughs, and Kurr scuttled out into the hall.

Returning to Emma's side, Dominic held her and rubbed a hand over her back, still keeping watch on their enemy who was now just outside the alcove, conversing with his cohorts.

"What do they want? Tell me!" she gasped.

"Rosetta. And more like her. They expect us to mate here in this room. Repeatedly. Producing more—" His brows slammed together as his eyes dropped to her belly. His hand reached toward it, hovering over her flat abdomen but not touching.

"You're with child," he said. It was a flat, resigned statement that revealed none of the turbulent mix of emotions he was experiencing.

She caught his eyes. Nodded.

"It's mine."

"Yes."

A fraught silence passed. "What—no questions? No recriminations?"

"I didn't understand what happened last night—how it happened. But I wanted it. I want you." She closed her eyes, her face turning to parchment. "I'm feeling a bit faint."

"Gods, Emma." He took her shoulders in both his hands, lifting her close, and she gripped his wrists, covering the manacles. "You've picked a hell of a time to—"

Sudden, absolute blackness came as a large, opaque net of some sort was cast over him. He'd allowed himself to be caught off guard. Emma snatched at him, calling his name, trying to hold on to him. Amid the clank of chains and the discordant voices of his assailants, his muffled words to her doubtlessly went unheard. Within minutes he found himself trussed and carried off.

Outside he was thrown to the temple's marble steps, where he rolled and bumped his way down all nine of them. When he landed at the bottom, he began to fight clear of the fabric that cloaked him. Above him at the exterior facade of the temple, the demon lord was preparing to seal the impenetrable bronze gates.

"Wait! No!" Dominic stomped up the first few stairs, tripping over the chains still clamped to his manacles.

"You may go for the amulet. But the other two stay," Kurr

calmly informed him. "If you attempt a rescue, the mother dies. You have one week to return yourself and the amulet to us."

With that, the immense bronze doors clanged, shutting him out.

Every instinct urged him to storm the temple in an attempt to rescue Emma and Rose. Yet he would not win a fight against so many.

And because he had no idea where the amulet was, it seemed Emma would die within the week, either by the hand of the demons or by this world's slow poisoning of her.

He'd never felt this helpless in his life. This was what love had done to him. Given him a weakness. And a reason to live.

Wagering everything on the veracity of what the Facilitator had told him, he gathered the chains and slung them around himself so they wouldn't drag the ground, praying he was making the right decision.

Then he turned and loped for the gate.

25

An hour later, Emma waited on the pallet with Rose nursing at her breast. She was consumed with worry over what had they done with Dominic and what would happen to her child if she died. She had to escape—to go home and summon help.

She drew in a shaky breath that rattled in her chest, willing herself not to cough. Night had fallen, and most of the demons had left her and the temple, presumably to feed. Only one guard had been posted at the cell door, and he was eyeing the ElseWorld servant who'd been sent to see to her and Rose's needs, as if he planned to make a meal of her once she'd completed her tasks.

"In what direction does the gate lie?" Emma whispered to the servant when she ventured near.

"To the west, Signora, though its magic can be seen hovering in the sky from any distance. We don't hide our gate as you do in your world," she replied in subdued, broken Italian. Her frightened eyes darted to the demon. "You should've stayed there. You'll die here soon enough. We all will."

Growing impatient, the demon came closer, growling. After

checking Emma's restraints, he ushered the servant from the cell. When they'd gone, Emma unfolded the fingers of the hand in her lap and stared at the object she'd stolen from one of Kurr's bracelets.

A key.

Wrapped in her handkerchief.

Though the square of linen had once been white and appeared to have been repeatedly laundered, it was threadbare and stained. When they'd wrested Dominic from the room, she'd been holding his wrists and had inadvertently pulled it from his glove in her efforts to keep him with her.

She ran the pad of a finger over her embroidered initials. Four weeks ago, he'd secretly taken this—this memento. For that's what it must be. He'd kept it close all this time as if by doing so, he'd also sought to keep her close.

This sweet, precious knowledge lent her strength when she most needed it, for all was quiet in the temple now. It was time.

Tucking the handkerchief in her pocket, she poked the key into one manacle and then the other. With muted, rusty screeches, they opened, and she shook them off. Though this world had made her ill, it also seemed to have magnified the miniscule amount of magic she possessed, transforming it into a marginally useful talent. Allowing her to manipulate certain objects. Allowing her to filch the key from Kurr.

A horrible shriek sounded from somewhere in the temple, and Emma jumped from the pallet with Rose in her arms, her heart pounding. The servant. She was being attacked.

Dashing from the alcove, she found the mammoth bronze doors at the front of the temple with little trouble, but they appeared to be an insurmountable obstacle. With Rose in the crook of one arm, she attempted to lift the enormous latch with her other hand. It easily held against her puny efforts.

The sounds of ripping flesh and cracking bone echoed off the temple walls, making her fingers tremble. Setting Rose at her feet, she pressed both palms flat over the latch, concentrating, desperately summoning whatever magic she possessed. Long, terrifying moments later, she watched in amazement as it released and the door flew open. Grabbing Rose, she hastily departed the temple.

As she'd been told, an aura of magic swam in the westward distance, indicating the location of the gate. Though she saw no one, the sounds of mayhem were everywhere. Demons.

She hurried down the steps and headed toward safety. Home.

A half hour later, yet another coughing fit struck her, and she put a hand out, resting against a trunk of a tree. Rose was crying. Emma herself was exhausted, sick. Scarcely able to draw air into her lungs. If not for the child she carried in her arms and that in her belly, she would have given up then and there. With a murmur of reassurance to Rose, she roused herself and moved on.

Sometime later, when she drew closer to the gate, she was felled to her knees by another racking cough. This time, it drew unwanted attention. Dozens of demons who had gathered near the gate's entrance now turned her way, their jaws and chests splattered with the blood of their hapless victims.

They came close, shadowing her, surrounding her. Claws snagged her bodice, ripped her skirts. Reached for Rose.

"No!" she wailed, holding on to her child as best she could. Knowing all was lost. That she'd failed Rose. Would never see her family again. Or Dominic.

"Dominic."

Then, as if in a dream, everything began to change before her eyes!

She and Rose were unhanded. Looking disoriented, the demons began jerking and moaning. As their movements grew even more uncoordinated, they began stumbling and bumping into one another and then falling to their knees.

Scarcely able to credit her good fortune, Emma gathered

Rose close and escaped them. The gate swam in her clouded vision, just ahead, only a hundred feet or so away now.

Behind her, the demons turned to wraiths, writhing on the ground. And then in groups of two, then five, then by the dozens, they crumbled to nothingness, their evil dissipating as if it had never been.

Somehow she managed to make it to the cave she sought and drag herself through its tunnel and then through the gate itself. This time, if its magic stung her, she was too ill to notice it.

And then she was through, and she and Rose were falling into Dominic's arms on the other side.

And she was breathing in the fresh, sweet, life-giving air of her own world.

"I have them," Dominic told Nicholas and Lyon. Not expecting the brothers to entrust Emma and Rose to his care, he was surprised when they only nodded and continued through the gate to determine the state of things in ElseWorld.

The chains he wore and encounters with demons had slowed him, and it had taken far too long to reach the gate. Having learned of Rose's illness from the servants and been unable to find Emma, her family had concluded she must've gone to him in ElseWorld.

Therefore, two of the three Satyr lords had already been in the cavern when he'd arrived, preparing to cross over to search for Emma while Raine remained behind to protect the rest of the family and the estate. They had helped Dominic cross in this direction, whereupon he'd quickly informed them of the Facilitator's demise and his shocking revelations, and of Emma's whereabouts.

He'd been attempting to resign himself to the agonizing task of waiting while they ventured into his world. And then Emma had come bursting through, and now she lay across his lap. Cuddled in his arms. Safe.

"I'll take Rose to the *castello*," said Jane, who'd accompanied her husband to the brink of the gate. "I called a physician to see to them when they arrived, just in case. You'll bring Emma?"

At Dominic's nod, Jane took the fussing child from her sister's lax arms and made to go. Hesitating, she turned back to him and lay a hand on his shoulder. "Thank you. For—" Her voice broke with emotion. "For everything." Then she and Rose were gone.

Emma's eyes opened, and her lips curved into that gentle smile that so fascinated him.

His heart surged at the love in her eyes. Never having seen that particular emotion directed his way by anyone before, it took him a moment to recognize it for what it was.

"How are you feeling?" he asked gruffly.

"I love you," she whispered.

Love. She loved him. With that single word, she was telling him he could have her in his arms every night. In his life every day. That he could be a father to Rose and to their unborn child. That he could work her land, tend its ancient grapevines, bringing forth life instead of death.

Not waiting for a response, she sat up within his embrace, looking almost miraculously recovered. "I heard what you told Nicholas and Lyon. I can attest to the fact that your absence from your world seems to have had the beneficial effect you desired. It felled the demons and allowed me safe passage." Laying her head on his shoulder, she gazed up at him. "But now that it's no longer safe for you to reside in your land, will you come home with me? Stay here with us?"

When he still didn't reply, she turned teasing. "You'll have little choice, I'm afraid, now that Jane has accepted you. Nicholas gives her anything she desires, so if she wishes you to remain here . . . I warn you he's a formidable force."

With every fiber of his being, Dominic wanted to agree to

her proposal, but life had taught him not to trust. To take nothing for granted.

He lifted his gloved hand, forcing her to acknowledge it. When he spoke, his voice was rough and low. "I will always carry this evil within me. It's part of me."

She curved a soft palm to his cheek, shushing him. "Only a good, strong man would carry such a burden to keep his people safe. A lesser man would have released the pain of it and left those who depended on him to fend for themselves. To die."

Tugging at the laces of his glove, she held his eyes as she slowly unfettered that most despicable part of him. Beneath the threaded leather, the skin of his hand was pale, unused to light, sensitive. Untouched by anyone save himself for his entire adult life. She brushed her fingers over its back, and he moaned at the sensual thrill it sent through him, his eyelids drooping to half mast.

Turning his hand, she studied the pool of silver at the center of his palm. Then she cupped his hand in both of hers and brought it closer.

"Emma." His voice was tortured, wary, choked with suppressed emotion.

Her breath came, warm and sweet upon the mirror, heating it, misting it. His pulse tripped erratically, and his entire body tightened in rejection, not wanting to subject her goodness to his vileness. Yet craving her acceptance. Craving what she would do.

Her lips touched him then, butterfly light. Caressing the hard, cold surface of his palm.

And at her kiss, something wounded in him was mended. Something frigid was melted. Evil was defeated by love.

26

Satyr Estate in Tuscany, Italy
EarthWorld, six months later

Emma paced the library of the carriage house, anxious as she always was when Dominic took Rose on their regular excursions to ElseWorld. Though they left her only for a day and a night each month, it was a dangerous time.

Dominic told her little of what went on there in that other world. She knew only that Rose was kept sequestered in the temple and that its heavy bronze doors remained locked and guarded while he did what he could to protect his people. There was pride in his voice when he'd told her that no matter how the demons howled and battered at the temple walls in frustration, their daughter didn't cry.

Understandably there was some resistance to their visit among his sect because their presence caused the demons to temporarily rise. Yet the two of them needed to cross to ElseWorld periodically, or both would sicken for the lack of breathing its air.

Fortunately Dominic's world was well aware that it benefited greatly from the tithe of wine this estate provided and the regular exchange of vines and grapes that enriched both worlds. This ongoing trade was necessary to secure the health and survival of all concerned, for without it, all would wither and perish. So an uneasy system continued in which Dominic's people grudgingly accepted the necessity of his and Rose's coming.

Negotiations had been initiated, and it was hoped they would lead to a permanent interworld treaty. When the subject of the missing amulet had surfaced as a point of contention, an exhaustive search for it had been undertaken upon the Earth-World estate. However, it hadn't been found and was presumed lost.

Emma ran a finger along one of several dozen bookshelves, over the gold-leaf bindings of ancient tomes Dominic had brought her from his world. Always he lavished her with fascinating gifts of books, urns, jewelry, parchments, toys for the children, and exotic perfume and clothing, as though he still didn't believe himself to be gift enough to keep her love. As though he didn't want her to rue her decision to stay with him rather than go to London.

She took care to reassure him that she had more than enough to occupy her mind and spirit here now—two children, a flourishing vineyard, and a growing collection of books and artifacts. When Jane teased her that her home would soon be transformed into the museum that Nicholas's *castello* was, Dominic had simply responded that they would enlarge their accommodations if necessary. In fact, Dominic and Nicholas had become close friends, with much in the way of common interests.

Her eyes fell on the object she'd had framed and positioned prominently on the fireplace mantel in their growing library. She went and picked it up, studying the threadbare, dingy square of linen behind glass. Her handkerchief.

To some it was a shocking eyesore. But when anyone questioned her about it, her gaze always found her husband's as she informed them that it was a reminder of what a good man she'd wed.

For she now knew him to be a man who bore a terrible burden, yet who carried himself tall and straight and met every conflict, every duty with bravery and honor. A man who loved his family and made certain they knew it.

Arms came around her, strong and solid.

"Dominic!"

Her husband was home.

VINCENT

PROLOGUE

Satyr Estate in Tuscany, Italy
EarthWorld, 1839

He was a boy of twelve years, teetering on the cusp of manhood, when he first discovered the object on the floor of the
olive grove.

While playing a game of soldier with the other children, he
had gone where he'd been forbidden to wander. To an isolated
area of the estate where employees of the vineyard and even the
children of the Satyr lords themselves were not allowed to trespass.

How innocuous the object had seemed that day! It was
small, round, and flat. He didn't think much of it initially, only
slipped it in his pocket and carried on with his game.

But that night, tucked up in his bed, he'd remembered it.
Lighting a candle, he'd pulled it out for closer examination.

It was the size, shape, and burnish of an old coin, and it had
an antique look about it. He'd turned it over in his palm, growing excited. Could it be a treasure left here on this ancient land

by Etruscan or Roman soldiers? He scraped it with his thumbnail, removing some of the grit.

It was gold!

With escalating enthusiasm, he scrubbed it clean. On one side was a low-relief likeness of Bacchus, the wine god. And on the reverse was a depiction of vines and other markings—words he wouldn't manage to decipher until years later when he was grown.

Putting it in his pocket again the next morning, he carried it there for several days, considering whether he should give it over to his father. He'd been a sweet boy then. A good boy and a smart one. One with a bright future and a family who loved him.

But the amulet, for that's what it was, slowly and inexorably became the center of his life to the exclusion of all else.

It began to call to him, softly at first. Beckoning him to do things he knew he oughtn't. Things he knew were dishonorable. In the beginning, it was only simple, naughty things. Stealing a friend's favorite toy. Lying to his mama.

Then it escalated to acts far more sinister.

After each transgression, the satisfaction was intense, providing a sexual thrill he could obtain by no other means. He would tug at himself until he spilled, knowing it was wrong to get pleasure from such things as he'd done. And he was always repentant afterward.

But the mesmerizing, ever-present voice of the amulet drove him to commit such acts again.

As time passed, he began to keep to himself more and more when it became clear that his development from boy to man was occurring at an unnaturally slow pace. The matter of a male organ's size was important, he knew, because others began to tease him when he pulled out his pitifully small sausage to piss. It wasn't his fault that the thing in his pants had never grown larger like those of other boys. Eventually he began to suspect that carrying the amulet in his pocket so often had cursed him with this malformation.

Furious, he'd tossed the golden disk away countless times. Buried it occasionally. But he always retrieved it again, for something in him knew the amulet wouldn't have asked such a sacrifice of him without giving him something in return.

The years passed, and he kept it close, telling no one of its existence. Waiting. Waiting for it to reveal more of itself. Waiting for it to guide him toward the glory he'd convinced himself was his due.

And then, one day, he finally discovered its purpose. His purpose.

Resurrection.

1

Satyr Estate in Tuscany, Italy
EarthWorld, 1850

Lord Vincent Satyr, firstborn son and heir of Lord Nicholas Satyr and his wife, Jane, gripped himself in an urgent fist and kneed apart the pale thighs of the woman who lay beneath him. He groaned as he fed the crown of his cock to the plump lips tucked high between her legs. Teasing himself back and forth, he glossed her erotic nether mouth with the first milky pearls of his pre-cum.

There was no need to rush this, for the entire night lay ahead, rich with the promise of carnal pleasure. He'd been anticipating his time with her all day. While his nose had been buried in the hefty tomes plucked from his library shelves, he'd been imagining this moment. This pussy. Craving it.

On the morrow he would travel to ElseWorld and gather nine bitter enemies together at one table in an attempt to catalyze peace between them. Negotiations would be delicate.

Crucial. Lives and worlds depended upon his skill as a mediator.

When he should've been concentrating on the careful construction of the treaty that would unite these disparate Else-World factions into a single governing body, he'd been distracted.

With thoughts of this woman.

His hand curved at her jaw, and sapphire eyes that were so like his father's drank in her flawless beauty. Her forearms were lax on the pillow on either side of her head, her elbows bent and her fingers loosely entangled in long waves of shining moon-blond hair. Pale blue veins at the underside of her wrists pulsed with need.

And with blood that ran cold.

"Watch me open you," he murmured, though it was unnecessary to say the words aloud. She would sense what he wanted.

The thick fringe of her dark lashes rose to reveal violet eyes that were the same rich color as the Sangiovese grapes he and his brothers cultivated in their vineyard here on the Satyr estates. She looked upon him with adoration, as though he was her entire world. And he was. Still, he avoided those startling eyes as he often did, not wanting to acknowledge that they were vacant, completely void of life.

Her gaze lowered obediently, and he watched her expression as he began his push. Felt her breath hitch and saw her skin flush as her slick furrow eased apart for him. For now, he was stingy, offering her only his crown and another inch, enjoying the hug of her plush labia as he rocked back and forth.

Her breasts gave against the hard muscles of his broad chest as he leaned closer. Her head fell back, and her long, white throat arched for his mouth.

His lips brushed the skin below her ear. "Do you want all of me inside you, *cara?*"

The question went against one of the primary tenets of successful negotiation. Never ask a question to which the answer required could be only either, yes or no.

But in this instance, her response was a foregone conclusion. It came as expected, tremulous and sweet.

"Yes, Vincent. Gods, please, yes." Her soft cheek nuzzled his granite jaw.

At the sound of her voice, an odd panic to drive himself deep inside her swept him. But he forced himself to go slowly. He wanted this to last.

Her fingers dimpled the bed pillow as he sought to further occupy the haven that was her body. She was delicate. A foot shorter than he when they were standing, and ninety pounds lighter.

And he wasn't a small man by any measure. Everything about him was big—hands, feet, shoulders, intellect. Cock.

It was the latter of these endowments that rendered him an object of awe, envy, and consternation among his peers. He knew his rod's measure well. So did half of Italy.

In fact, its dimensions were the stuff of legend—all because of a much sought-after courtesan he'd visited three years ago. Her bed had been comfortable enough, and after hours of fucking, he'd made the error of falling asleep there. Like some sort of conniving, nocturnal tailor, she had taken advantage of this lapse to measure him. From root to cockslit, she'd pronounced him to be possessed of eleven thick, ruddy, vein-roped inches. In circumference, he boasted seven inches, and his knob even fatter.

She'd been well connected, and word of his extraordinary size had spread through European society like wildfire. According to her tale, she'd swallowed the entirety of him in all variety of manners and had brought him to climax eleven times that night, rewarding him for each of his shaft's inches. Although he recalled matters differently, it made a good story, and he and his prick had become infamous almost overnight.

"It's good," his companion whispered as he plowed deeper, "so good."

Lifting his chest slightly, he fixed his gaze on the perfectly formed twin mounds that rose and fell in time with her shuddering breath. They were beautiful breasts, lush and high.

Touch them.

He'd barely completed the thought when her hands slid between their bodies. The curves of her palms cupped the underswells of those voluptuous breasts and began an erotic massage meant to tempt him.

She closed her eyes and moaned.

The sound shot a surge of lust straight to his groin, causing him to convulsively sheathe several more inches of himself inside her in one involuntary shove.

Her gasp was muffled by the sharp crack of a log snapping in the immense stone fireplace set in the corner of his bedchamber. Flames sparked higher, drenching her hair with Titian highlights and limning her pearlescent skin with gold.

In this light, she looked almost Human.

But she was not. No, the woman he lay with now was a expendable, lovely, necessary counterfeit.

A Shimmerskin.

With little effort on his part, he'd summoned her from the mists of ElseWorld tonight for a single, specific purpose—fornication. She was incapable of complaint or refusal. Incapable of experiencing a myriad of emotions Human women possessed. Anger. Fear. Desire. Love.

And the moment his body tired of this current occupation, she would be easily dispatched into the ether once again. It was a circumstance he took for granted, for all the Satyr had been accustomed to employing Shimmerskins in this way for centuries.

Transfixed, he watched her hands move on her breasts in an upward sweep that brought thumbs and fingers together to twist and tauten rosy nipples. She could lift those nubs to the kiss of her lips if he Willed her to. Could fondle them with the lap of her pink tongue and suckle them until they were reddened and stiff.

Later perhaps. In his current state, the sight of that would have him shooting off in her before he'd even managed to fully glove himself.

Lingering in the cradle of her thighs, he still teased at her, penetrating in slow increments, only to retreat and delve shallowly again. She would need time to adjust to him. And the voyage inside her would be as much a part of the pleasure as the eventual docking.

"The rest will go more easily," he coaxed. He wasn't sure if he was reassuring the remaining five inches of himself that, with patience, it would eventually find itself housed inside her. Or if he was reassuring her, as he had so many other females before her, that his sexual appendage would not split her asunder.

Like his brothers, he'd never had any trouble attracting women. Legions of them were intrigued by the sight of his broad shoulders and even more so by the bulge between his thighs. But he'd come to dread the moment they first lay eyes upon his manhood in its naked state.

Females almost universally claimed to clamor for a large cock. Yet, present them with one of his intimidating magnitude, and they quickly turned less eager.

A few more inches.

Ah, Gods, he was nearly in. Poised at the brink of ecstasy, his pulse thundered erratically. He cupped the rounds of her bottom in both hands, rocking himself deeper and deeper still in quick, staccato pumps.

"Mmmm. Yess." She murmured encouragement, her sexy voice at his ear urging him on.

It was a joy to fuck a female who didn't grimace as he pierced her, to know for a certainty his impalement wasn't causing her discomfort. His hands slid down her thighs and then hooked the backs of her knees, pulling until they were bent high and wide on either side of him. His palms planted themselves on the mattress alongside her so his muscled arms held her legs folded upward and apart.

As her hips tilted for him, he drove the rest of the way home. Seating himself deep, he luxuriated in the rare pleasure of finding the entirety of his shaft fully encased in a womanly passage.

Ahh . . . heaven.

She was warm. Tight. Slick.

He was hot. Hard. Hungry.

"That's . . . Fuck, that's good," he groaned as he ground his groin sensuously over hers.

"Good," she echoed.

Arching his back, he watched his corpulent prick retreat, newly slicked with her juices. Watched it spear her again in a long, determined stroke, thrusting so deep that the inky fur of his genitals embraced and enveloped her hairless ones. As her creator, he had determined that the only hair her body possessed would be eyelashes, eyebrows, and that on the top of her head.

He began rutting her in quick, hard strokes, relishing the sensation of repeatedly plundering the full, succulent length of her channel. None had ever brought him more pleasure than the silvery luminescent figure now under him.

He sought to prolong it.

But his cock had a mind of its own, and it twitched with the need to race toward its lascivious goal. Hard hips settled into a familiar thrust and retreat. He let her legs unfold, and her calves hooked themselves around the backs of his thighs. Mindlessly he worked himself in her, glorying in the massage of her inner tissues.

His elbows dug into the mattress, and his fingers dove into

her luxurious hair, holding her for his kiss. "How can you not be aware, damn you," he muttered against her lips. "You taste Human, feel Human, look Human—except for that skin."

Those remarkable eyes only blinked at him, devoid of emotion. Ducking his head, he grazed her throat with the rasp of teeth and mouth. It was because she was his favorite that he never looked too deeply into her eyes. He accepted insentience in other Shimmerskins as inevitable. However, something within him needed to foster the illusion that this female was fully alive. That she was capable of enjoying him as thoroughly as he did her.

"I am, Vincent," she assured him.

Though he knew it was only his unvoiced wish that had prompted her statement, it nevertheless ratcheted his need to a fever pitch. The lustful blood of the ancient Satyr thrummed hotter, a hectic, carnal drumbeat in his veins.

Her tender, naked pussy sucked at him, enticed him, nudging him all too quickly toward climax. *No!*

He wanted this first fuck of the night to last. If he could, he would prolong it indefinitely. If he could, he'd strap her to his chest and keep his cock lodged inside her day and night. If—

Soft fingers grazed his thigh, surprising him, for he hadn't requested such a caress. Though her touch was butterfly light, it was enough to make him lose the tenuous grip he had on his control.

His strokes turned more vigorous. Lengthened. Strengthened. The muscles of his biceps bulged, and his fingers raked into the bed linens on either side of her, crushing and twisting.

Flesh and bone slammed together in loud, rhythmic slaps that echoed in the stillness of the darkened room. Cum gathered in his balls, readying.

The sound of her breath as it caught in shallow, irregular gasps excited him. But still, he needed more. He needed her to . . .

Want me.

In this silent request, he wasn't asking that she only want his fucking, but that she want every part of him. Heart, mind, body, and soul. It was a ridiculous, impossible requirement. His brothers already suspected he was addicted to her. He was glad they weren't here now to witness how right they were. They wouldn't understand it. *He* didn't understand it.

She lifted a hand to his cheek and tried to catch his eyes, and fool that he was, he let her. "Yes, yes, Vincenzo, I want you."

The sentiment was undoubtedly false, but his body didn't care. Sapphire tangled with violet as his desire rose to a painful pitch. With broad hands he gripped her hips and angled her to receive one last, savage penetration that shoved them both a foot across the feather mattress.

Every muscle and tendon in his body wrenched taut as he hung on the precipice of ecstasy for a suspended, agonizing, blissful moment. Cum frothed and then sizzled its way into the thick duct along his root, coursing up his considerable length. And then finally, finally . . . it erupted from him.

A low, primitive sound escaped him at the glorious, indescribable sensation of imparting seed. An earthy moan rose in her, escaping her throat as a joyful, feminine cry that curled around his soul.

Like a row of talented fists aligned along his cock, her tissues milked at him, oiled him with the stimulating aphrodisiac of her body's cream. Forgotten for the moment was the fact that hers was simply an automatic orgasm response, that a Shimmerskin's release was infallibly triggered by that of a Satyr male.

He pulled back and drove home again. His body surrounded hers, moved with hers, over hers, and in hers. Again and again he gave his masculine gift to her in hot, fluid spurts. Distantly he heard her murmur to him, felt her inner tissues convulse as his seed soaked them, drenched them, flooded them.

Long moments later, he lay sprawled over her, still buried

inside her, his lust only momentarily banked. He experienced no belated concern that she might have communicated some vile disease or that she might have conceived his bastard. Her kind were incapable of doing either.

Her fingers played in his hair, combing it lightly, caressing his cheek, his shoulders, the smooth muscles of his back. Again he fleetingly wondered why she was touching him when he hadn't specifically Willed it, but for the moment he didn't care.

He raised on one elbow to gaze down at her, mesmerized by her remarkable beauty. He had only himself to congratulate for it. He'd given extensive consideration to her creation. His brothers rarely spent so much energy designing feminine receptacles for their cum, nor brought forth the same one more than a few times.

He'd first conjured her just over a year ago on his twenty-sixth birthday. Before and since then, he had called forth others of her ilk.

However, she was the only one he had ever summoned repeatedly. The only one who was constantly in his thoughts. By now, he had fucked her dozens of times. Hundreds. He should have grown bored with her.

But he hadn't.

It worried him on occasion. Sometimes he even denied himself, seeing how long he could go without her, but their eventual reunions only proved all the more urgent because of his abstinence.

He lowered his head, kissing her throat.

"Where do you go when I am done with you?" he whispered against soft, radiant skin.

"Away," she told him.

"To where? To what place?"

Her reply, when it came, was barely audible. "To nothing. To nowhere."

Hours later, he eased from her for a final time and fell exhausted upon the mattress beside her. His satiated penis lay half wilted on his left thigh, drained after countless climaxes. Even in repose, it remained partially tumid and embarrassingly majestic.

It pained him to know his companion would momentarily shimmer away into the ether, now that he no longer had physical need of her. He felt her flutter the coverlet over him as he drifted toward slumber.

"Stay," he commanded, knowing she would not.

2

The next morning, Vincent awoke to two realizations.

His cock was rock hard.

And there was a woman in his bed.

The first was far from an unusual circumstance. The second was extraordinary.

On all the previous occasions that he'd visited a bedchamber other than his own, he'd always been scrupulously careful to absent himself from it well before dawn. Without exception. And never in his twenty-seven years had he taken a Human female into his own bed.

He assessed his situation.

Her back was tucked to his chest. The room was dim, though the morning sun was already smirking at him through the uncurtained window, amused at his predicament. The ashes in the fireplace appeared cold. And his bed reeked of sex.

His left arm was slung around a sloping waist, and his hand reposed between a pair of voluptuous breasts. His fingers were entangled in long blond hair. All of which defined the body he held as unquestionably female. Crumpled bed linens draped her from the waist down.

His mind worked, trying to piece together the events of the previous night. He'd bedded a Shimmerskin. But the moment his mind had calmed with sleep, she would've disappeared. She couldn't have continued to exist without his conscious Will.

This woman must therefore be someone else. Someone Human.

When a man of his rank in society slid his cock through the ring of muscle guarding a decent woman's hymen, he may as well have slid a wedding ring upon his finger. Was he soon to be wed, despite his objections?

Did he owe her an apology? Had he forced her? Hurt her? Was she a prostitute who'd tricked her way into his bed?

Who the fuck was she?

He rose on one elbow to look down on her. Her long hair was a lush, pale tangle that obscured half of her face. The other half of her countenance was buried in the pillow. No help there.

Whoever she was, she must be removed, and quickly. He had a meeting today in ElseWorld. Negotiations were at a critical juncture, and their outcome was a burden he bore alone. The process had begun years earlier, initiated by numerous attorneys. However, all those had fallen by the wayside over the course of time. In fact, the last of them had met with suspicious, fatal accidents in recent months. Leaving him as the sole hope to broker peace.

His companion stirred, snuggled, and then stirred again. The pearly skin of her back brushed against his darker, more heavily muscled flesh, and his already stiff cock hardened further. Under the covers, his hand shaped her hip, unconsciously massaging as it traveled over the velvet warmth of hip, belly, rib, and then breast.

Damnation, if only he could recall her name. Women didn't

appreciate it when a man couldn't. Even prostitutes could turn sour over such a misstep. But his mind was a blank on this score.

The morning sun turned more persistent and shifted so it lit her body differently than before. Under its caress, her skin was pale, and more dazzling than perhaps it should have been. He looked closer, curious. Her skin wasn't just pale, he realized. It was *luminous*.

Pushing back the blanket, he slid his hand upward along the curve of her waist. In the wake of his touch, her flesh glimmered unnaturally. Her skin wasn't just luminous. It was iridescent!

She stretched languidly, sending a seductive wave of glistening pearlescence over her body.

"Fifty thousand hells!" he roared in shock.

The precise moment the woman realized she was not alone was almost comically obvious. Her entire body abruptly froze in mid-stretch. In a flurry of legs and arms, she bolted up on the mattress, twisting the covers into a tangle around her ankles as she scuttled away. Crouching on all fours at the far precipice of his massive bed, she swung around to confront him.

Her elbows were slightly bent, her knees spread, and her shoulders hunkered. It was a classic pose of fight-or-flight readiness.

They stared at one another with identical expressions of horror.

"You!" burst from each of them simultaneously.

"You're the Shimmerskin," he accused. "From last night."

Confusion entered her expression, but she didn't respond.

His gaze roamed her body. That she had remained with him after coitus was completed between them last night was a circumstance unprecedented in the entire history of the Satyr. It was impossible!

Yet here she was. A Shimmerskin. His *favorite* Shimmerskin.

A foolish spurt of joy rose in him. How many times had he privately wished for this very occurrence?

His gaze captured hers and saw that her purple eyes were no longer vacant. They were wild with a shock that matched his own. And with something else. Fear.

Her gaze darted around his bedchamber as though seeking an avenue of escape.

"I don't understand. How can you still be here?" He reached out and touched her arm, intending only to determine for an absolute certainty that she wasn't a figment of his imagination.

She flinched and recoiled from him, rubbing the place he'd touched as though it hurt.

For a long moment, they stared at each other, transfixed.

"Say something," he ordered at last.

Her expression turned annoyed. "Farewell," she told him.

With that, she leaped from the bed and scampered for the door, kicking off the sheets as she went.

"Demons take it, woman, get back here!" Vincent shouted.

His eyes flicked to the clock on the mantel.

Wonderful. He would need all the time left to him to prepare himself and his arguments prior to the meeting that would take place in the adjacent world in two hours. As daybreak had come here in this world, dusk would have arrived in ElseWorld. Because the various factions who would convene there with him today were a mix of nocturnal and diurnal creatures, his meetings with them were scheduled at all hours.

And now there was a naked female cavorting about in his home.

He donned his dressing gown but didn't bother to give chase. She would return. Shimmerskins always obeyed a Satyr's every command. Without exception.

Seconds ticked by. She did not return. The realization that she had no intention of doing so was slow to sink in. When it finally did, it was nothing short of astounding.

It was a simple matter to track her scent down the hall. She'd gone into the adjoining bedchamber—the one that would someday, in the distant future, house his wife. And possibly Landon's as well.

His long robe billowed behind him as he went in after her. At the sight of her shapely, naked backside, he ground to a halt. She'd opened the window and was leaning out, surveying the verdant landscape below.

"I wouldn't advise it. You'll break an ankle or worse," he informed her, guessing she had escape in mind. Though he'd kept his voice calm, she whipped violently around at the sound of it. Her eyes were dilated, frantic.

As he began to stealthily stalk her, she cast another look out the window and then apparently decided not to chance it. Together they performed an uneasy dance, him advancing and her retreating and neither of them sure what would happen when they met.

Eventually she allowed him to back her into a corner at the far side of the bed. Then she made a desperate, calculated lunge over the mattress, rolling across it toward the door and escape.

Quick as a whip, his arm lashed out and caught her waist, hauling her off the bed and back against him. Whirling to face him, she pushed an arm's length away, yanking ineffectually at his hold.

His eyes swept her nude body. Bacchus, she was beautiful. Two hours was actually quite a long stretch when he considered it. Perhaps they could squeeze in a time enough for . . .

"No fuck," she said fiercely.

His head reared back, and a bark of surprised laughter escaped him. "What?"

Her eyes held his for a long, accusatory second, and then they dropped to gaze pointedly in the general direction of his genitals. He hadn't bothered to fasten the sash of his dark satin robe, and it hung open. His huge penis jutted from the divide in its front gap, fully engorged and ready. Almost threatening in its size.

He let go of one of her wrists to fold his dressing gown over himself. It tented ridiculously over his distended rod.

"My apologies," he said. "It's just that—" He waved his free hand between them, intending it to encompass the entirety of her. "You're beautiful, and . . . and naked. And we've lain together before. It's natural that I would react to you physically."

An affronted silence greeted him. Poised on the balls of her feet, knees flexed and shoulders tensed, she appeared ready to flee or to attack at the slightest provocation.

"I go," she announced at last.

"Go?" His brows raised. "Go where precisely?"

She gazed beyond him and then around the room, growing ever more agitated. Her eyes returned to his, and she seemed to force the fear away. Her shoulders squared to defy him. "I go."

"Whether or not you go is my decision," he informed her, crossing his arms. "And you're not leaving until I get to the bottom of this. Until I'm certain you have someplace safe to go. Do you understand?"

She shot him a disgruntled look.

It shocked him almost more than did her presence here. Before today, he had never seen so much as a whisper of a negative emotion on her beautiful countenance in all the months since he'd first created her. Her eyes had held only varying proportions of lust, adoration, and subservience when they'd gazed upon him.

"Why didn't you return to the mist from which you originated last night as you always have before?" he demanded.

She shrugged, her expression mutinous.

The silence deepened, but he waited her out. A natural negotiator, he'd long ago harnessed his patience and honed skills that helped him sway others into accommodating him.

"Change. I change," she blasted finally.

"Change? How?"

Her hands gestured in a futile way as she sought the words to explain. "You bring me. Times many. Last times I change."

"Are you telling me you can no longer return to . . . wherever Shimmerskins come from? Because I somehow changed you?"

She nodded once and then looked perplexed and shook her head instead. "I don't know."

"Did I conjure you to service me too many times? Is that what made you real?" His eyes drifted over her. "*Are* you real?"

She looked away. "I go."

"There's something you need to understand," he told her, his tone sharper than he'd intended. "You won't be going anywhere for the present. You're naked. And you glow. Normally Humans can't see Shimmerskins. But you're not a true Shimmerskin anymore, are you? Which means you may be visible to Humans now. And if you're noticed, your existence will lead to questions that will endanger my family. I can't allow that."

He wasn't certain how much of that she understood. Perhaps all of it, for she now looked even more distraught.

"Come with me." He left her, moving to stand in the doorway. Glancing along the corridor, he made sure no servants were about, and then he beckoned her, doing his best to appear unthreatening. No easy task for a man of six and a half feet. "Come back to my bedchamber. We'll talk."

"No fuck," she insisted.

"No," he agreed solemnly. "No fuck."

"You want," she said, gesturing toward his turgid cock.

He looked down at the male appendage she found so offensive. His robe had fallen open again, and it hung in the divide. It was so heavy it couldn't support its own weight, so it didn't bob skyward like those of most men. Instead it swung at a lower angle, thick and heavy between his thighs and curving very slightly leftward like some sort of erotic cutlass.

"I suppose that's obvious." He casually tucked himself away and reclosed his robe, firmly tying its sash. "Nevertheless, you may trust my word that I won't force myself on you."

She looked skeptical.

Red singed his cheekbones as he hurriedly embarked on an uncharacteristically feeble attempt to explain his past behavior toward her. "What I mean to say is that you have my apologies if I've forced myself on you previously. But I didn't know . . . That is, you weren't supposed to feel anything when I . . . when we . . ."

She came toward him then, pausing only when she drew even with him in the doorway.

"I feel," she murmured softly, not looking at him.

Like a queen, she swept past him. He followed, considering the implications of her curt confession until they were back in his private chambers. Firmly closing the door, he stood with his back against it and contemplated her.

"Did you 'feel' all those times we f—"

Her eyes shot sparks.

Breaking off, he gave her a mocking half bow. "Ah, I gather you come equipped with the usual odd female notions of propriety. Which means that you may employ certain words to describe our previous liaisons, yet my use of them is deemed offensive. My apologies. I meant to inquire regarding whether or not you've been aware during the times I've engaged you in 'carnal relations'?"

She stared at him a moment and then averted her eyes to her fingers where they toyed with the twisted-silk fringe edging his bed curtains. "Only last."

"Only last night?"

Her shoulders rose and fell. He barely heard her whispered, "And."

"And other times as well? How many others?" he demanded.

The eyes that lifted to his were wounded, full of secrets untold.

"Ten?" he prodded, not wanting to know but needing to.

She shook her head.

"More?"

Again she shook her head.

"I will have the answer from you, however long it takes."

A great shuddering breath slowly heaved from her lungs like the exhalation of a bellows.

"*Tre*," she whispered, speaking in Latin.

Instantly his mind traveled back, retrieving and sifting through recollections of the last three times he'd conjured her. Last night. A week earlier. And the time before that had been— Moonful. A Calling night.

He drove taut fingers through his dark, blue-black hair.

Hells! The first sex of her life that she could actually remember, and it had been an eight-hour Calling fuckfest? He scarcely remembered what acts he'd engaged her in that night as he'd gathered with brothers and cousins in the sacred glen that lay hidden in the heart of the Satyr Forest.

Shimmerskins had been everywhere. They'd been quickly and easily brought forth from the spectral mists that clung low and thick to the verdant landscape of the glen. Since the beginning of time, it had been assumed they were insentient. That Bacchus had created them to act only as vessels for the lecherous ejaculations of legions of Satyr males. No one had ever thought to question the tradition.

He looked at the woman who stood before him and saw memories of that night shift in her eyes.

Between her luminous sisters and his relatives, there'd been a crowd of nearly two dozen on the last occasion of Moonful. Spirits and cocks had risen to greet the arrival of the whole moon that signaled the culmination of Bright Half. The blood of his ancestors had pumped hot and hard in his veins. Wine had flowed freely. As had semen.

Matings had been rigorous and guilt-free. He'd been inside her and inside others like her in every way possible, and they'd all arduously dedicated themselves to accommodating his passions.

Each orgasm had been swiftly forgotten as the search for the next began. It had been an orgy of epic proportions. In other words, a typical Calling night in the Satyr glen.

"Do other Shimmerskins . . . feel?" he asked in dawning realization of what this could mean to the males of his breed. If all Shimmerskins had the potential for sentience, they could no longer be used in good conscience in the way his family had utilized them for centuries past. Under such circumstances, to continue on as before could only be deemed heinous. Criminal.

She shook her head slowly and flattened a hand between her breasts in emphasis. "Only."

Relief swamped him at her admission. His fraternal relatives had no idea what a narrow escape had just been handed to them. There were still questions, but . . .

His eyes glazed over as they fell to the hand between her naked breasts. Breasts that were full and perfect and crowned with nipples that were pink and pointed. Under his robe, his sex twitched.

Both her hands dropped to fist at her sides. "No fuck."

"What? Stop saying that! I have no intention of attacking you."

She looked skeptical.

He sighed. She had reason to mistrust him. From her point of view, it must seem that he had used her sexually without her consent in their past associations. He should consider himself fortunate she remembered only the last three. But, damn, why did one of them have to be a Calling night?

He closed his eyes and rubbed the heel of his hand to ease the sudden tension in his forehead as he tried to recall more of the Moonful they'd shared. He had been drunk with wine and lust.

If Landon had been there, they would have passed her between them. Taken her together against the base of one of the ancient statues that ringed the glen. As they had a year ago, the night he'd first conjured her. The night Landon had been on leave from the war in ElseWorld.

A night she couldn't remember.

Suddenly he had to know.

"Did I, we, *anyone* hurt you during that Calling two weeks ago? Or since?"

A gamut of emotions flitted over her face—bewilderment, wariness. Then she stiffened and looked past him. "I go."

When he didn't move from the door, she glanced toward the window.

"As I said before, I'd advise against it. We're on a *piano superiore*. You understand? An upper floor?"

Unwilling to admit whether or not she comprehended, she only crossed her arms, inadvertently showcasing breasts that plumped heavily on them like ripe, delectable fruit displayed upon a platter.

His cock throbbed, hungry.

"Let's put some clothing on you. Then I might not find myself constantly hard."

"Clothing?" She brightened instantly.

He smiled, absurdly glad he'd pleased her. "You wish for something to wear?"

She nodded.

Locating a pen, he briskly scribbled a cursory note to his brother Marco. Then he stepped into the hall and, seeing a manservant downstairs, he tossed the missive to him, summoned his bath, and instructed him to have the note delivered to Marco's home, which was less than twenty minutes ride from his own on the expansive Satyr estate.

Returning to his chamber, he withdrew one of his shirts from the armoire and gave it to his guest. Though it had been cut from the costliest of woven linen fabric and had been fitted and handstitched by the finest tailor in Florence, she studied it at arm's length, clearly disappointed.

"Do you require assistance?" he asked, uncertain of the reason for her displeasure.

She sent him a glance that told him she considered his attempt to get his hands on her both transparent and pathetic. Frowning in concentration, she slid her arms into the sleeves.

The garment was huge on her, its cuffs flopping to her knees, and its tails drooping even lower. He rolled the ends of the sleeves back to reveal her hands, and then kissed the backs of each. She tasted just as she always had. Delicious.

She snatched her hands back, rubbing them as if washing them together.

"Does it hurt when I touch you?"

"Hurt blankness."

"That, of course, makes little sense, but we'll sort it out later. My shirt will have to suffice as clothing for the present. I've sent word to one of my brothers' homes for the loan of something more suitable. A dress and other fripperies should arrive within the hour."

At this, her eyes sparked with keen interest and slowly smiled into his. In the sunlight streaming through the windowpane, they were bright amethyst jewels brimming with delight.

He'd seen that smile of hers many times. And it had reached her eyes before. But now something about it was far more appealing.

Abruptly he realized what the difference was. It was no longer a false curving of lips he'd instigated in her by his Will.

This was a smile, freely given, by a woman with a Will of her own.

His gaze roved her features and roamed lower. Damn, she was beautiful. Sweet. To hell with clothing. He took a step toward her. He needed to . . .

"No fuck," she warned, her smile dimming.

He stopped short, biting off a silent curse. "Apologies yet again. I momentarily forgot the new rules."

Rules were something he understood. Bending and arranging them to suit his preferences was part of any negotiation and was a business at which he excelled. It was only a matter of time before she was in his bed again.

He could wait.

A while. His eyes slid over her again.

A short while.

3

Convincing her to remain hidden while jugs of steaming water were delivered and poured into his claw-foot tub proved easily accomplished. At least, once he'd posed it to her as a game.

Upon the departure of his servants, he took the precaution of latching both door and windows before sinking into his bath and commencing his ablutions. At the sound of his splashing she crept out of hiding.

She came closer to stand by the tub, observing his every move with a critical eye.

"I'm bathing."

"Bathing."

"Yes. In order to become clean."

She wrinkled her nose. "Unclean?"

He frowned. "No, I am not unclean. . . . That is . . ." He stumbled to a halt, glad his law professors at the University of Bologna were not in the room to witness this fumbling for words of their most lauded and exalted magna cum laude student. "It's rude to stare," he archly informed her. "Sit over there on my bed where I can keep an eye on you."

Though she moved away at that, she ignored his directive and instead chose to roam the perimeter of his bedchamber, peeking into the armoires, his shaving mirror, behind the privacy screen, and generally inspecting the surroundings with the diligent curiosity of a child.

Eventually she paused at his bedside table to ponder the stack of ancient leather-bound legal tomes he'd borrowed from an administrative library in ElseWorld. She hefted one in her hands, appearing surprised at its weight, and she nearly dropped it to the floor before managing to maneuver it atop his bed.

"It's a book. Open it," he suggested.

"A book. Open it," she mimicked softly, as though wanting to experience his words on her tongue.

Sitting on the mattress, she unfolded the volume on her lap, whereupon she began leafing randomly through its musty parchment pages. Now and then, she paused, seeming to study a passage more intently.

"Can you read?"

A shrug was her only reply. However, the book seemed to occupy her for the moment, and for that he was grateful since it freed him to consider other more pressing matters.

It was a mere fifteen minutes to the gate on foot, which left him well over an hour's time before he must depart. It was too dangerous to take her with him to ElseWorld. Therefore, though he was reluctant to do so, he would have to leave her in the care of someone. But who?

After a moment, she lay the open book flat on his bed and settled on her stomach to continue her perusal of it. His shirttails slid higher on her, revealing the curves of her bottom and her long legs below. Practical considerations left him as he studied her, lying there amid bed linens that had been tangled by their nocturnal passion. A passion that still rode him this morning.

"Gods," he muttered. For just a moment, he was tempted to

take himself in hand, but it was her body he wanted sheathing his cock, not his fist. In an abrupt move, he stood from his bath, and she glanced up.

Water cascaded from him—a slick sheet racing down his chest, torso, belly. There it was forced to part, forking around the thickened, florid cock angling from his groin, before it could sluice down his legs and back into the pool.

She sat up and closed the volume, her fingers marking her place as though she'd actually been reading with comprehension and planned to return to a particular sentence where she'd left off. Standing it on end across her thighs, she folded her forearms atop gilded binding that was four inches thick.

Then she commenced to observe his every action as he reached for linen toweling and began to dry himself. The sensation of her gaze moving over him was every bit as tangible as the stroke of his towel-draped hand. Predictably his cock swelled to ever-greater dimensions. There was little rush to dress, for it quite literally would not fit in his trousers in its current state.

"It has a mind of his own," he muttered, making no attempt to disguise his erection. "I'll be damned if I'll apologize yet again for it."

"Damned if I'll apologize," she echoed.

Stepping from the bath onto the sheepskin rug, he was arrested by the smug smile that flitted across her lips. Though she'd refused him earlier, some part of her still took pleasure in his body's response to her. Her eyes had darkened, and a flush tinted her cheekbones. She wasn't as immune to him as she'd led him to believe.

He tossed the towel away and took a step in her direction. Without quite realizing how he'd gotten there, he found himself beside the bed.

Then he was drawing himself over her. And she was lying back, allowing it.

He reached between them to shove aside the legal tome and

the obligations it represented. His body relaxed into hers, and it seemed the most natural thing in the world for his knees to press hers wider and his groin to nestle in the warm, feminine notch between her thighs.

"It's poor manners to stare," he scolded, his voice low and velvet. His fingers threaded her hair, dark against light. "Especially at a naked man to whom you are not wed. In fact, in this world, such unseemly behavior would commonly be construed by that naked man as an invitation."

She screwed up her expression in way that implied she was utterly at a loss to understand him.

Brushing her mouth with his, he made it simpler. "No Human woman would stare so brazenly unless she meant to invite a man here." His cock gently nudged her. "Between her legs."

"No Human." She touched her own cheek, indicating she referred to herself.

His interest sharpened at the confession, and he instinctively transitioned into the role of the interrogator he'd been trained to be. "Then what are you?"

A terrified confusion seeped into her eyes at the question but was quickly snuffed by the sweep of her lashes.

"I am . . ." She sought words to define herself but failed to locate them.

A rivulet dripped from his damp blue-black hair onto his collarbone and then made its way down his chest. Her finger caught it, tracing its path on his skin.

"I am unwet," she decided softly.

Her unexpected response and the dazzle of her jeweled eyes as they peeked up at him temporarily blinded him to all looming responsibilities.

His head lowered. "A state more commonly referred to as 'dry.'"

Gazes and lips caressed and clung, and her hands lifted to stroke the damp slopes of his shoulders. Though their bodies had loved before, all was now changed between them. They were new to one another, yet not strangers. The circumstances of their liaison had altered irrevocably with the coming of dawn. He wanted a new joining. Wanted to remind her that she wanted him. Needed to brand her as his, lest she'd forgotten.

His fingers went lower, parting the tails of the shirt he'd given her to find the warm, slick heart of her. Her eyes fluttered closed, and she arched into his touch. His thumb pressed delicately at her clit, and two fingers delved inside her and then out again in an erotic stroke. She'd been wrong about one thing— she *was* wet. For him.

She moaned softly, and her fingers clutched his arms.

"Look at me," he told her, hearing the need in his own voice. She complied, and at the same time drew up her legs on either side of his until her calves hugged his hips. Her slit coddled his balls. She was open, ready.

How was it going to feel to drown himself in the depths of her amethyst eyes—now that they were *aware*—at the very same moment he drowned his sex in hers? The thought turned the thump of his pulse even more urgent, more passionate. A fevered lust heated his blood—a blood endowed unto him by centuries of lecherous, fornicating Satyr ancestors.

Beads of pre-cum formed at his tip, and they painted a thin, silvery line down her belly as he led the crown of his cock to her opening. There, it spread lips that were already slippery with feminine desire.

"Please," she whispered at his ear. It was the sound of a willing, wanting woman.

"Gods. Yes." Muscles bunched in his buttocks as he flexed his hips, beginning to part her.

At that very moment, a brisk knock sounded on the door.

Her breath hitched, uncertain. Their eyes caught and clung.

"A hundred thousand fucking hells!" he bit out through his teeth.

Someone was in the corridor outside his room. Throughout the entirety of the estate, it was an unwritten rule that servants were forbidden to disturb a Satyr male in his bedchamber. The reason for this break with tradition must be an important one for a member of his household to risk dismissal over it.

His cock was poised at her gate, dying to breach her, to taste her. Their joining could be consummated so, so easily. They needn't linger over it. He could . . .

She tilted her hips, luring him deeper. His crown slipped inside her.

His hands planted themselves on the mattress on either side of her as he plumbed an inch deeper, and deeper still. He'd achieved little more than several inches of ingress, and already his balls had lifted taut, quivering with the need to ejaculate the seed they brewed.

The clock on the mantel at the opposite wall began to bong mournfully, another insistent reminder of duty. It was nine o'clock.

A slew of curse words filtered through his mind, and he faltered, his expression grim. Never had he wished his obligations further away. But the fact remained that he was due to depart this world in a little over an hour.

Forcibly defusing the escalating need between them was one of the hardest things he'd ever done. Muscles clenched again as his hips lifted, reversing the direction of his cock.

"No," she pleaded, clinging as he quit her.

"Another time," he murmured against her lips. "Soon, I promise."

"Promise," she echoed in a forlorn voice.

As the ninth bong sounded, the knock came again, louder this time.

"A moment!" he roared toward the offending interruption.

He considered explaining himself to the woman under him, but the gap in their communication skills was so great that doing so would take too long. Straightening away from the bed, he stood, carrying her with him to the edge of the tub.

"Your turn."

She stared down at the pool, somewhat surprised at the novelty of the suggestion he'd presented. Reaching down, she tested the bathwater with her fingers, swirling them curiously through its fluid warmth. Then, without protest, she allowed him to lower her the rest of the way into the tub until she sat, submerged to her chest.

"Remain there, *quietly*, while I answer the door," he told her, placing a finger to his lips in emphasis. "Don't speak. You understand?"

At her nod, he grabbed his dressing gown, donning it as he crossed the room, whereupon he yanked the door open with the full force of his frustration.

As he'd expected, it was one of the servants. She looked a bit taken aback at his thunderous expression and even more alarmed when he crowded her backward and stepped into the hall with her. She'd no doubt have fled with her apron flung over her head if he hadn't had the presence of mind to forcibly secure the crest of his turgid cock under the waist sash on his robe as he'd tied it closed.

"Well?" he demanded as she only continued to gape.

She quickly remembered her place and her mission and bobbed a curtsey. Doing her best to tamp her curiosity when they both heard the splashing sounds issuing from the room behind him, she announced, "*Scusi*, Signore, I apologize for the intrusion, but a package has arrived."

"Well? Where is it?" he inquired impatiently, noting the woman's empty arms.

"Why, it's in your brother's hand, Signore. He asks me to inform you that he awaits you downstairs."

"Damnation! Tell him I'll be down directly." Dismissing her, he stepped back into his room.

The Shimmerskin was bathing just as he'd left her, stroking over her arms and shoulders and essentially imitating the way he'd washed himself earlier. While he'd thought she'd been engrossed in his book, she'd apparently managed to pay close attention to his toilette as well. The water rose higher on her smaller frame than it had on his. Her breasts bobbed along its surface, full and rosy.

Bacchus! His erection would never subside if he didn't manage to get himself under control. He turned to make himself ready, trying to block out the subtle sounds she was making behind him.

"Finish your bath," he told her as he jerked on his boots over his trouser legs. "I'm going downstairs to fetch suitable clothing for you, and then I'll return."

Without awaiting her reply, he took her assent for granted and strode to the door, shut and locked it, and then stalked toward the staircase still buttoning his shirt.

4

Halfway down the grand staircase, he froze.

It appeared that not one, but two of his brothers had come in response to his simple request. And Landon had accompanied them as well!

Marco and Anthony, two of the twenty-four-year-old fraternal triplets that comprised the whole of his male siblings, stood at the foot of the stairs, their dark eyes twinkling. Marco wore his banker's suit, and Anthony, who managed the Satyr Vineyard accounts, wore similar tailoring that marked him as a man of business.

Several yards beyond them stood Landon, Vincent's closest friend. Five years their senior and two years older than Vincent, he wore his usual taciturn expression, along with a supple leather jacket, work-worn trousers, and scuffed, muddied boots, which indicated he'd just come from toiling among the vines.

"Why aren't you ready for departure?" Anthony demanded in outrage. "Have you even reviewed the list of negotiation points for the meeting before you make your way through the gate to Julius?"

Vincent ignored this outburst and eyed the package under Marco's arm, which no doubt held the items he'd requested for the Shimmerskin in his quarters.

"I wasn't aware it would require three grown men to deliver one small parcel," he remarked coolly, loping down the remainder of the dozen or so steps between them. "I suppose I should be glad Julius awaits me in ElseWorld and Daniela is abroad, or you'd doubtlessly have invited our other two siblings along to assist in so onerous an endeavor."

Though all four brothers served the Satyr in their own way, none had been gifted with the calling to work the land as their father, Nicholas, had. Only Daniela, Vincent's younger sister by one year, had grown up to surprise them all by doing so.

During her temporary absence, she'd requested Landon's help, although she had difficulty in turning the reins of responsibility for her patch of vines over to any man, even one so qualified for these duties. Entirely of ElseWorld blood, Landon had immigrated to this world ten years ago and was now employed to oversee all the brothers' sections of vineyard.

Marco made a show of examining his surroundings. "Where is she?"

"Who?" Vincent asked innocently.

"The woman upon whom you wish to hang this garment." Marco shook the package he held meaningfully. "It's not every day my eldest brother sends his servant to me with orders that I'm to filch a dress from my wife's closet and deliver it to his bachelor household. Caused quite a stir. Millicent awaits details," he said, referring to his wife.

"Exactly as you say," said Vincent. "I ordered a dress. Not the lot of you."

"I'll remind you that I live here," Landon offered with a rare touch of droll humor.

He'd been standing apart from them with his hands on his hips, but now he ambled toward them. His left leg was stiff and moved awkwardly, a result of three years of service in the war that still raged in ElseWorld. Though he'd never spoken of those days, they'd injured him in more ways than the physical.

"I offered to see the package safely delivered in your hands," Landon informed him, stationing himself comfortably against the newel post at the base of the marble stairs. "However, Marco wouldn't give it up without an explanation for its contents. Anthony was anxious to ensure you get through the gate in time for your endless discussions of legalities. Together they proved an unstoppable force."

It was a ridiculous statement. Though all four of them were of massive size and stature, Landon topped even Vincent by an inch or so and was slightly broader of chest.

Ignoring him, Vincent made an undignified grab for the package.

Marco was ready and snatched it away, tossing it to a startled Anthony. "Come now, just show her to us, or at the very least give us a name, and we'll be on our way."

"There's no woman, I'm telling you. If you've come hoping for a show, you've come for naught. I need the dress because I'm required to attend a costume ball in ElseWorld," Vincent fibbed easily.

"Anthony?" Marco looked to their sibling.

Vincent glared at Anthony as well, daring him to expose the falsehood he'd uttered.

"How am I to know? It's Julius who keeps track of the details of Vincent's obligations, social and business."

Marco eyed him, undeterred. "A facile lie, big brother. But the prospect of you in my wife's gown? Its hem would barely reach your knees. Confess. Who's it really for?"

"None of your affair." Vincent made another grab, but Anthony, who'd caught the spirit of the game, dodged and tossed his package back to his brother.

"Landon! Don't just stand there, traitor. Assist me," said Vincent.

Landon lifted both hands, palms outward. "You're on your own. I admit I'm growing as curious as your brothers."

Marco held the bundle behind his back. "Come, Vincenzo. If you didn't want us to know, why ask me for the dress?"

"Because Daniela is unavailable? Because you're the only married brother I have?"

"Why didn't you put your request to Mother?" Anthony put in. "I believe she possesses one or two gowns in her many closets."

Vincent's brows rammed together, and though he knew that his mother, the well-mannered Lady Jane Satyr, had accompanied his father and sister abroad, he nevertheless lowered his voice as if he feared she might be eavesdropping. "This matter is best kept between us. For now."

A look of smug amusement lit Marco's face, and he shoved aside the collar of Vincent's shirt. "Aha! You're marked, there on your throat." He poked a finger in Vincent's chest. "You *do* have a woman here! Where is she? In your bedchamber?" He craned his neck, straining to look around Vincent's bulk to the stair landing above.

Vincent shifted his collar higher, hiding the bruise the Shimmerskin had left. "All right, yes! I am entertaining a woman here. Are the three of you sufficiently satisfied? Now stop wasting my time. Will you just—"

Marco snickered. "Wait until Mother gets wind of this. She'll have you engaged and—"

When Vincent made another grab, Marco flung the box toward Landon.

"Not so fast," said Landon when Vincent turned on him. Holding the parcel out of reach, he flattened a work-toughened hand in the center of Vincent's chest, gray eyes skewering him for a potent moment as only his incisive gaze could. Whatever he read in Vincent's face had him sobering. "Well, I'll be damned."

"Gods!" Marco gasped at the same time.

"It's *her!*" Anthony chimed in, pointing up the stairs in astonishment.

Vincent swiveled, knowing full well whom he was likely to see behind him. As he'd suspected, the Shimmerskin was now standing at the top of the steps, her hand on the banister, and one high-arched foot poised on the first descending rung.

Fresh from the bath, she'd donned his shirt again and wore it like an unbelted, unbuttoned robe. Her luminescent, shapely legs were long and bare beneath it, and her lustrous hair spilled down her back and shoulders like tumbled moonbeams.

Somehow she'd unlocked the bedchamber door and escaped. Or in order to penetrate it had she managed to momentarily dissolve back into the enchanted mist from which she'd originally issued?

All four men stared, mute and transfixed, as she gingerly made her way toward them. As if she were a youthful queen who'd forgotten to don her royal raiment and slippers, her every step displayed a length of thigh and more than a hint of belly and breast. Two rungs above him, she stopped, a hesitant smile on her lips as she first studied him and then took in each of his companions in turn.

Marco gaped. "You conjured her yet *again?* How many times has it been now? In the name of Bacchus, Vin! I'm growing ever more concerned that you may have a problem."

"I do indeed have a problem," Vincent gritted. "Three of them in fact, all loitering here in my vestibule and pestering me when I've got a critical meeting to convene in less than an hour's time."

"I believe the correct term might be an addiction," Anthony remarked to his triplet, overlooking Vincent's interruption.

At Landon's continued silence, Vincent shot a glance in his

direction. Prurient interest flashed in his friend's dark, solemn eyes as they swept the woman on the stairs, but it was swiftly doused, and he looked away, aloof again.

But Vincent had expected such a reaction. Had in fact hoped for it. He and Landon had always gravitated to the same women ... before the war.

Whereas Vincent had served a brief stint of active service prior to going on to attend university, Landon had spent much of the last three years fighting a war that had been raging on for twenty-seven years. Just shy of a month ago, he had abruptly left his regiment for good and returned here through the gate. As far as Vincent knew, he hadn't had a female since he'd come home.

Having tired of her contemplation of the men, the Shimmerskin was now surreptitiously testing the nap of the carpet runner with the curl of her toes, like a gypsy determining its worth.

Seeming oblivious of the giant males who looked on, she folded her legs beneath her and unceremoniously sat upon a tread. Tracing the subtle, woven pattern with her fingertips, she then leaned down to rub the rich weave with her cheek, catlike. Her lashes drifted closed, and a blissful smile curved her lips. "Ummm."

All humor fled the four men in an instant, leaving a smoldering tension to fill the void. Vincent felt the others' sexual interest roil as if it were his own. Knew they would discern the ramping of his pulse as well.

Through all the centuries past, it had been this way between Satyr males. This preternatural dissemination of carnal awareness among them was an inalienable part of their makeups, and it had the happy effect of exponentially heightening their enjoyment of lascivious engagements.

Marco and Anthony shifted beside him, and a hint of ruddy color tinged Landon's cheekbones. The Shimmerskin sat there, seemingly oblivious to the undercurrents.

"Just give me the damned dress." Vincent took the box from Landon's suddenly lax fingers. The Shimmerskin's arm luminesced under his hand as he pulled her upright and smacked the package to her naked belly.

"Put this on," he told her, amazed to feel possessive of her.

Her brow wrinkled, and she cocked her head, uncomprehending.

When she made no move to grasp his offering, he folded her arms across it. But when he let go, she allowed it to slip heedlessly to the floor.

As the parcel tumbled down a couple of steps, the ribbon tied around it loosened, and its wrapping shifted askew.

Her eyes lit with interest when a dusky red ruffle appeared. A pair of stockings slinked haphazardly from among the jumble to lie on the stair, and the heel of one shoe and the toe of its twin burst from the paper.

She seemed to recognize all this for what it was, for she immediately whipped his shirt off. Blithely tossing it over the balustrade behind her, she knelt beside the unexpected bounty.

Vincent could almost hear Landon's inner predatory growl at the sight of her like this. He and these men had shared numerous Shimmerskins in the course of their lives. Satyr rituals at Moonful were such that they'd all seen one another and their mates unclothed and locked in passion many times before.

However, it was one matter to have Landon and his brothers view this woman in a state of nakedness when they'd gathered in the glen for salacious purposes. Having them ogle her on his stair, in his home, in broad daylight was quite another.

Breasts that were too voluptuous for her frame bobbled gently with her motions as she stood again and lifted the dress high to admire it. Her face was heart-wrenchingly awed at the simple gift.

He put a hand on her shoulder. "Do your dressing upstairs in my chamber," he heard himself order.

Marco frowned at him.

He'd sounded jealous. He *was* jealous. Gods, was it possible? Of his own brothers? Of Landon? Men with whom he'd grown up and easily shared dozens if not hundreds of other women?

With one leg in the dress and the other poised to join it, the Shimmerskin looked inquiringly at him. "Why?"

"What the hell?" Even Landon straightened from his usual slouch at this, dumbfounded by her question. By the fact that she'd asked it.

Vincent took the garment from her, lifted it over her head, and then began brusquely adjusting it to fit.

"What the hell's going on?" Marco demanded. "A Shimmerskin questioning our instructions? And requiring dresses? Where in hellfire did she come from?"

"I summoned her in the usual way, for the usual purpose." Vincent paused and then admitted significantly, "Last night."

"*Last night?*" Marco echoed.

"And she's *still here?*" asked Anthony.

"As you see. It seems she has achieved sentience. And I assure you she is more confused about how this has happened than we are."

"But that's impossible," Anthony said slowly. "Shimmerskins never outstay their welcomes. They don't have such impulses. They aren't . . . real." His hand lifted toward her as though to test the truth of his assertion.

Vincent nonchalantly pulled her out of reach. "Apparently if you conjure the same one once too often, she can become so."

"You fucked her sentient?" Marco chortled in spite of himself. "That's quite a feat, even for your monumental cock."

The Shimmerskin paused in her examination of the gown's bodice to glare at him.

Vincent winced inwardly as he worked at the fastenings along the back of the dress. His brothers had never fully appreciated the difficulties brought on by the proportions of his masculine appendage but rather had assumed his dimensions were something in which all ladies took delight. "I'm pleased that my predicament amuses you."

Fingers brushed his arm. The Shimmerskin. She'd turned before he'd managed even one closure, and the gown's bodice gaped, exposing her. His eyes searched hers and saw she'd meant the gesture to comfort him. Somehow she'd guessed his vulnerability.

Like a bolt of lightning, a shocking realization came to him. This impulse to hide her stemmed from the fact that he was unsure of her. Unsure of his hold on her. He'd created her. But if she was truly sentient, she could choose to leave him.

Taking her shoulders, he turned her and then gave her a little push upstairs. "Go. I'll join you momentarily to help you finish dressing."

She rolled her eyes, eliciting a gasp from Anthony at her audacity.

"Upstairs!" Vincent ordered, pointing in the direction he wished her to go.

Looking a trifle wounded by his rebuff, she nevertheless bunched the skirts around her waist and made to go, pausing only to gather the shoes and stockings.

"What are your plans for her?" Landon asked dragging his attention from her as though it were a supreme effort to do so. "Besides the obvious."

"She's not interested. In the obvious."

"A Shimmerskin not interested in fornication?" Marco scoffed. "Unheard of."

"Yet true. And it leads me to speculate that other rules common to Shimmerskins may not apply to her either."

"You don't suppose Humans will be able to see her, do you?" Anthony interrupted.

The ear-shattering clang and clatter of a tray crashing to the ground drew all attention to the landing at the top of the stairs. An elderly servant was poised there, her face blanched and her gaze on the glimmering, disheveled, half-naked woman ascending the expanse of staircase between them and her.

"If it isn't Lady Godiva herself, returned from the dead!" she squeaked, crossing herself.

"I suppose we may consider that sufficient answer to your question," Landon muttered.

Taking the stairs two at a time, Vincent lifted the Shimmerskin in his arms and then smoothly reversed his direction, heading downstairs with her. Glancing at Anthony as he descended, he jerked his head in the servant's direction. *Deal with that*, his expression ordered.

Anthony immediately understood and deferred to him, as all the brothers did in serious matters. Once Vincent had quit the stairs with her, Marco and Landon trailed him into his study.

From somewhere behind them came Anthony's voice, speaking to the flustered servant. No one lingered to see him stretch out a hand to her shoulder as he murmured, thus initiating a bespelling that would obliterate from her mind any recollection of the female apparition she'd witnessed.

Vincent inhaled, enjoying the warm, sweet scent of the woman he carried. It was a scent he'd created to appeal to him on the basest level possible.

Once in his private library, his eyes went to the treatises and legal documents he should have been poring over at this very moment; then they shifted to the massive clock on the opposite wall. He had to leave within the quarter hour.

He set his pretty burden on her feet and cupped her cheeks in his hands, concentrating in order to initiate a temporary bespelling. It would render her skin's appearance normal in the eyes of the servants, though not to his family.

When it was done, he stood brooding over her. His brother was right. She could become a danger to him if he let her. Anything a man in his position wanted this much couldn't help but put him in jeopardy of blackmail. Or, as Marco suspected, at the very least she could prove a distraction from the negotiations.

Marco stepped closer then, separating their tangled gazes. "Please tell me you aren't imagining some bizarre set of circumstances that might enable you to keep her here with you. Among the family." His voice seemed oddly distant. "Vincent! Did you hear me?"

Vincent blinked and stepped back from the Shimmerskin, glancing at the others.

Landon had already comfortably ensconced himself in the chair he often occupied in the evenings and crossed a booted ankle over his knee. And when had Anthony had rejoined them?

How long had they all been gathered there, watching him gaze at her in this besotted manner?

"I go," said the Shimmerskin, obviously sensing she wasn't wanted.

"There, you heard her," said Marco, gesturing toward her as if matters had been settled to everyone's satisfaction.

"Where would you suggest she go, precisely?" Vincent reached for her again and twirled her around so he could close the fastenings at her back at last. Though Marco's wife had an excellent figure, the dress was large on her, particularly in the waist, even without the benefit of a corset.

"You really don't know how to send her back?" This from Anthony.

"No, and she doesn't know how to get herself back either. Shall I open the door and shove her out to fend for herself? Or perhaps one of you is willing to drive her to Florence and drop her from your carriage into the street? You can imagine what would become of her."

"You're going to the council in ElseWorld today, are you

not? Why not take her with you through the gate and deposit her there?" Marco suggested.

Landon spoke for the first time, and though his voice held little force, it commanded. "That's hardly different from dumping her in a foreign city here on our side of the gate."

"Marco's idea is sound," said Anthony. "The magic from which she emanated is thick on the other side of the gate. Perhaps she'll be reabsorbed somehow."

"And what if there are complications? My attention must be on negotiations. No, she stays here, for now. And she can't be left without supervision until we know more of what to expect from her. One of you must take her for the day."

"Define 'take,'" murmured Landon. His tone was shaded with a hunger for her that he appeared to be having surprising difficulty repressing.

Hearing it, Vincent's own lust surged. His mind formulated a completely impractical scenario in which he would usher Marco and Anthony out and then bend her over his desk. And then he would lift the back of that ruffled red skirt she so adored and enter her from behind while she took Landon in her mouth.

His eyes lifted and snagged hers. Saw they were filled with a doelike awareness of his erotic imaginings.

Slowly her head turned toward Landon, meeting his gaze. Gray eyes heated, dilating.

"Right." Aware that Landon's unwitting attraction to her might well overwhelm him were he left alone with her, Vincent had no intention of allowing that to happen. Not yet.

So, instead, he surveyed his brothers. "Normally Julius would be my choice as caretaker since he's the most virtuous when it comes to women. Unfortunately he'll be with me today, which leaves the two of you. And as you are wed, Marco, you are hereby crowned with the dubious title of the most trustworthy brother I possess."

"And how am I to explain her to Millicent?" Marco protested.

No one cowed Marco, save his wife, a fact that Vincent privately found humorous in view of the fact that she was surely little more than half his strength and bulk. But as they were all well aware, Marco was happily married and would not stray. Even under a full Moon, he'd remained true to his spouse of two years.

"Your wife has gone to Florence until tomorrow, has she not?"

"Yes, and only think how delighted she will be to discover upon her return that I've housed a naked Shimmerskin under her roof as a favor to you."

In spite of the protest, Vincent sensed his brother's capitulation. "It's settled then. I must be off."

With that, he turned to the Shimmerskin and kissed her forehead. "I must go. For the entire day," he told her. "My brother Marco will see to your needs. Stay with him until I return."

She flicked a glance at Marco, hesitant.

"Stay," he said, realizing it was the last word he'd said to her the previous night.

She smiled slightly as if she, too, recalled, and then she inclined her head in acquiescence. "Stay."

"*Grazie*, brother," Vincent threw behind him as he departed the study. "Anthony. Landon." With these brusque farewells, he slipped out the door to make his way to the gate.

Marco followed him and caught his arm on the front steps.

"She's a danger to you," he warned. "To us all. When you return, I urge you to find a way to get rid of her."

Behind them, the Shimmerskin stood in the window of the study, listening to that which no Human ear could've overheard through distance and glass. Placing a palm on the windowpane, she watched Vincent cross the courtyard.

"Danger," she whispered. "Rid of her."

5

ElseWorld

Minutes later, Vincent arrived in the midst of the ancient forest that lay at the heart of the vast Satyr estate. There, he slipped through the secret gate that joined EarthWorld to ElseWorld and then made his way through the mist-laden channel until it expelled him in semi-darkness some fifty feet farther on. As day dawned in his world, night was falling here.

His brother Julius, the most serious of the triplets, stood waiting at its far end. Looking vastly relieved at the sight of him, he nevertheless irritably slapped a sheaf of carefully arranged and clipped documents against Vincent's chest.

"You're late," he said by way of greeting.

"Unavoidable."

"I traveled through war-torn territory this evening yet managed to arrive on time," Julius groused. "Don't think I didn't sense what you got up to last night. Now we will both be made to appear tardy on the most important day of negotiations."

Vincent drew back to read the documents with which he'd

been accosted. "There's more to it than what you imagine, but I'll explain later. What's all this?"

"The usual. Disagreements over ultimate ownership of fertile lands, seaports, vineyards. Petty dickering with regard to the redrawing of borders and the tithe we pay from our wine cellars in EarthWorld."

"Two hundred thousand casks of the finest vintage in existence is hardly a petty matter," said Vincent, skimming the first page.

"Signores Vincenzo and Julius! Welcome, welcome." It was a Facilitator come to greet them, though his real purpose was to ensure their safe passage to the meeting place. The elderly man would accompany them alone, for it was assumed none would dare to attack them while they were under the aegis of such a sacred and revered figure.

His gnarled hands waved them forward. "It is indeed an honor. A pleasure. Step this way, please. Yes, that's it, that's the way," he said as he directed them both toward a uniformed brigade of what appeared to be military personnel.

"Is this meant to be some sort of official welcome?" asked Vincent, eyeing them. There were at least fifty of them in all, forming an impenetrable wall and blocking the path to their destination.

"They're inspectors," he was told.

"Why so many? And so heavily armed?" Julius stroked the ebony mustache he'd been cultivating for the last month with two fingers, looking concerned.

"Do not be offended," the Facilitator rushed on, sensing his discomfort. "Extra precautions are necessary. All who come this way must be searched. There have been threats."

"Of what sort?" Julius demanded.

"Threats against your lives and those of the leaders who will gather on this side of the gate with you. Some in our world cannot bend with the winds of change."

Vincent flicked his hand in a gesture meant to end the discussion. "We're late, remember? And it grows dark here in this world. Let them do as they will, brother, so that we can move on."

As they approached the regiment, three men and one woman stepped from the ranks and came toward them. Vincent sat on one of the benches and allowed them to remove his boots. When he was directed to, he stood, raising his arms to be patted down. With a huff, Julius followed suit. Fingers combed through their hair and rifled through their pockets and boots, presumably searching for weapons or contraband.

And all the while, Vincent paid them little heed as he continued to scan the information that had taken Julius days to research, collate, and put to paper.

A hand slipped between his thighs, startling him, and he grabbed the arm attached to it in a harsh grip. His eyes met those of the sole female guard.

"What is it?" another of the guards called to her, sensing trouble.

"A suspicious bulge."

The guard laughed. "He probably stuffs his trousers to impress the ladies."

"I'm not impressed," she said, sober faced.

They'd spoken in an ElseWorld dialect, obviously and erroneously assuming he wouldn't understand.

The Facilitator drew near, trying to smooth matters over. "For the duration of the talks, a thorough search will remain customary," he said, attempting to placate Vincent.

"I have nothing to hide." Vincent released the female guard's arm. Her hand worked at the fastenings and then dipped inside the front of his trousers, unceremoniously groping him. Her eyes darted to his, widening at what she'd discovered.

He smiled at her and raised his brows. She blushed, something he'd never seen an ElseWorld guard do.

"Can we hurry this along?" Julius complained from behind him. Presumably he was being searched himself, something he would hate, for he was less free with his person than were Vincent and his brothers.

The female removed her hand and nodded to the other guard. "It's all him."

The male guard gaped and nudged another of the guards, whispering. A mild stir rippled through the rest of the ranks, swiftly gaining momentum. It seemed his reputation was about to spread to this world as well.

The search completed, Vincent and his brother restored their clothing and then set off for their destination, accompanied by the Facilitator.

"I hope you enjoyed yourself back there," Julius said when they were out of earshot.

Vincent smiled. "The perks of our travels to this negotiation are few. Allow me to enjoy those that come our way."

They crossed a boundary, whereupon a second Facilitator joined them. The two elders met their palms, murmuring to one another in a cursory greeting. Their trio hardly broke stride as the second continued on with them, and the first one departed.

Their new escort led them across a devastated landscape. A temporary cessation in fighting had been called, and the sounds of weaponry fire had ceased. Even in this city, the closest to EarthWorld, which was comparatively unharmed, there was evidence of widespread destruction.

"What's all this?" Vincent waved a hand toward the building that lay ahead gleaming in the darkness, high on a bluff. Though modest in size, it was constructed of fine marble that had been detailed with high-relief sculptures of flora and fauna native to ElseWorld. High turrets lit with torches bracketed each of its four corners, and two armed guards were posted in each.

Skipping with every third step to keep pace with their longer strides, the Facilitator spoke haltingly in broken Italian as they approached it. "It was built specifically for this new round of meetings. In honor of the treaty negotiations."

Vincent shook his head, amazed at the expense that had been gone to. "A tent would've done as well."

Without thinking, he'd spoken in the Facilitator's first language rather than in his own native Italian. The man brightened at his use of the dialect that was more familiar to him, and he lapsed into it as well. "No, no, a more fortresslike environment was necessary." His voice lowered, hushed with unease. "Demons have been sighted."

Vincent's brows rose, and he shot Julius a confounded look.

"What is he saying?" Julius inquired, juggling papers as he sought to keep up.

Vincent translated briefly. A natural linguist, he was fluent in two dozen EarthWorld and ElseWorld languages and could read several more, though he'd devoted little time to their study. "Did you know about these rumors?"

Julius shrugged. "A recurring theme. I assume they're simply based on fear and not to be considered seriously. We all know the demons' reign of terror ended over a decade ago when Dominic made his home in EarthWorld."

The Facilitator obviously understood enough of that, for he rushed in. "Except for the hours of black surrounding Moonful, when the demonhand returns to us. Then the demons stir. And now some say they begin to come to them again in their nightmares."

"Gods! We don't need this," said Vincent. "If the factions have been stirred up by this talk, they'll be in no mood for agreement."

"Let's hope they've all been searched for weaponry as thoroughly as we were," said Julius.

Catching the gist of his statement, the Facilitator rushed on.

"Let me endeavor to reassure and pledge unto you that all desirable and necessary safeguards are in place, including surveillance, barricades, and guards with armaments. I trust you'll be pleased at our unrelenting efforts of perpetual security and will—"

Vincent interrupted his assurances when they showed no sign of abating, putting a hand to the Facilitator's chest to halt him as they neared the meeting premises. "My brother and I need time to speak privately before we enter the meeting chamber. As we are running late, we'll bid you farewell here. We thank you for your efforts on behalf of the negotiations." He took the Facilitator's pale hand in his, giving him a gleaming smile and offering the traditional phrase that served as both greeting and leave-taking. "As the moon reflects the sun."

"As the moon reflects the sun," the Facilitator echoed, obviously disappointed that he would not be admitted to the meeting itself, for all wished for a glimpse of the room where the negotiations were to be held. Julius added his own cursory salutation and a half bow before moving on in Vincent's wake.

The swell of voices raised in conflict reached the two brothers before they had even crossed the threshold.

"Tantrums already?" muttered Vincent.

"I told you it wouldn't do to be late," said Julius as they ducked into the elaborate structure.

"Cease your worry. I assembled the primary points I wish to make here weeks ago, as well as my supporting arguments," Vincent returned. "All that remains is to present them and see what unfolds as a result."

"And regarding this new question of the demons?"

"The only thing that everyone in this world fears and despises with equal fervor are demons. Therefore, if the matter arises, we will turn it to our benefit and use it as a unifying factor."

And then there was no more time for discussion, for they were admitted to the conference room. Inside sat an assemblage of six men, two women, and one androgyne, all of whom were more bestial than human. Nine adversarial factions, all coming together for the first time since King Feydon had departed their world leaving behind mischief and mayhem, but no successor.

Though the glass table at which they were gathered was round, it had taken some doing to find an arrangement of seating that kept dire enemies apart.

One chair remained empty. Vincent's. Julius would be seated several feet behind him on a low dais, joining other occupants of the room who would not participate directly in the talks. Each delegate had brought a food taster and an entourage of personal guards and servants. The sound was overwhelming as voices clamored to be heard.

Taking his place, Vincent stood, gazing out over the room.

There had been other meetings like this one between smaller groups of dignitaries over previous years, and much had been resolved. Now there remained only a few, last, difficult points of contention.

Over the coming days, he would make his arguments, soothe tempers, and persuade others to see reason. His reason. Bringing varied personalities and egos to a meeting of the minds was an art in which he not only excelled—it was one in which he reveled.

The burden was heavy, the consequences of failure dire. Yet he was exhilarated. In his element. A determination rose in him to make this work. By the end of the month, he hoped to have a signed treaty.

He raised a hand, commanding and receiving quiet.

"Delegates, these negotiations are officially open."

The Feroce leader immediately leaped to his feet, slamming a fat fist on the table. "I wish to put forward a proposal that the gate between our worlds be forever sealed."

Matters proceeded downhill from there.

6

―――――――

EarthWorld

Darkness had fallen by the time Vincent arrived on his brother's front step. Only the ethereal creatures who acted as night servants were left on the estate, for all Human servants had been banished to their quarters outside the grounds at dusk.

As he entered the house, the subtle, delicious smells of dinner assailed him, along with his brother and his closest friend.

"Thank the Gods you've finally returned," said Marco, looking unusually frazzled.

"Here," Vincent said, presenting him with a tacky bit of precious jewelry and Landon with a bouquet of bizarre, long-stemmed blossoms. "Gifts from our ElseWorld relations."

With doubtful expressions, the two men eyed what he'd given them and the bounty of other presents that overflowed his arms.

"Did all go well?" asked Landon.

"No," Vincent informed him baldly, leading them into the nearest salon where he dumped the rest of his armload upon the first chaise he encountered. "As the meeting opened, the Feroce delegate brought forth a motion to seal the gate between our worlds."

"Gods! Why?" asked Anthony, overhearing as he joined them.

"To prevent Dominic from crossing over to stir the demons." Vincent randomly chose a foot-high, ribald statue of Bacchus and two nymphs, which he handed to Anthony. "For you."

Anthony rolled his eyes and set it aside.

"But he and Rosetta will die without periodic visits to Else-World," said Marco.

Landon frowned, slapping his bouquet against his thigh so pollen dusted the leather of his trousers. "Don't the Feroce realize another demonhand will simply rise up on their side of the gate when that happens? That things will return as they were before, with demons running rampant every night instead of just one?"

"And what of the vines . . . ? Our families? Neither will survive a sealing off of the conduit between our worlds," added Marco.

"Exactly. I've calmed the waters for now. But the seeds of suspicion toward us have been carefully and well planted by someone. In fact, we are accused of having a vested interest in keeping the demons alive."

"What would we have to gain by that?" asked Anthony.

Vincent shrugged. "Ask the Feroce. Other than that, it was the usual day of tantrums, chaos, and sporadic moments of forward momentum countered with intermittent instances of the opposite. And here?" he asked, glancing around in an effort to determine the Shimmerskin's whereabouts.

"I would describe matters here in much the same way," said Marco.

"Where is she?" Vincent asked, and all knew whom he meant.

Marco went to the door of the salon and bellowed. "Cara!"

"Cara?" Vincent parroted.

"Your protégée's name. She has intimated that you bestowed it upon her yourself."

In spite of the day's rigors, a chuckle escaped Vincent. "I suppose I should deem myself fortunate she chose that endearment from among those less salient I might've called her in the throes of—"

"Why are you shouting, Marco?" Millicent inquired, entering the room. Noting his presence, Marco's wife smiled and came closer to accept the brush of his lips on her cheek. "Welcome, Vincent! Where's Julius? We so rarely see him these days."

"Millicent! You've returned sooner than expected I see." Vincent shot Marco an apologetic glance, knowing he wouldn't have relished explaining the Shimmerskin to his wife.

"Yes, and we've both been enjoying our unexpected houseguest," Marco said, his expression indicating that the exact opposite was true.

"She's been no trouble," Millicent politely assured him, "for once she discovered the library, she hasn't left it."

"It seems she can read," Landon informed him.

"Interesting," said Vincent.

"Julius isn't with you?" Millicent inquired again.

"Our brother sends his apologies. The meetings are to reconvene two days from now, and he has remained behind to do some covert investigation before I return."

"He is away so much I begin to suspect he harbors a fondness for someone in that world," Millicent mused.

"Really?" Anthony's interest sharpened.

"Don't tease him about it," Millicent scolded. "You should be pleased if a female has recognized your brother's many fine qualities and he reciprocates her affection. And, Vincent, I'm glad you've come. I'll set another place."

"But—" Vincent began.

"Cara!" Marco called again, stepping on his demur as Millicent departed. This time, the Shimmerskin appeared almost before her name died away, joining them from the direction of Marco's study rather than the library.

"Vincent!" she shouted with delight when she saw him. She went straight to him, sliding her arms around his neck and drawing his face down for her kiss. Pleasure at the sight and feel of her swept him, and his arms automatically enfolded her in return.

The yield of her soft body against his harder one felt so right. A sweet joy filled him. She was still here. Still aware. Still his. Yet something about her was different. Cupping her jaw, he brushed his thumb over her cheekbone eliciting only a faint shimmer. Over the past ten hours, her skin's iridescence had significantly diminished. She was becoming more Human.

He glanced at Landon over her head. He'd been watching them, and the same realization was in his eyes.

"What were you doing in my study?" demanded Marco, breaking up their embrace.

"In my study," she echoed, pulling away.

"She only does that to annoy me," Marco fumed. "I've discovered she can speak well enough when she so chooses."

Suddenly Cara's expression lit with awe as she spied the pile of gifts on the chair. Sinking to her knees before the colorful abundance, she began picking through it with the excitement of a child.

"Treasure," she breathed.

Vincent watched her fondly. She'd asked nothing of where he'd been or why he'd been gone so long. A Human woman would have been all over him with curiosity.

Aside from the diminished glow of her skin, there was something else different about her, he noticed. Her overall appearance was somehow more refined. Millicent must've taken her in hand in the short time he'd been gone, for her golden hair had been tamed in flattering twists and curls, and her dress had been altered to better fit her.

Marco pointed at her where she still rummaged through Vincent's booty. "I'd keep a close eye on her. She steals."

"She does *not* steal," said Cara, irritated.

"What do you call the hoard of objects you've amassed in the corner of my library in less than a day's visit?" He pointed up the stairs. Her eyes followed the length of his arm and then lost interest.

"What do you call the hoard of objects," she mocked, pointing in imitation of him and clearly not comprehending the concept of ownership.

"I call them *my* belongings!" Marco shouted. "And what were you doing in my study just now?" He stood back, eyeing her as though to trying to detect any lumps and bumps on her person that might indicate the presence of contraband.

"Belongings? I don't belonging."

Marco smacked his hand to his own forehead, appearing to be at his wit's end. "Gods, it's been this way all day. Her, speaking gibberish. Half the time I suspect she does that to irritate me as well."

Smiling slightly, Cara shrugged, and the red dress slipped off her shoulder, affording them all a glimpse of the upper curve of a full breast. Marco's voice dwindled off, and a taut silence filled the room.

Landon cleared his throat.

Vincent shifted. The groin of his trousers was suddenly far too tight. He reached for her. "I'm pleased the visit went well, but I think it's best that we take our leave of you. Tell Millicent—"

"Nonsense!" Millicent reentered the salon. With a smile she appropriated Cara's arm, leading her away. "We can't let you go home to a cold house after your long day, Vincent. I'm sure you must be ravenous. Do join us for dinner."

As Vincent stared after them, feeling as if his favorite toy had just been taken from him, Millicent's voice floated behind her. "And Cara's to stay with us for the next few days. For propriety's sake. You can't have an unwed female living in the home of two bachelors. How would it look?"

Cara sent him a saucy, innocent smile over her shoulder. "How would it look?"

7

Somewhere around the end of the third course of bread and brie and the presentation of sorbet and strawberries for dessert, Cara found herself abruptly taken out of herself. Though no one fully understood this description when she was later questioned, it was the only way she would be able to characterize the bizarre experience.

One moment she'd been sitting before the white damask-covered dining table at Marco's home, gathered there for a repast prepared by his wife and her servants.

And a moment later, she'd found herself somewhere else entirely. Two men—both strangers—had taken her there, holding her captive in sumptuous, elegant surroundings that were completely foreign to her.

They thought her stupid. Worthless. Only good for fucking. They expected absolute obedience. Something she no longer wished to give.

Before she was taken, she had been sitting at that immaculate table among familiar faces, smiling because she wanted to. Because she felt happy. She'd been in the company of Vincent and two of his brothers, Marco and Anthony, and the other man they called a friend, Landon.

She'd been closely observing Millicent, the only other female at the table, in order to determine the uses for each of the utensils that had been precisely stationed alongside her plate. Never having dined in a formal setting, all this was new to her.

A plate, she'd surmised, was the appellation for the flat, opalescent disk with a thin circlet of gold around its outer edge. Periodically, these disks were whisked away by servants in crisp black and white, only to be replaced by another dish, with a similar design, containing delectable food of another kind.

Most recently, a fluted bowl encrusted with pearls had arrived, set before her by servants who seemed to work as diligently at making themselves invisible as she sought to make herself the opposite. It was filled with a pink, mushy substance and plump strawberries.

Vincent's handsome face smiled at her, and he pointedly lifted a pronged utensil, indicating she was now to employ it, the smaller of the two remaining pieces of cutlery that had been placed in careful readiness before each diner.

Cara lightly ran a fingertip along the slender, gleaming smoothness of a handle, then a neck, then onward to the part of the instrument that drew her. At its tip, it divided into four tines. They were sharp.

"It's a fork," someone whispered to her. Millicent. The female. Wife of Marco.

Somehow she'd already known what the utensil was called. Words seemed to be coming more easily now, though from where they came she didn't know.

Still, she smiled her thanks at the woman and lifted the fork, finding it cold in her hand. She turned it in her fingers, strangely mesmerized. Candlelight flickered off its golden sheen, momentarily blinding her.

"Cara?" It was Vincent's voice. Vincent, the beautiful male

who filled her with himself and who gave her his seed when he pleased. The one who had given her a dress and whose eyes were blue and intelligent and kind. The one who kept her safe. Her creator.

Though he raised his voice when she didn't respond, the volume of it seemed strangely muted. She touched his lips with her fingers as he repeated her name, wanting to hang on to his voice, to him.

He took her upper arms in his hands and shook her, his face growing ever more concerned. He repeated her name, but the sound of him faded away. . . .

. . . Silenced by new voices.

Her finger hurt. She looked down and saw she still held the fork and had pressed the tip of her finger to the tips of its tines, applying constant and steady pressure. Suddenly they pricked and broke her skin. Four points of blood welled.

Then, with astonishing suddenness, she found herself gone. Whisked away from Vincent and his family and their table.

Now she inhabited another place that was dreamlike and eerie. She was standing in a pool of soft light. Candlelight. There were nine silver tapers in the candelabrum on a small, bare table. Wax melted down their lengths, like pricks slowly ejaculating.

It was as if only the immediate vicinity in which she stood existed in this world, but nothing further. No distance.

Two plants that were strange, with long arms, undulated into her vision. Somehow she sensed they were poisonous.

And then she saw that the plants were in fact two men seated upon cushions of a black velvet chaise longue. Though she felt them studying her, for some reason she could not clearly see their features in return.

"Like Sleeping Beauty in Perrault's tale, she pricks her finger and falls to slumbering once again," the larger of the two men said.

He wanted her. She scented his desire even amid the cloaking scents of incense riding the air.

The other slender, olive-skinned one was less interested in such things, but his gaze was riveted on her, too, in a way that frightened her even more than the other one's.

The larger man rose and stood before her, his palms covering her breasts, massaging them through the fabric of her pretty, ruffled red dress. The dress Vincent had given her.

She tried to curl her fingers and claw at his face. But to her dismay, she instead found herself sliding her own palms up the front of his red satin vest.

He stroked her hair, and she could smell his awful need to bend her to his Will. "Take off your gown."

"You're wasting time," the slender man on the couch told him.

But the man beside her continued to stare at her with his black eyes. "I want her to take it off. For me."

She opened her mouth to refuse but instead felt her lips curve into a beguiling smile. She wanted to push him away, but could not seem to act against him.

Tilting her head at a coquettish angle, she lifted her hands to the fastenings of her dress and began to do as he'd bade her.

It was then she realized to her horror that things had reverted to the way they'd been before, back in the time when she'd existed without Will. Before Vincent had brought her to life.

Before she'd become Real.

Now, as in that uncertain time before, she existed only to serve.

With each garment that fell, her heart fell a little further as well until she was naked, heartbroken. And as each part of her anatomy was uncovered, the man with the black eyes touched it, tainting her with his fingers and his mouth. He was unhurried, certain of his ability to hold her here in this terrible limbo as long as he Willed it.

"*It's true then,*" *he said in growing excitement.* "*She shimmers, yet she's Human.*"

Human.

She turned her head and saw the table that was covered in pristine white, neatly set with plates and golden cutlery. The others were still there. She could see herself seated there as well, fully dressed, still and deathly silent.

Vincent was speaking urgently to her, trying to wake her. His brothers, Landon, and Millicent were as well. They had all gathered around her, looking so concerned.

The flat of her persecutor's hand slapped her right buttock, snapping her attention back to him. As it slid up her back to grasp her nape, his other hand slid down her belly and slipped between the front of her legs. Without warning, a thumb drove inside her feminine slit, and a middle finger rammed inside the muscled ring of her anus, lifting her a few inches from the floor.

His face drew near to hers. "*You're a sweet little cunt. I can see why he wants you.*"

"Cara!"

Hands came. Warmer, kinder hands from that other, better place in EarthWorld. They clutched her shoulders and stroked her cheek. Trying to woo her back. She swayed, wanting to go.

"*Listen to him, calling for you,*" *whispered a harsh voice at her ear.* "*But you don't want him. You want me, don't you?*"

"Yes," *she breathed. Her voice was lilting, well modulated, and pleasant, as it had been designed to be.*

"*That's good. A good girl. Kneel for me.*"

He turned her then to kneel on the couch, her knees straddling the outsides of those of the slender, olive-skinned man who was still seated there. A hand between her shoulder blades pushed her forward, toward him. To keep from toppling down upon him, she braced her hands on the high back of the couch on either side of his shoulders.

The slender man blinked up at her, and his eyes flashed silver and then ruby, startling her. She saw then, as she hadn't before, that he was naked, garbed only in circlets of leather clasped around his waist, neck, and wrists, all of which were adorned with various charms. Between his legs his thick, sallow-skinned cock stood high, its tip angled menacingly toward her slit.

Behind her, clothing rustled. Another man's cock found its way between her legs, cold and prickly—a shock to her warm skin.

She wanted to close her legs but found she couldn't. The strange creature before her had spread his knees wide between hers and stretched his arms outward on each side of himself along the back of the couch. His ruby eyes gazed up at her, enjoying her helplessness. Yet unlike the other man, he seemed in no hurry to join himself to her.

And then, like the sting of some cruel insect, the fat cock of the man behind her drove into her pussy. Her pink, fluted nether lips opened for him in a silent, panicked scream. He retracted almost immediately and then returned to sting again and again. She hadn't been mated to him before. She would have remembered. His rod was squat. Stunted. A third the size of Vincent's.

Her traitorous body willingly adjusted to hug its puny shape, and her cream saturated her feminine passage to make his sojourn within her an enjoyable one. Her agonized heart contracted with shame even as her vaginal walls contracted, forming a sheathe that would better suit so small a male appendage.

She was a Shimmerskin, after all. Eager to please.

"That's it, little puttana." Bone slammed, bruising bone. He wanted to hurt her. To own her like Marco wished to own things. Why?

High along the insides of her thighs, his balls jounced and thumped, bloated with seed he planned to force on her. Her channel clenched in rejection, but this only excited him. He slapped her rear again and bit the slope of her shoulder like an animal.

The creature before her observed all this, his expression now a combination of mild curiosity and boredom. His hand went to his prick, idly stroking it with clawed fingers.

"Gods. Oooh, Gods!" The man behind her shuddered over her, moaning. Within seconds, he spewed into her, flooding her tissues with his repulsive, unwanted gift. His arms wrapped around her waist, and he held her close, gasping over her.

Eventually he lifted away and something cold touched the plateau of her lower back, making her jump. She glanced over her shoulder and saw that her punisher had placed a round, golden disk there.

"I love you," he whispered, rubbing it in circles over her skin.

She wasn't certain for a moment if he was speaking to the coin or to her.

But shameful words forced their way into her mind and instantly trembled on her lips before falling from them to ride on the air.

"I love you," she echoed.

"Soon you'll be mine," he told her. "I'll take you from him."

And then she knew why she had been brought here.

This man hated Vincent and planned to hurt him. Somehow. Through her.

Lips kissed her neck. Ugh. Bristle. His upper lip was furred. Like his crotch.

"Soon," he whispered.

She nodded. Died a little inside as she did.

His cock slithered from her, soggy and deflated. Taking his coin, he placed it in the small pocket of his vest, stepped back, and let her go.

She straightened. Felt his cum dribble from her slit onto her inner thigh.

The olive-skinned male on the couch before her spoke again at last.

"Have you remembered your purpose?" he demanded.

She looked down at him. "What?" she whispered.

"Cara!" A masculine voice called to her, offering protection from those that would harm her. Vincent.

She reached out to touch him but felt only the smoothness of the fork on the table at her place setting.

Hands shook her, desperate to wake her. "Cara!"

"Your purpose. You will return to us again and again until you remember it," she was told. A clawed fingertip poked her midriff, drawing a line downward toward her . . .

She stepped back. "And if I remember?"

Ruby flashed silver. "Then all will be well."

"I'll no longer have to come?" she asked desperately.

"Come where? Cara?"

Flickers of light blinded her. Dozens of golden candles danced before her now, blazing merrily.

She was back. For this was the ornate candelabrum on Marco's table, not the silver-candled one in that other, strange place. She sat very still, barely daring to breathe, afraid she might be snatched away again.

Vincent was next to her, his hand clasping hers.

Without conscious will, she began to speak. "The thought came gently and stealthily, and it seemed long before it attained full appreciation; but just as my spirit came at length properly to feel and entertain it, the figures of the judges vanished, as if magically, from before me; the tall candles sank into nothingness; their flames went out utterly; the blackness of darkness supervened; all sensations appeared swallowed up in a mad rushing descent as of the soul into Hades. Then silence, and stillness, and night were the universe."

The scrape of a chair. A gasp. Low conversation.

"Her verbal skills have certainly improved," someone muttered. Landon.

She turned her head, gazing into his solemn gray eyes. His was a deep sadness he sought to hide. Her heart wanted to reach out to him, to tell him she, too, had been wounded and understood. But she couldn't seem to gather the wherewithal to stir.

"She's quoting a passage from Edgar Allan Poe's tale, *The Pit and the Pendulum.*" This from Marco.

Millicent shuddered. "A frightening story."

"But where would she have come across it?" asked Anthony.

"Perhaps she and the author have just met in the ether," Millicent proposed with a shiver.

Marco slipped a comforting arm around her. "More likely in the *Broadway Journal.* There's a copy of it in my library."

"How the hell would she have committed such an excerpt to memory in one day when she can barely speak full sentences?" asked Vincent.

Marco raised and lowered his shoulders, appearing equally baffled.

Vincent clapped his hands before Cara's eyes, and she jerked, instantly and fully aware. Shoving back her chair in a burst of energy, she leaped to her feet. Locating him among the others, she flung her arms around him and curled herself onto his lap.

"Thank Gods!" he whispered into her hair, folding her in his embrace.

His entire family was staring at her, their expressions filled with varying degrees of suspicion, dismay, and sympathy. The scent of incense was gone. As were those horrible men and that room.

What would these kind people think of her if they knew what had just occurred? Perhaps her kidnappers hoped she would tell. Hoped she would help them to hurt Vincent in the telling. No, she wouldn't speak of it. She didn't want to. She wanted to forget.

She snuggled into Vincent's shirtfront. He smelled of masculine goodness, of safety.

"What happened?" she mumbled.

Vincent's head whipped back in surprise.

"She's asking *us* that?" someone marveled. Anthony.

"You faded," said Landon from somewhere behind her.

She straightened at that. "I disappeared? As I used to before?"

"Not exactly," said Vincent. "Your body was still a warm and solid presence, but it became translucent, and you appeared to be in some sort of trance that lasted . . . ?"

"Eight minutes," Landon supplied.

"Where did you go?" Vincent asked.

"To nothing. To nowhere," she murmured. The same words she'd given him in response to a similar question the previous night.

"Did you see anything during that time? Hear anything?"

"No! Stop!" she railed. "I don't remember. Nothing happened. One moment I was eating, and then the next, you were all staring at me. As you are now."

Uncomfortable at being the center of so much attention, she shifted on his lap, feeling the bulge at his groin. High between her thighs, she was wet with the leavings of another man's defiling.

She wriggled from him and stood, announcing, "I have need of the chamber pot."

Without a word, Millicent took her hand and accompanied

her to a room, where she found basins, fresh toweling, and a brass chamber pot. The latter was an item that had fascinated her since this morning when she'd first seen one. Her need of it now seemed reassuring. A symbol that she was Human, though this was a notion Millicent had earlier advised her was best kept to herself.

As she thoroughly washed herself, questions swirled in her mind. If the man in her vision had given her seed that was real, it followed that he must be real as well. Which meant that her visit to him hadn't been a dream.

She trembled, terrified anew.

When she left the room, her privates were once again pristine and parched of semen. Still she couldn't seem to erase the sensation of powerlessness and debasement. Or the fear that what had occurred might happen again.

"Shall we put this unpleasantness behind us and continue with our meal?" Millicent suggested when she eventually exited the room.

Put it behind her? Impossible! She'd been damaged. Abused.

"Of course. Thank you," she told the other woman, linking arms with her and unconsciously mimicking her cultured voice.

Back in the dining room, Cara parted from her. Going to sit in her former chair, she smiled at the others. They'd stopped talking when she'd entered, and she was certain they'd been discussing her. Wondering what to do with her, their problem.

"Shall we put this unpleasantness behind us and continue with our meal?" she said, parroting Marco's wife. With that, she lifted the golden fork, speared a strawberry, and placed it in her mouth.

Eating. It was what Humans did. Therefore it was what she wanted to do. Become truly and thoroughly Human. Real. Safe.

Now that she'd tasted "real"—smelled it, lived it—she couldn't bear the thought of going back to the nothingness of before.

"I think this meal is over," said Vincent, pulling out her chair and helping her to stand.

Stealthily she slid the fork she held into her sleeve, not knowing why she did it. But when he took her forearm, he felt its slender, lethal presence within the fabric and took it from her, holding it high between them.

"What did you intend this for?" he asked softly.

"I don't know," she whispered in bemusement. Her eyes turned up to his, a desperate plea in them. "I don't know."

His gaze met Landon's over her head as he took the fork, slapping it in Marco's palm. "I believe this is yours."

With that, he and Landon each grasped one of her elbows. Like two giant oaks towering over her willowy frame, they ushered her toward the door.

8

"Take my carriage," Marco offered as he and his wife trailed the three of them to the *portico*. "I ordered it made ready for you earlier."

"Shouldn't Cara stay here with us?" Millicent protested but less forcefully than before, Vincent noted. Cara's bizarre stunt had made her as wary as Marco.

"This is a thornier circumstance than we at first surmised," Marco answered. "Let her go with Vincent and Landon for now."

"Yes, Millicent," said Cara, touching the other woman's hand. "Let her go. Thank you for the lovely dinner. And for this." She lifted the small tapestry-covered traveling case containing a donation of garments, which Millicent had left for her by the door.

Without further farewell, Cara slipped ahead of the men and down the steps. A light fog had gathered, and her mildly luminescent figure cut an eerie swath through it, appearing almost to float along the ground like an ethereal wraith.

Vincent and Landon made to follow, but Marco caught Vincent's arm, stalling him. "Tonight has done nothing to diminish my misgivings regarding the wisdom of keeping her here. She's unstable. And a thief," he said, exhibiting the golden fork she'd tried to steal.

"Your concerns are duly noted. And appreciated."

"And ignored?"

Landon had paused on the steps just beyond them, looking impatient as he watched the driver assist Cara into the carriage.

"Keep an eye on her," Vincent told him, knowing he could trust Landon to make sure she didn't disappear.

"Marco's right," said Anthony, joining them. "I cannot help but find it strange that she would achieve sentience in your bed on the very eve of your negotiations in ElseWorld. And then to have your efforts thwarted on the first day in such a suspicious manner?"

"You think her some sort of Trojan horse, purposely sent to infiltrate us and derail the treaty?" Vincent asked.

"In light of everything, is it so ridiculous?" said Marco. "All that aside, as a practical matter, I agree with Millicent that the two of you simply cannot keep an unattached female under your roof for any length of time."

Vincent glanced at Landon and followed his gaze over the lawn. Saw Cara sitting in the carriage. Her head whipped away. She'd been watching them. He shifted slightly, turning his back to her, suddenly wondering if she might be gifted with the ability to read the speech on his lips from a distance.

"We'll take what you've said into consideration," he said, and then he turned down the stairs. Landon joined in step with him, and together they made for the carriage.

Marco's voice floated after them. "See that you do."

"I'll drive," Landon called out when they reached the conveyance. The driver looked somewhat taken aback but readily relinquished the reins and jumped down as Landon swung up.

Vincent left them to it and joined Cara inside. As they embarked on the journey to his estate, he settled back against the plush squabs, contemplating her.

She slipped something from the tapestry bag. Another golden fork. She turned it in her fingers, holding it between them, openly and wordlessly admitting her guilt in taking it.

Vincent's eyes flicked to it and back to her face. "Thievery is a lamentable and unnecessary pastime of which I hope to cure you. I assure you I'm wealthy enough to purchase however many forks you require and whatever else you desire. And you may avail yourself of anything I own as well."

"Own. Yes. It's the moving of objects to locations I prefer that affords me ownership. As you did when you brought me here. Moving me from Nothing to Real. Own."

He frowned. "Sentient beings don't own one another. They choose to remain in one another's company, as I choose be in yours."

She shrugged, not debating him on the issue of whether or not she was sentient as he'd expected, but instead saying, "Your brother thinks more of ownership than of choosing."

"Marco? He's in banking. In charge of the family coffers, so I suppose matters of ownership and belongings are an important part of his professional purpose."

"What is *my* purpose?" she asked quickly, pondering the utensil she held as if expecting it to reply rather than him.

His gaze brushed over her figure.

She stilled under the visual caress. Understanding slowly colored the eyes that darted to his. Lifting the front of her skirts high, she half stood and came over him. Sliding her knees onto the seat on either side of his hips, she settled herself on his lap facing him. He slumped lower, grasping the bones of her hips and adjusting their fit so her unguarded slit aligned itself perfectly with his wool-encased shaft.

Her body undulated sensuously, riding him. "This?" she whispered close to his ear. "Is this my purpose?"

Though his mind worked on her question, his hands caught her motion and gladly assisted her in it.

"Only this?" she insisted. She combed the tines of the fork down the side of his neck, sending a chill over him. His rocking of her slowed, and his hand caught her wrist, drawing it carefully away.

"No. Of course not." But he heard the ambivalence in his voice. Knew she would hear it.

"Then fuck me," she murmured. The fork hit the seat cushion beside them with a barely discernable thud and then bounced from it and clattered to the floor.

"Cara—"

"Give me your cock," she begged softly, wrapping her hands at his nape. "Help me serve my purpose."

He hesitated, wanting her. Yet wanting to make things right.

But her knees had already lifted her away just enough to allow her nimble fingers to free the fastenings of his trousers. He groaned as she quickly released all eleven inches of him. Need overrode thought. Words could wait.

She quickly settled close again, using her weight to flatten his shaft against his belly. Resuming her ride but not yet inviting him inside her. Holding his gaze, she stroked her flesh against his. Sliding soft, plush lips along his length in long, hot drags. A labyrinth of veins rose along his cock in her wake, so abruptly he could almost feel the sensation of them popping forth.

"You're dry," he muttered against skin that was as fine and flawless as a baby's.

"Make me wet," she urged in that breathless voice that never failed to lure him toward climax. "Fuck me. Fill me, Vincent. Spill inside me and make me wet again. Clean again. Please."

Something was wrong. She sounded desperate, almost frightened. He held her away so he could examine her face.

The curtains at the carriage door swayed, and moonlight

turned her violet eyes to jewels. Shaded with lambent desire, they were hungry for him. And more beautiful than he'd ever seen them.

Simply because they were aware.

"Come inside me."

"Gods, yes." Slamming the soles of his boots wide on the edge of the opposite seat, he drew her higher against his chest with one hand wrapped around her ass. She pushed upward with her knees, spreading her thighs, offering herself, begging him to pierce her.

Reaching between them, he took his cock and plowed its crown along the length of her slit, parting her. She quickly flowered for him, her velvet, rose-colored petals opening, turning slick.

The carriage began to falter and its pace to decline, as if its driver had suddenly forgotten to steer. He wondered how Landon's brawny frame would fit were he to decide to join them inside the conveyance. It went without saying that when he entered her, Landon would know. His brothers would know as well. Satyr blood bound them all, and any carnal engagement one undertook stimulated the others' need for such things, no matter how distant their respective locations.

Though clucking over what he would consider an error in Vincent's judgment, Marco would no doubt be lifting Millicent's skirts soon enough—a consequence of Vincent's current physical engagement with Cara. Anthony and Julius would likely be using their fists or conjuring Shimmerskins soon as well. All benefitted when one experienced pleasure.

And if matters proceeded as he expected, Landon would benefit far more directly from this than would the others.

Cara sank over him, and he let gravity and the gentle sway of the carriage guide her lower. She seemed oddly smaller than he'd fashioned her to be. But at his initial entry, she began to reconform, her fit adjusting to him.

"Tell me if I hurt you," he said.

"A good hurt," she murmured, quickly caught up in her enjoyment.

He pressed his mouth to the hollow of her throat as her body swallowed his crown and several inches in one gulp.

From outside the carriage, Landon's sudden, terse call to the horses reached him. And then they were off again, hurtling homeward at a furious clip.

"Another wants to take me," she whispered. The admission fell from her, and she ducked her head against the side of his face as though she immediately wished it back.

"Yes," he groaned, assuming she'd guessed she was meant for Landon as well. He rocked himself deeper. Just a few more inches. "Are you willing?"

"Willing?" she echoed, shaking her head. "Don't send me back."

"Send you back?"

Her eyes misted as they snagged his. Damn Marco. His talk of returning her to the ether had terrified her.

"I swear to you I have no intention of sending you back to your former situation. Or anywhere else." As she took another inch of his length, it was the furthest thing from his mind.

She looked dubious.

"Fucking is easily had, Cara. Even before, you were more to me than *this*." In a wordless defining of his reference, he bucked his hips, sending another inch inside her. "I want you, no other—in this and in my life. You were made for me."

"Made for me." She smiled into his eyes, appearing deeply affected. Then she turned her head slightly, angling her chin in the general direction of Landon's seat at the front of the carriage. "And."

Intuitively she seemed to understand her purpose. At least the one he'd originally intended her for. As a mate for him. And for Landon.

The notion had him pulling her higher on him and then ramming her down the final inches of his shaft. At last, at last her passage took all of him.

"Gods, Cara." The feeling of being thoroughly sequestered inside her was indescribable. Addictive. A momentous homecoming. Pleasure crested at this affirmation that she could still encompass all of him in spite the fact that she was no longer fully a Shimmerskin. Real or unreal. At the moment, he didn't care what species she was.

His hands slid under her skirts, up her thighs. Shaping the rounds of her ass, he worked the delicate clasp of her up and down his length, using her body on him as he might have his own fist.

Their lips clung, their moans and breath twining. Her fingers threaded into his hair.

The pace of the carriage increased dramatically, rocking them together and apart with its rolling gait. The fucking became almost effortless as the conveyance's momentum alternately drew her away and then buried him in her to the hilt again.

"Oh, Vincent." Her voice was pure anguished need. Her head fell back, and he gazed at her smooth white throat. At the heave of breasts quivering within her bodice. And then he felt her channel begin to squeeze him in a shuddering rhythm that milked him from groin to cockslit. Once. Twice. Never in all their prior joinings had she come first. Another sign she was changing, for a Shimmerskin's release could only be triggered after her partner's had begun.

His head fell back and every muscle in his body clenched taut as a tremendous orgasm rolled over him, surprising him with its ferocity. He spurted deep, deep inside her, each coming of semen matching that of thunderous, driving hoofbeats.

And then the carriage was slowing. Lurching, it came to a

halt so abrupt that, had his boots not been braced on the opposite seat, he and his delectable rider might've both been pitched to the floor. He heard Landon call out to a night servant with curt instructions to unhitch and stable the horses.

They were home.

The carriage door was peremptorily flung open, and a pair of heavily muscled, masculine arms reached inside. Cara's eyes widened at Landon's ravaged expression, but she nevertheless loosened her hold on him.

Vincent considered it the height of self-sacrifice when he allowed Landon to take her, hoisting her over one shoulder without a word. He watched through the half-open door as Landon's long stride ate up the distance across the courtyard. He took the marble steps two at a time, and then he was inside their *villa*.

He and Cara had both still been coming when she'd been so decisively wrenched off him, so he remained in the carriage briefly, finishing himself off by the use of his own hand. With the last pump of seed, he was already sliding a few buttons home to seal his trousers. Then he jumped from the conveyance, following in Landon's wake and calling out to the servant to see to the bag of clothing Cara had brought.

The front door had been left open, and inside he found Landon had pinned Cara to the wall behind it with his body. His mouth was on hers, his legs between hers, and his hand was working at the fastenings of his trousers.

"In the study, Landon, for Gods' sake," chided Vincent, nodding toward the bevy of night servants who'd gathered to stare.

Landon only snarled at him, but he didn't react in kind, likely because he'd just climaxed and Landon had yet to. It had been a long time since he'd seen this man so desperately at the mercy of his cock. Some thought Landon cold, but he was warm enough, given the right circumstances.

"Fuck me," Cara coaxed, her eyes seducing Landon's. She slipped her hand to his groin and boldly cupped him. With a randy grunt, he ripped the front of his trousers open, popping buttons.

"Landon! Not here!" Coming between them, Vincent swung Cara into his arms and carried her into the study. Hard on their heels, Landon was swearing ripely. He kicked the door shut behind them, fairly growling with need.

Taking Cara from Vincent, Landon set her on the edge of the desk, flipping up the front of her skirts and shoving his trousers just low enough to expose himself.

"You shouldn't have waited so long," Vincent told him, propping a shoulder against the door to watch.

"Waited so long," he heard Cara murmur against Landon's throat. Her eyes found his over the other man's shoulder, and he saw them darken as Landon breached her.

Her ankles rose to clasp behind him, catching atop the bunching of trousers slung low at his hips. With a mighty shove, Landon slid fully inside her, his way paved by an erotic blend of Vincent's seed and her natural cream.

Her dark lashes fell shut, and her head fell back. Her arms locked straight behind her, hands braced on the desktop.

Sleek muscles at the sides of Landon's buttocks clenched as he thrust inside her, hard, his big hands anchoring her ass for his taking. The immense desk lurched several inches across the floor. Papers, books, and pens scattered. A dozen violent pumps later, his massive frame was shuddering over hers.

Gods, he'd known Landon to go an hour before finally coming if he set his mind to drawing out the task. How the hell long *had* it been for him?

Without glancing his way, Landon moved from the desk, taking Cara with him and sinking to his knees on the plush carpet. Lifting her away, he turned her and set her on her knees before him, her back to his chest and his calves between hers. Shoving his trousers lower on his thighs and rucking the back of her skirt up, he quickly retook the same passage he'd just enjoyed.

Her back arched as he speared up into her. Her fingers rose to brush his jaw, and his lips turned into her palm as he began to rock her again, every bit as hungrily as before. His broad hands came over her breasts in a massage that matched the rhythm of his stroke. Though Landon didn't acknowledge him in any way, he'd settled them facing him so that Vincent could observe what they did this time. And so he could easily join in.

Cara smiled in his direction, issuing the overt invitation Landon would not. Vincent's cock twitched, demanding he attend to it. Unclasping his trousers again, he discovered he'd misbuttoned them, inadvertently showcasing more of himself than decorum dictated for anyone who'd cared to look as he'd made his way into the house.

Going to the couple on the rug, he knelt before Cara. Landon's hands released her, grasping the bones of her hips as she went down on all fours. Licking her lips, she encircled Vincent's root with a fist and led him closer.

All three of them groaned in a salacious harmony as he entered her mouth and began to ride her tongue, even as Landon plowed on in her furrow.

"This ought to put Marco in a severe snit," Landon said an hour later as he drew on his trousers. Seeming only then to realize he'd ruined their fastenings beyond repair in the vestibule, he gave up and let the front placket of his pants lie open to expose him in a lurid vee.

"He knew to expect exactly this, as did Millicent. Why else do you imagine they sought to confine Cara in their home?" Vincent countered as he attempted to refasten his own trousers, using his sole available hand. Cara was leaning against him, and his other arm was curved around her waist.

"He may have expected this of *you*," said Landon. "But he knows I have more restraint."

"Oh, really?" Vincent glanced pointedly at the destruction his friend had wreaked on his desk in his rush to plunder their woman.

Cara yawned.

"May I suggest we adjourn to my bedchamber?" Vincent offered.

"Bed," Cara echoed. With her head on Vincent's shoulder, she smiled sleepily at Landon and lifted her hand toward him, beckoning him to join them.

When he didn't respond, Vincent swung her in his arms and turned to go. After a long moment, Landon followed them.

Much later, as dawn approached, Landon stood from the bed and made to leave them. Distant again and brooding, he stared at Cara where she still lay draped over Vincent's body. His hand was rubbing her back, and his cock was still buried in her, leisurely pumping the last of its semen. Though she was still coming as well, she was already half asleep.

"I'm glad this happened," Vincent told him.

Gray eyes shot to his.

Something had damaged Landon in ElseWorld, though Vincent never expected to learn exactly what it was. He'd always been withdrawn, but now there was a raw look in his eyes, as if witnessing so much killing in the war had wounded him internally where his injuries could not be seen or mended.

"I didn't create her only for me. Didn't you guess?" Vincent went on, softly so as not to wake Cara. "Didn't it strike you as odd that her body was specifically designed to harbor my dimensions as well as yours? How many females, even Shimmerskins, could do that?"

The two men stared at each other across the bed, across the woman both wanted. The woman that tonight both had tacitly agreed to share.

With a barely discernable inclination of his head, Landon made to go, but Vincent stopped him again. "The situation in

ElseWorld could turn ugly at any time," he said with necessary bluntness. "If anything should happen to me, you'll watch out for her?"

Landon froze in the doorway, his back to him. Then he nodded slowly and took his leave.

9

Normally Vincent was exhilarated by the prospect of work. But the following morning there was a distraction in his study. A female one. Cara.

She was unwrapping and examining all the silly gifts he'd brought with him from ElseWorld, *ooing* and *ahhing* over each in turn.

Across the room, Landon sat in his usual place when he wasn't in the vineyard, making a pretense of reading a reference treatise on viniculture while his hungry eyes tracked Cara's every move.

Upon opening a long, slender object, she suddenly leaped back from it, looking frightened for some reason. He and Landon both half rose from their seats, preparing to go to her aid. Then both sank again as they noticed the harmless nature of what she'd uncovered—a foot-tall painted wooden soldier with a black hat, lying on its side.

"It's a nutcracker," Vincent informed her.

Still looking inexplicably horrified, she sidled closer again to study it. "What is its purpose?"

Landon went to it and, opening its jaws, he revealed a void in which he set one of the nuts that had been sent along with it. Pounding downward, he then pulled out the meat and shattered shell. "There, you see? To crack nuts."

She stared at it, transfixed. Then with a forefinger she drew an imaginary line across the base of her throat. "Death."

Landon laughed, and Vincent looked his way, surprised. He hadn't heard the sound of his full laughter since he'd returned from the war. He sat back in his chair. "I suppose it does have a rather evil, guillotinelike aspect about it."

"Evil," she pronounced with a nod.

Having apparently lost her taste for exploring more gifts, she came to perch on the edge of Vincent's desk. The same edge upon which Landon had taken her the previous night. "What is your purpose?"

"By that, I assume you are asking me about my business pursuits? I'm in the profession of law."

"Law."

"A system of codes that govern behavior and determine regulations for how a people live. The rules of society here are based on the Justinian code in Roman law, which sought to lay down clear, concise, understandable rules of government."

"As your body has governed mine . . . before."

He was surprised at her understanding. "Somewhat similar. Yes."

"What are the rules of government between us now?" she inquired.

He shifted, growing uncomfortable with the direction of her questions. "They are changing. We must alter them to suit us."

She leaned closer. "To suit us? Or to suit you?"

He looked to Landon for help, but he only raised his book higher, shielding himself. Vincent gathered the distinct impression he was stifling more laughter.

"Both, I suppose."

Her brow knitted. "How did you arrive at your choice of purpose?"

"I suppose it began with my talent at mazes and puzzles. Wading through the intricacies of law is much like solving a puzzle. One gravitates toward that at which one excels."

She looked confused.

He eyed her, suspicious. "It's odd the things you understand and those you don't."

She nodded. "Odd."

"It's also odd that you can speak perfectly complete sentences when it suits your purpose."

"Yes!" she grew suddenly more excited. "My purpose. What is it?"

He stared in exasperation. "Ask Landon. I believe he may be better able to answer you, for I am preoccupied with thoughts of ElseWorld and my meeting there tomorrow."

She turned on Landon, and he straightened in his chair, looking alarmed. "What is my purpose?" she demanded.

Vincent kept his head down, leaving Landon to fend for himself.

"Whatever you wish it to be."

This seemed to annoy her. "What is *your* purpose?"

"I tend the grapevines on the estate," Landon replied.

"Why?"

"Because it suits my disposition, I suppose."

"Why?"

"Because I enjoy making things grow. All of us here on the estate work toward one purpose—to keep this land safe in order to protect the Satyr legacy, the vines, and the gate."

"That was more information than anyone else has been able to draw out of him in the weeks that he has been home," Vincent informed her. "Perhaps your abilities lie in the area of interrogation."

"Interrogation?" She screwed up her face, confused again.

"I'm teasing, Cara. Landon and I have had all our lives to determine what our purposes are," said Vincent. "You've had two days. Give yourself time. There's no rush. You'll find a purpose."

She ignored his somewhat patronizing smile. "But I *am* in a rush. I wish to find my purpose. Today. Where am I to look for such a thing?"

"Look to your interests, as we have. Or look to the needs of others and determine if you can make yourself useful to them," Landon suggested.

"Why this ongoing interest in finding a purpose?" Vincent asked.

"Another wants to take me," she whispered, repeating the phrase she'd used in the carriage.

His eyes narrowed on her, wondering now if he'd misinterpreted those words last night. "Landon, do you mean?"

"No," she admitted after a moment. "When I was taken last night. There were two men."

He straightened. *When she'd been taken? What the fuck?* "What happened?"

He went to her, but she refused to look at him. "One of them hurt me—the one who resembles a nutcracker. Then the other one asked if I had remembered my purpose. He said he'll continue to take me until I remember my purpose."

"Gods!" This from Landon, who'd dropped his book and slowly risen to his feet.

Cara turned to Vincent and put a hand on his shirtfront, her eyes desperate. "What is my purpose?"

His big hands covered her small one.

But he had no ready answer.

10

The second time Cara was taken out of herself, it was worse.

For she was lying in bed. Vincent's bed, where she'd believed herself to be safe.

She sat up in the pitch of night, unaccountably afraid, and spread a hand over the sheets next to her. They were cold. Vincent, her protector, must have gone to that other world. For law. His purpose.

Across the room, the nutcracker grinned at her, its teeth leering white under its coal-black mustache. It had grown taller, as big as a man.

"Landon," she whispered, drawing her knees up and wrapping her arms around them. He was only a few doors away, down the hall.

She turned to leave the bed and seek him out, but someone stood there, blocking her way. Looking upward, she saw then that her persecutors had come again. And this time, there would be no one to see or hear. No one to call for her or worry over her as there had been at Marco's home.

The dimensions of the room abruptly shrank to include

only the three of them, and again she saw the dripping silver candles, but now there was no couch, only the bed. The larger man—the nutcracker—was dressed in the usual crimson vest and was drinking from a wine bottle that was only a third full. Drunk. The other olive-skinned one was naked and watchful, waiting for whatever was to happen to unfold.

She tried to remain calm, to pay attention this time. Tried to notice details as Vincent had suggested she do this morning, if this happened again. This, after he'd drawn from her a complete confession of all that had occurred during her first taking.

The nutcracker pushed her to lie on the bed and lowered his green bottle, sliding it smoothly under her gown and between her legs, nestling its tip at her brink.

No! The word resounded in her mind. These were her private parts. Vincent had spoken with her about this as well—had said these parts were inviolate. That she could choose who touched her there. She struggled to say no to him, yet she could not.

The bottle pressed higher, its smooth green mouth and then its neck slowly invading her soft, pink flesh. It went deep, and then he tilted it, douching her feminine tissues with the spill of wine.

"Drink," he told her. "And let it cleanse you of *his* seed before I take you. Before I butter your buns for *him* instead of the other way 'round, for once. He's always gotten everything handed to him. So easily. So unfair."

With an abrupt movement, she swept her arm out, pushing him and the bottle away. When she sat up, wine stained the sheets under her like a pool of blood, as if she'd hemorrhaged. But still she couldn't say the word *no*. Couldn't make herself leave them.

The nutcracker looked angry at being thwarted. But the olive-skinned one ventured closer and wrapped his arms around him from behind, dipping his hands inside the front of his trousers to stroke his stunted cock and soothe him.

Over the nutcracker's shoulder, ruby eyes peered from olive sockets, burning over her. "Your purpose. Have you remembered it?"

She shook her head at the dreaded question. Then something clicked in her brain, telling her what she must do to please him instead. Scooting across the bed, she crouched on the floor to look underneath it. Spying the tapestry bag Marco's wife had given her, she pulled it out. Taking it onto the mattress, she sat in her former position and opened it.

The garments she'd been given now hung in the armoire. The only item the bag contained was a large square of linen that had been folded with almost ritualistic perfection in order to conceal its contents.

The nutcracker's black eyes had fallen shut, a blissful look on his face as another's hand masturbated him. But the olive-skinned one's gaze was keen as he watched her unfold the linen and fondle the hoard of injurious objects within. Forks, knives, writing instruments, and more—she'd stolen them all from those who cared for her, having no idea why she'd done so.

She selected one from among them—an ancient dagger she'd taken from a glass case in Vincent's library. Its solid, silver handle was as fat as two fingers and was carved with vines and bunches of grapes that wound over the muscular torso and furred haunches of a mythical satyr. At the rounded end of the decorated handle were his cloven hoofs. Near the middle of the knife, the satyr's silver tongue extended from his mouth, flattening to become a long, sharp-tongued blade.

Lying back, she poised the blunt tip of the handle to nether lips, where the bottle's mouth had been. Her hand shook with the effort to stop herself from the impulse that held her in its thrall. A single tear fell to her temple, dampening her hair. "No." she whispered. "No."

The olive-skinned creature's ruby eyes snapped menacingly. His clawed fingers reached into the pocket of the nutcracker's vest. Pulling out the golden coin she remembered from before, he laid it over her lips with a gentle menace that sapped her will and rendered her mute.

Straightening, he unfastened the nutcracker's trousers and shoved them lower. The bottle fell from the nutcracker's hands to the floor, and his body arched as he was brutally entered him from behind.

Three gasps mingled as cold, blunt silver pricked her at the same moment. Her knees rose, and the soles of her feet dug into the bed linens. She didn't want this, but another will guided hers now and she was helpless against it. As the dagger's handle navigated deeper, her body caressed it, conformed to it. Loved it. Until it was entirely embedded in her and only the blade protruded obscenely from her slit.

As the figures rutted next to her, they seemed to merge into one another, slowly and eerily. Until two became one. Except for the ruby eyes and olive cast to his skin, the nutcracker looked the same as before. But she sensed he was different now. More lethal. He leaned close, his lips at her ear.

"When next I come to you, I will fuck you where your satyr has been," the amalgam said in the nutcracker's voice. "I'll leave my cum behind for him to discover. You will ask him to place his mouth on you there afterward, that he may taste my leavings.

"And when he does, you will plunge this very dagger into his broad back. Kill him as he's tasting me, so that I will be in his mouth forever." A clawed finger scraped along the blade that protruded from her.

Her lips sealed with gold, she could only gaze at him with wide, terrified eyes. Heat pricked over her, washing her with numbing panic. *No. Please. No.*

And then the coin was abruptly plucked from her lips and secreted in the vest pocket again, and then her persecutors were gone.

"No! Please, no!" As she pulled the dagger from her body,

the words shrieked from her, quaking the air and echoing off the walls.

"What!" Almost instantly, Landon filled the doorway, blinking at her. He was naked. Muscular. Fresh from his bed.

Vincent joined him a second later. Handsome. Strong. Concerned. "Cara! Are you all right?" He made to pass Landon and go to her, but Landon put a staying hand at his chest as he noticed what she held. The dagger.

She turned to face them then, her expression solemn. "I was sick, sick unto death, with that long agony, and when they at length unbound me, and I was permitted to sit, I felt that my senses were leaving me. The sentence, the dread sentence of death, was the last of distinct accentuation, which reached my ears. After that, the sound of the inquisitorial voices seemed merged in one dreamy indeterminate hum. . . ."

"It's another passage from *The Pit and the Pendulum*, almost verbatim," muttered Landon.

"Why are you reciting these texts? What does it mean?" asked Vincent.

"Mean," she said calmly. "I have discovered my purpose."

She lifted both arms high, hands clasping silver. And then in a single, fell swoop, she stabbed the blade of the ancient dagger she held into the mattress where Vincent would normally lie in sleep.

"Death." Violet met sapphire. "Yours."

Then she burst into tears.

11

"Where were you?" Landon asked him over Cara's head a few moments later. Vincent had just removed the knife and discarded it, and Landon sat on the mattress, holding her on his lap.

"Downstairs in the study," said Vincent. "Preparing for my journey to ElseWorld."

Both looked at Cara as she began speaking gibberish. "Bottle, bottle. No."

Vincent grabbed her shoulder, shaking it. "Stop that. Speak properly so we can understand. So we can help." His tone was gruff with worry.

"Words here," she said, tapping her temple. "Sometimes not come," she said, tapping her mouth.

"I think the 'taking' experience may be garbling her speech for a time after it happens," Landon suggested.

Vincent took her shoulders urgently, willing her to help them. "Cara. What did the men who 'took' you look like?"

"Nutcracker."

"Both?"

She shook her head. "One had olive skin and red eyes."

Vincent and Landon exchanged alarmed glances.

"A demon?" Landon hazarded in disbelief.

"But he merged himself with the other one," said Cara, her voice rising. "Now both are the nutcracker!" She put a hand on Vincent's arm. "They wish to stop you from reaching your goals. Law. I am to help."

"What else?"

"A gold coin. He worships it." She put two fingers to her lips, remembering its cold hardness.

"What does it look like?"

"Grapevines on one side, Bacchus on the other," she told him.

"The amulet," both men said at once.

"Gods! If the demons have found it, they'll be resurrected regardless of the demonhand," said Landon. "Dominic will have to go back to his world, to his old way of life. And then Rose . . . The fighting. Hells."

"Even worse, if the Feroce succeed in sealing the gate, Dominic and Rose will die on this side." He stood. "I'm due in ElseWorld soon. I'm taking Cara with me to see if she can point to her abusers. And I think the faction leaders will find what she has to tell them quite interesting."

"I'm coming," said Landon.

Vincent nodded, having expected his words.

ElseWorld

"Go back," a stern voice ordered.

The trio had hardly crossed the gate into ElseWorld when they were stopped in the tunnel by a hoard of guards who awaited, their every weapon trained menacingly toward them.

Immediately spotting one of her persecutors, Cara backed away, pointing. "Nutcracker."

Because the word had become her favorite euphemism for all things unacceptable, Vincent and Landon didn't at first realize what she meant.

"Julius!" Vincent called.

Why was he speaking to her enemy in such a familiar tone?

"Nutcracker!" she insisted.

"*He's* your nutcracker?" asked Landon, finally understanding.

"Kurr, actually," the creature said, speaking in the nutcracker's voice. He stepped into the circle of light emitted by the portal through which they'd just passed, and Vincent gasped, seeming to recognize him yet be put off by his appearance.

His skin was a mottled olive-green color, his eyes flashing ruby and silver, his mustache and boots pitch black. A blend of two males—just the way she remembered.

"You must turn back," one of the guards insisted. "We're under orders. The gate is to be sealed today, by command of the Feroce. There will be no treaty. No more passage between worlds."

"Julius, listen to me," said Vincent, speaking to the nutcracker. "Once the demons have everything they want from you, they'll kill you and take another host."

"He doesn't hear. He's ours now," the nutcracker replied. "The amulet led your brother to us only recently, though he found it years ago, not long after it was lost. He was weak, easily taken as a disciple and then a host. And even better, he has now given me the opportunity to take something from you. From your family, who have done my kind so much harm."

His clawed fingers reached out, beckoning her. "Come."

In a fury of muscles and curses, Vincent and Landon lunged toward her, trying to stop him from taking her. Guards wrestled with them, and it took five of them to restrain each of her protectors.

She stared at the nutcracker's clawed hand like it was a viper.

No! she wanted to scream. But, dreamlike, she left her companions and went to him.

"Cara!" Vincent's enraged, worried voice seemed distant.

Her arms hung limp at her sides as her nemesis enfolded her and held her to him, pressing her face into his vest and stroking her hair. "She comes with me. You see, something of your brother does remain within me." He thumped his chest in emphasis. "His jealousy of you. Because the gate is to be sealed, I've decided there's no need to kill you after all. I'd rather think of you in your world, worrying over her."

His face bent to hers, and he kissed her throat with lips that were dry and fleshy. Abhorrent. Ruby eyes watched Vincent over her head, relishing his jealous anger.

Vincent and Landon thrashed within the holds of their captors, who struggled valiantly to control them. In the confusion, Cara's fingers crept up crimson satin and stealthily dipped into her captor's vest pocket, finding what was secreted within. Stealing. But she doubted Vincent would mind this time.

Above her, the nutcracker's laughter taunted him. "How does it feel to want something so badly your very entrails ache for it? But for once a woman prefers me over you, brother. After the gate is sealed, know that she'll be fucking me. Servicing me. Every day and every night." With an arm around her, he turned to lead her away, to his world.

"No," she whispered, finding her voice and her will. "No."

He paused at that, and those hideous eyes looked down at her, mildly surprised. "You can't say no to me. You're an insentient. Not meant to control your own destiny."

"No!" Wrenching away, she pivoted and hurled the powerful amulet she held safely through the gate. As she tried to reach Vincent and Landon, sharp claws raked her back. Stinging. Poisonous. She fell, dizzy.

Behind her, the demon shrieked as his last hope of resurrection fell into enemy hands. Falling to his knees he began to writhe and convulse, spewing vile curses and impotent enchantments. Then he went limp and slowly, very slowly he fizzled into benign nothingness.

Having lost their leader, the guards let Vincent and Landon go, uncertain what they were to do next. As none from Else-World could permeate the portal from this direction without an invitation, they simply stood there, confused.

"Cara!" Vincent lifted her in his arms, and Landon watched his back, ensuring that their passage through the gate was a safe one. On the other side the two men turned homeward, where they assured her over and over they would find an antidote for whatever poison the demon had imparted.

Violet eyes opened, gazing into sapphire, and Cara began speaking in a rush, quoting yet another verse of *The Pit and The Pendulum*.

"I had swooned; but still will not say that all of consciousness was lost. What of it there remained I will not attempt to define, or even to describe; yet all was not lost. In the deepest slumber—no! In delirium—no! In a swoon—no! In death—no! even in the grave all is not lost. Else there is no immortality for man. Arousing from the most profound of slumbers, we break the gossamer web of some dream. Yet in a second afterward, (so frail may that web have been) we remember not that we have dreamed."

She blinked up at him. "I have discovered the problem with being real," she said, a slight smile curving her lips. "Pain."

Then she fainted, lying unconscious for the next day and a half.

12

Satyr Estate in Tuscany, Italy
EarthWorld, 1850

The front door of the *villa* slammed.

"In here!" Vincent shouted in answer to Landon's hail.

Downstairs, footsteps thundered toward the base of the grand staircase.

"Boots off!" Cara called.

The steps paused. They heard two clumps as a pair of boots struck the marble floor.

Her eyes alight with wry humor, Cara twisted to smile back at Vincent from her seated perch atop him. "It's taking Landon a considerable time to accustom himself to the fact that yours is no longer a bachelor household. I've told him that when he returns from the vineyard, he must endeavor to leave the muck outside."

He'd taken her feminine channel from behind this time, and though his cock twitched inside her, eager to get on with the business of fucking, Vincent ignored it for the moment and returned her smile. "Old ways die hard."

He and Landon had wed Cara one week ago today in an ancient ceremony that was attended by all the EarthWorld family and even some dignitaries from ElseWorld.

The footsteps drew closer, and Cara turned around again, affording him a view of a slim back draped with silken mooncolored tresses that tumbled past her hips to dust his belly. Four thin stripes that were several inches long marred her shoulder, reminders of the demon attack. They were largely healed, but the sight of them never failed to send a chill through Vincent at the thought that he'd almost lost her.

She was watching the door to the corridor, which lay to their left, and pursed her lips in disappointment when the footfalls beyond it only continued down the hall.

"Here!" Vincent called out.

Almost instantly, the door burst open. Wearing his usual garb of leather trousers and a dark linen shirt, Landon appeared, looking shocked to see them in his room. In his bed.

Vincent had wondered if it would anger him that they'd chosen to invade his private sanctum for the first time.

But the emotion smoldering in Landon's eyes wasn't anger. Instead he stood in the doorway, beholding them with a poignant sort of awe, as though he wanted to savor every detail of the loving scene before he became part of it.

Vincent lay there with his head on Landon's pillow and his hands on their wife's ass, letting him look. Her body already rode his, her back to him and her shapely legs bent alongside his outer thighs. Lodged as deep inside her feminine throat as it was possible to go, his cock was an eager iron fist of quivering nerve endings.

Though she was undeniably Human now, Cara still retained much of her Shimmerskin intuition when it came to carnal matters. And now, as if she knew precisely how best to prolong Vincent's ecstatic agony, she chose that moment to tease both men. Flattening her hands on the mattress between his thighs, she rose onto all fours, keeping her knees so widespread on either side of his hips that she released only a few of the eleven inches he had recently worked so hard to plow inside her.

Vincent glanced downward between them. Framed in the inverted vee of her thighs was the length she'd relinquished. Though his crown was still safely nestled inside her, six or seven inches of ruddy cock stood exposed between them. High and glossy with her juices, it poled up into her, connecting their bodies like an erotic umbilical cord. Her nether lips were stretched wide, embracing its exceptional circumference with a trembling, openmouthed kiss.

Vincent's hands found her hip bones, and he gritted his teeth, forcing himself not to return her bottom to its former seat. He'd have her again soon enough.

Her face was still turned toward Landon, where he lingered in the entrance to his own room. She'd angled her jaw toward Vincent as well, ensuring that he would witness her rapt expression as she gazed at the other man.

A pink tongue peeked out, wetting her lips.

His eyes shot to Landon, who was staring at her like some sort of ravenous beast.

"As you can see, the timing of your homecoming is excellent," Vincent informed him.

At his words, Landon abruptly snapped out of the concupiscent thrall in which Cara had held him and sprang into action. Flinging off his jacket, he didn't bother with the buttons of his shirt but only crossed his bent arms overhead to grip the fabric at his shoulder blades and strip it off as he came toward them. At the bedside, his hand fell to the placket at the front of his trousers.

Cara watched those long fingers rip at the fastenings of his pants, and Vincent saw a smug, feminine smile curve her lips. She was well aware that though their male bodies might be larger and more dominant, she possessed an equal measure of control in these matters of the flesh.

Landon made short work of his final garment and moved to join them on his bed.

"Come, husband," she beckoned. Her hand reached out, running over Landon's sculpted chest, her thumb teasing a flat nipple. Even as she did so, Vincent felt her nether throat slide lower on his prick to encase another inch of him. Then she released half of that measure, beginning a stroke that would eventually have her retaking all of him. No matter whose bed they lay in, she never forgot that her love was for both men.

The far end of the mattress depressed under Landon's knee.

Letting him take some of her weight, Cara slid her palms upward along the center of his ribs, over breastbone and collarbone, where they diverged to clasp his nape and pull his lips down to hers.

As their embrace deepened, Landon's hands smoothed down her back on either side of her sleek spine. Grasping the twin globes of her rear, he caught the motion of her stroke on Vincent's cock, pushing slowly until she had been fully impaled and then lifting her just as slowly so she was forced to release some of what she'd taken. And then again. And again.

"Gods! Enough." Displacing other hands, Vincent gripped her hips and took over, thrusting his greedy rod high inside her, then pushing her away, then yanking her down and thrusting again. Fucking himself with her beautiful, perfect body.

In this position, the thick, veinlike duct that ran the length of his cock's underside would tease her clit with every stroke he gave. Soon it would deliver his sperm into her, but for now he rutted with care, giving her just enough to stimulate but not yet allowing either of them to come.

Landon's eyes turned dark as Cara moaned encouragements

and pleas meant for another husband against his mouth. Driving his fingers into her hair, he pulled away, separating their lips. He sat back with his legs folded under him, knees widespread, leading her head downward.

Eagerly Cara bowed forward over his lap, her spine forming a smooth seductive curve. Landon gathered the fall of her hair back with one hand, twisting it at her nape so Vincent could watch if he chose. Gray eyes lit with anticipation as Landon stared down at her. Vincent knew the moment she took her other husband's cock in her mouth, for he arched his throat high and sucked a sharp hiss between bared white teeth.

The time for talking was done.

The atmosphere quickly turned tense and sultry and was permeated only with harsh grunts and groans, the humid slaps of heated flesh, and the creaking of bedsprings.

Their coming together was even more passionate, more meaningful, now that vows bound them and bands of glistening gold graced their fingers. Never again would he and Landon view Cara as an expendable vessel for their seed, and the days when they'd considered her as such seemed distant. She was their wife and held their hearts now as she held their cocks, cherishing and worshipping both tight and deep inside her as if she would never let them go.

Vincent felt her feminine throat pulse gently, its muscles rippling along the length of his prick in a way that presaged her orgasm.

His balls throbbed in response, heavy and hardened by the viscous weight of the semen that had collected within. Soon it would burst forth and funnel through his cock to fountain into the welcome of her body.

"Landon," he murmured.

"I'm close," came the low, masculine reply. "Very close."

Landon's chin was angled low, his slitted eyes watching Cara minister to him, her head bobbing over his groin. The sinuous muscles of her shoulder and back undulated in time with her head and with her hips, which massaged Vincent's prick in an age-old carnal rhythm.

Vincent stuck a finger deep in his mouth, moistening it along his tongue. His other hand spread the cheeks of her rear, and the wet finger pressed at the prissy, puckered moue it found there. At his touch, her hips slowed in their fucking of him, and the globes of her buttocks trembled in wary anticipation.

Gently his finger screwed at her until the reluctant O of muscle gave. Then he penetrated and sawed shallowly within the ring's clench until he heard her moan around Landon's cock. At the sound, Vincent sent his finger deep, in one smooth push, feeling her entire body wrench taut in reaction.

And then the world shattered around them, and three jubilant shouts broke from throats that were hoarse with emotion.

Seed blasted forth, and hard, masculine muscles bucked and strained with its giving. The saddle of Vincent's hips lifted its rider from the bed, and Landon's white-knuckled fingers threaded her hair, holding her skull. Cara's mouths took and took from them and swallowed and gulped and gasped for more. And still it went on and on for long moments, during which their connected bodies seemed to cling together in a suspended sort of ecstasy.

Afterward there was time for cleansing in stone basins that sat ready for them, and for low, murmured words, and then soft touches, and then the loving began again, continuing far into the night.

There was no need to curtail matters. In fact, this night was something of a celebration. Several days ago, the amulet—missing for thirteen years—had been returned to the statue of Bacchus in the sacred temple.

And earlier this very day, each of nine adversaries in Else-World had reached a consensus and had sent a single representative to scratch their names upon one parchment—a treaty that would end the war that had begun with King Feydon's death twenty-seven years earlier, the very year Vincent had been born.

"Love," Cara whispered much later as she reclined on her back, her head resting in the nook of Vincent's shoulder.

Her fingers drifted idly up and down the length of his shaft, and then she sighed deeply and arched her back, drawing up her knees. This, of course, was Landon's fault, for his mouth was busy between her legs.

"Yes," Vincent returned, toying desultorily with a rosy nipple at her breast. "This is love."

He'd designed the female body he now held in his arms over a year ago. Designed her to need two specific men and to satisfy them. In the making of her, he'd ensured that she would bring them joy in carnal matters. But even he could not have foreseen the infinite pleasure she would eventually bring to other aspects of their lives.

For she was real now, and the love that existed between the three of them was just as real. It was a love born of loneliness, loyalty, sacrifice, and passion. The kind of passionate love that would last for their entire existence on this Earth.

Their time together was destined to be rife with fucking and laughter and satisfying occupations. And Gods willing, children.

Three hearts—three lives—bound into one.

Cara turned on her side, savoring the soft convulsions of yet another orgasm Landon had just supplied. Her lips brushed Vincent's ribs, and then she kissed her way downward, beyond his belly, to nuzzle his cock with her cheek. She took it in gentle fingers, finding the joyful tears of pre-cum he'd wept at her touch and rouging them over his tip with the pad of her thumb.

Violet smiled into sapphire across the long, ridged expanse of his muscled torso. Her head lowered. Those beautiful pink lips opened, preparing to take him in.

He closed his eyes, anticipating.

Ahhh!